ALSO BY DAVID JOEL STEVENSON

THE SURFACE'S END
The Surface's End
The Dirt Walkers

VICTOR BOONE
Victor Boone Will Save Us
Victor Boone Must Die (Coming 2018)

ADAM—

VICTOR
BOONE
WILL SAVE US

DAVID JOEL STEVENSON

THANKS 5 much!

[signature]

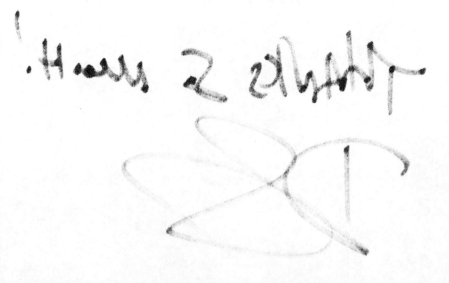

CHAPTER ONE

I hate this part.

We're surrounded by masked men with several guns pointed at hostages. Any normal human being would try to lay low for one of two reasons.

Reason one would be because they could use the element of surprise, waiting until the criminals were distracted, in order to execute a somewhat thought-out plan. Reason two would be because they simply didn't want to get shot.

But I personally hate it because I'm an invisible *sidekick* to an arrogant megalomaniac with no powers. And his mouth has opened.

"You douchebags are in for a load of hurt, you know it?"

Ah, the poet speaks.

"Did you really expect to just walk in here in the middle of the day—in *my town*—and wave guns around without seeing the great Victor Boone?" He says his own name with reverence. "What really gets me, though, is that you grab the hottest chick in this city before I get a chance to."

He gives the buxom woman a wink, then flashes a flex of his bicep. I'm kind of surprised he still even notices women, and doesn't simply stand shirtless in front of the mirror, winking at himself while he stares at his muscles.

And, as always, the beautiful girl blushes and smiles sheepishly, as if they're the only two people in the room. As if there isn't a guy holding her by her red hair and zip-tied wrists.

I don't get women.

They all say that they want a nice guy – a guy who buys them flowers and is sensitive to his own feelings and all that. But every single last one of them fall for Vic. He's never bought a girl flowers.

"You're not fast enough, Victor Boone," snarls one of the masked men as he scans the barrel of his gun across the innocent civilians strewn about the floor of the bank.

Crap – there are even kids in here.

Most of the people on the floor also have their hands zip-tied, which is fairly strange. I'm not sure why the thugs would've taken the time to tie each hostage up if they were planning on an in-and-out robbery. In my experience, very seldom does a random person fight back in a situation like this – the yells from behind firearms are generally enough to restrain would-be heroes.

But, you know – not *super*heroes.

Or, maybe I should say superhero. Singular.

"Me? Not fast enough?" Vic taunts. "I'd like to see one of you stupid mother fu—"

Idiot. That's definitely on my list of cues.

Before he can finish saying the word, I quickly hug Victor—as lightly as I can—and fly through the closed doors of the bank, shielding his fragile face from the broken glass with my transparent body. We both shoot up a hundred feet in the air, out of range of camera microphones and normal human ears.

"Vic, what's your problem?" I ask him as calmly as I can, which is difficult at the moment. To the rest of the world he's hovering mid-air, having a conversation with himself. No one has a clue that I'm here—the awkward, overweight guy who is defying gravity and doing all the heroic deeds while hidden with invisibility.

"You heard that jerkwad," he screams at my face. "He said I was slow!"

I can assume that he doesn't realize that my face is literally an inch from his because even *he* can't see me. But the fact that he's yelling when he knows I can hear things from a mile away kind of makes me want to drop him.

"Regardless of what he said, you need to act like a hero," I say for the millionth time. "That includes the words you use – especially in front of kids. Even the word 'douchebags' is more than I'm comfortable with when you're representing us. And would you *please* respect women?"

Even if no one else knows I exist, he speaks for both of us. It might be his face on every social media post and news bulletin, but it's my powers that put him there. And my standards are much higher than his.

"Blobby, you are a pushover," he enunciates each word with a scowl on his face. "You might be okay with people making fun of you, but I don't stand for that kind of thing."

I take a moment in order to keep my words calm, especially after hearing his nickname for me. I could spend the next twenty minutes talking about him calling me Blobby again, but it's never helped before and we have bigger problems on our hands. Or, on my hands, at least.

"Vic. First of all, if they're trying to provoke you by saying you're slow, they're talking about me," I reluctantly explain. "You *are* too slow. You're a normal person. You can't even outrun a football, let alone a bullet. And second of all, he didn't call us slow – he said we weren't fast enough. There are at least fifteen guys with guns in there, and under most circumstances I'd say he's absolutely right to assume at least a few bullets would meet their targets. Regardless, cut the frat boy language out, okay?"

I don't wait for his response because I can hear the thugs start to talk amongst themselves, wondering if the great Victor Boone ran away. I can also hear some of the news cameramen telling their tethered reporters that everyone's hero must be having one of his "schizophrenic episodes" again. I need to figure out a better way to keep Vic on a leash if we're going to keep working together – fleeing the scene to have a brief come-to-Jesus meeting is starting to get really old.

Of course, I'm not sure why I even think the word "if" when I consider getting a new partner. Unfortunately, I'm stuck with him. And *he* knows that, too.

As we quickly lose altitude I hear one of the hostages whisper, "Victor Boone will save us," to the person next to her.

We're coming, ma'am. We're coming.

Vic stretches out his arms, holding his fists straight in front of him, trying to add to the effect of *his* flying. He might not have any powers, but he does spend a lot of time perfecting his showmanship.

We swoop back into the bank through the freshly-broken glass door. Another piece of property damage that I'm hoping insurance will cover. Sorry, folks.

I kick the gun out of one of the criminal's hands while simultaneously punching him in the gut and setting Vic down. The guy flies across the large room and hits the wall. I've gotten pretty good at knowing just how much force to use to knock a thug out without killing them. I've never killed anyone, and I'm pretty proud of that fact because it would be incredibly easy to do so. Especially considering what some of these villains do.

But that's a job for the justice system. Otherwise, how would I be any different from them?

"Miss me, *dirt bags*?" Vic puts incredible emphasis on the name calling to let me know he's only using the tame words sarcastically. He also combs his hair back. People probably think it's to show that he's calm and in control, but I'm pretty sure it's because he's obsessed with his hair being perfect. The split second flight probably shook it out of place.

Before anyone responds, one of the thugs pulls a trigger.

Crap.

I focus for a nanosecond, then rush toward the sound before the gunpowder ignites. I grab the end of the gun and point it towards the ceiling. A bullet bounces off my hand while I'm in the process of bending the barrel, and a second shot is fired.

Crap crap. These are fully automatic weapons. I should have noticed it before now, but I've been distracted by Vic's bro speech. I hope I actually am fast enough.

Luckily, only one more bullet hits my hand before the gun leaves the criminal's grasp. My foot connects with his face and he slides into a loan officer's large wooden desk. He's going to have a major headache when he wakes up in jail, because I'm pretty sure the desk is made of solid oak. Or, really I don't know what kind of wood it is – tree identification is not one of my powers. But he really hit it hard and it didn't fall apart.

I toss the gun and fly after another henchman, throwing him out of the bank's entrance where the cops are waiting for him.

I glance over at Vic, and he's doing what he usually does in moments like these: holding his hands out in my direction and scrunching his face in concentration. I guess there's nothing else he can do in these situations; there's really no other way to explain why his feet are stationary a few yards away from chaos. Telekinesis isn't far fetched when it seems like he's always flying around inside an invisible force field. But Telekinesis is something I unfortunately don't have.

The thing is, sometimes he gets a little preoccupied with his theatrics and he starts pointing his hands where he thinks I *should* go, rather than where I actually am. I sort of hate to embarrass him, but I have a hard time taking his direction.

Well, that's a lie – I don't mind embarrassing him. I wish I could do it more often, to try to keep him humble. Which is an impossible task.

"If any of you amateur cameramen have your cell phones out, make sure you're filming in landscape mode," Vic says while concentrating his hands incredibly hard on nothing in particular. "In case you want your shot to make the news. You'll need the wide angles."

That man loves being on the news.

Another trigger is pulled and I rush toward the guy holding onto the redhead. A bullet ricochets off my forehead before I slip the firearm out of his hands and smash it on the ground. I gingerly punch him in the face so that I don't hurt the girl in his grip. She smells nice.

There are still several bad guys with guns pointed at people, so I kick my speed up a notch to prevent any casualties. Apparently these guys are out for blood, and again that puzzles me. Usually, after seeing their companions flying through the air or skidding across the floor, guys like these start running away to try to save themselves.

I don't have time to consider their intentions, though. Each trigger that's pulled in my vicinity becomes my next target, and the nanoseconds start to disappear. I'm in a frenzy making sure the guns are not aimed at the hostages before their bullets leave a barrel, with masked men flying unconsciously through the air.

However, there's one trigger not in my immediate vicinity. My hands are still full of hot metal and what I thought was the last evildoer's face when I turn towards the sound.

The gunpowder has already ignited and the bullet trails down the barrel. When I realize what's happening, halfway to the gunman, the projectile has already left the weapon and rips through flesh.

"No!" I scream as I rocket my large body into the gunman, rage boiling over me like a volcano. "NOOOOOO!!"

Something clicks in me. I force the scumbag through the exterior concrete wall of the bank, then change direction toward the asphalt once we're outside. I'm punching him in the face as hard and as fast as I possibly can, which is *very* hard and *very* fast.

Before I know what I'm doing, the tattered, bloody man is twenty feet below the street, lying in the shadows of the sewer. His head is barely still there.

I have killed him.

I don't care.

After noticing my invisible hands hovering over his corpse, outlined in red, I wipe his blood from my fists with his shirt. I fly up through the hole in the road that I created with his body, and stand on the sidewalk in front of the bank. Either no one else knows what's going on, or time is still passing so slowly for me that they haven't had a chance to move, but I walk into the bank as restrained as I can and no one is in the way. My focus is unsteady and I struggle to remain invisible.

The chaos of the bank has ceased. The hostages are timidly looking up, discovering that no gunmen are left to hold them down. The red-haired girl is running towards the center of the room in slow motion.

We're headed for the same destination.

In the center of the room is a body with a single gunshot wound to the head, lying in a pool of his own blood.

Victor Boone is dead.

CHAPTER TWO

"The crime rate seems to be skyrocketing without our beloved superhero, Victor Boone, despite the city doubling its police force. Robberies are up six hundred percent from last year, drug-related homicides up two hundred and fifty percent, and random assaults seem to be springing up everywhere. Most of the recent crimes are going into a pile of unsolved cases, which is leaving many of our citizens still using a slogan that gave us so much hope not long ago: *Victor Boone will save us*."

The news reporter's voice overlays a video of yellow crime scene tape, apartment building fires and small-scale riots. Capital Vs are spray-painted on brick walls throughout the city using crude stencils. The final scene before I turn the TV off and crush the remote in my hand is a child dressed in Victor Boone pajamas with a cardboard sign, also echoing the slogan *Victor Boone will save us*.

Many people have accepted that the great Victor Boone is dead. The bank—after the forensics team dusted for every possible print and the damage was repaired—turned into a memorial of flowers and cards drawn by children. Weirdly, there were also a number of women's undergarments strewn about the tributes. The bank took a while before it officially opened for business again because they wanted to respect the people and Vic's memory – but rather than lay everyone off and convert their building into a bona fide museum, they eventually started participating in daily commerce once again.

It only took a day or so for an official statement to come out about why Vic's murderer died, although it was a bit far-fetched. They're saying that when Vic was shot through the head, all of his power left through the entrance wound and was unleashed onto the gunman. I'm not sure of the exact science of it—how his *power* would change directions as soon as it exited through the bank's walls to drive him underground, and why it would leave fist indentations all over his body—but I prefer it to everyone finding out the truth.

Everyone who refuses to believe that he's dead is clutching to a number of theories that are circulating. Some believe it was all an elaborate charade, and Victor Boone had to go undercover to track a criminal mastermind, so he hired actors to help him fake his death. Others believe that he only *seemed* dead, and that his body was switched with a double for the memorial service.

A number of people are even convinced that he did indeed die, but he's actually immortal and will burst through the grave when his energy returns. Because of that, there's a fairly steady crowd at his graveside around the clock.

The special crazies think his body is truly dead, but his spirit somehow jumped into someone who was nearby at the time, like some sort of possession. Several of them have been given restraining orders because they were stalking hostages from the bank, waiting for signs of the reincarnation of their beloved superhero.

I might be the only one in the world who knows that he's absolutely and permanently gone.

Victor Boone had been the face to my vigilantism for several years now. I never really intended on it happening that way. He was the one who took the credit when people so desperately wanted to give it. I guess to a certain degree, he saved *me*. There is no part of me that is interested in getting my sweaty, ugly face on a TV camera—masked or not—and recognition was inevitable. There was bound to be some situation where merely turning invisible wouldn't hide me from the world, and Victor Boone was more than happy to wear a spandex suit and look impressive.

It's been over two months since Vic was murdered, and I can count on one hand how many times I've left my apartment. I suppose you could say I'm adding to the crime rate, because each of the nights that I have ventured outside I've opted to be invisible, sneaking into stores and bringing back grocery items in bulk with a blanket over a seemingly self propelled cart. I leave money on the counter—more than enough to cover the items that I take—but I can't be sure that some greedy clerk won't simply pocket the cash when they open the store in the morning.

I just can't bear to show my face.

Not that it even matters. No one knows who I am. No one knows that Victor Boone was simply the handsome front for a superhero who would rather not be seen. Any time there was a need for a hero, my invisibility would kick in before I even planned on it. He was the very public secret identity for my secret identity.

I could go to any grocery store, lazily gather dozens of frozen pizzas and prepackaged cinnamon rolls, then nonchalantly pay at the register. I could even slip the bag boy a hundred-dollar-bill tip and he wouldn't recognize me as the overweight, invisible *sidekick* of Victor Boone. No one would know.

But I would know.

I thought I could do some good with the weird powers that just fell in my lap. Invisibility was the icing on the cake – I could still help people without fear of having people look at me or talk about me. But I ended up letting my city down.

Worse than that, in this case, I let Vic down.

I should've known better. I should've never let him get involved, as if that were possible. He was a normal person. Smooth and persistent as he was at getting in front of a camera after one of my first moments as an accidental savior, he was still just a normal person that I should've kept at arm's length. But instead, I embraced him. Put him in front of the cameras.

I don't see how anybody would blame me. In contrast to my oversized flabby gut, patchy facial hair, and persistent sweat stains, Vic was the perfect specimen. Chiseled jaw, bulging muscles, confidence. He was what a real superhero looked like.

Heck, I still question why *I* was the one with the powers when guys like him are obviously the ones who deserve them.

I keep picturing the moment over and over; the moment when a bullet slowly passed through his cranium while I was focused on everything else. And when I say *slowly*, I mean slower than any slow motion video you could've ever seen. For some reason my mind and body process time almost like it doesn't exist when I'm focused. And at that point I was crazy focused on watching the bullet move.

And less than a tenth of a second later, my focus was on the murderer behind him. First, I see his eyes widen, as if he sees me, and the next thing I know he's buried underneath the street's concrete, all but decapitated.

Part of me hopes the killer *did* see me in that tiny sliver of a moment before he died. I hope he realized that he unleashed a hurricane of vengeful pain on himself, even though I'm sure that he was unconscious before even going through the concrete wall of the bank.

But then the other part of me—the louder part of me—is sick to my stomach.

I'm a murderer.

I try to tell myself he deserved it, not just because he murdered Vic, but because he was prepared to murder a bunch of innocent civilians. I've been telling myself that for months. But his blood is on my hands.

Not only that, I wasn't thinking clearly at that moment. Even if he really *did* deserve it, I lost control. That's the scariest part for me, because it means that I could easily kill more people—a lot of people—if a situation got out of hand. If *I* got out of hand.

That's the reason I have to hang up my proverbial cape. I simply can't be trusted with it, or the power that I have. Not that I actually have a cape; they're silly and have no real purpose – and since I'm always invisible, it wouldn't even add any sort of effect.

I look down at the crushed television remote on the floor, continuing the thought of me getting out of hand. Exhibit B, I suppose. I pick up the now useless piece of mangled plastic.

I head over to the computer and, after looking at the model number on the destroyed remote, I order another one. I don't even choose the two-day shipping option to punish myself just a wee bit. Getting up to change the channels for a few days is small penance for losing my temper.

The moment I tap the confirmation button, there's a noise at my door.

Knock knock knock.

That's weird.

I hadn't been focused on the hallway so it's not the sound itself that gets me. I haven't ordered any food, the rent is paid for at least three years, and my only friend is dead. And he wasn't really a friend in the definitive sense.

My body tenses. I don't like surprises, especially after everything that has happened. The last surprise resulted in Victor's death and an ensuing chaos in the city. If I open the door and there's a box with a dead cat in it, I'm going to throw up on myself.

In times like this, I wish I had X-ray vision, but I suppose that's a lot like a billionaire wanting just *one more* billion. Instead, I focus and listen to the breathing and the heartbeat outside my door.

Nervous.

Kind of an *is-this-the-right-door* feeling, or possibly a *what-am-I-even-doing-here.* Not necessarily sinister. More like the times I heard the heartbeats of boys and girls asking each other out on dates in school. Not that I was ever on the giving or receiving end of those conversations. But I paid attention.

Singular.

There's no backup waiting in the wings, ready to pounce when I open the door. Only the breathing of one individual person, who I can most likely take down with almost no powers.

Small.

Okay – so even if it's someone with a nefarious purpose, the stranger is probably less than a third of my size, and can't be too dangerous. Unless they maybe have a Taser.

Feminine.

Oh crap. It's a girl.

And she smells pretty. Not like the kind of woman that douses herself in perfume because she's trying to hide her armpit sweat or chronic halitosis, but a subtle sweetness. A mix of vanilla and a bit of coconut.

It reminds me of a really cute girl in college who seemed nice, until she shallowly jumped on the Victor Boone bandwagon. Then, anytime I awkwardly tried to make conversation, she would just ask about Vic.

Of course, in her defense, my conversations probably weren't much more than stuttering her name and then drooling a bit.

This is the worst possibility. A pretty-smelling girl who probably doesn't even want to be here just knocked on my door.

Knock knock knock.

Crap! I thought time was going slower than it was, but apparently my focus is flustered, along with my cheeks. I look around the room, making sure there's nothing there that would implicate or embarrass me.

Fat chance… Frozen pizza boxes piled up, empty soda cans on every available horizontal surface, and a piece of plastic the shape of the inside of my fist on the desk beside me.

I can hear my grandma saying, *if you would just pick one thing up every time you walk through your room, you wouldn't have such a mess to clean up all at once.* Man, was she right.

Luckily, I'm stupid fast.

I fly around the room, shoving trash into oversized garbage bags and doing what I can to make it look like I'm a normal guy who leaves his apartment as often as a normal guy leaves his apartment. I heap the bags into my bedroom closet, assuming that isn't the first place the pretty-smelling girl will want to look.

When I'm done with that, I brush my teeth for the first time in a few days. I'd take a shower, but I can't speed water up; I'd just be spinning naked around the inside of a glass cage waiting to get soap off of my blubbery skin with leisurely falling

H_2O molecules. My shower stall isn't really big enough for a guy my size to bathe at light speed.

Perhaps ten seconds later, I'm standing at the door, questioning what I'm wearing when the sound arrives again.

Knock knock knock.

I can wrangle a bunch of thugs with guns, restrain crazy people with kitchen knives, and slow down speeding derailed trains all with my bare, invisible hands. But opening the door to a pretty-smelling girl throws me into a panic attack.

Taking a deep breath, I twist the doorknob and swing the thing open, carefully.

No way.

It's her.

"Mmmaa... Maria?"

My voice sounds stupid. Have I ever talked before? Well, I guess I haven't talked very much in the last couple of months, so maybe I'm just not warmed up.

Her green eyes look exactly as I remember them. Her curly dark brown hair catches a draft from the hallway, and a few strands caress against the silky smooth skin of her cheek. She brushes it behind her ear with a fragile hand like in a scene from a romantic movie.

I definitely should have taken a shower, not that it would have made me feel any more confident. Hopefully she doesn't have a super sensitive nose like mine.

"Hey Blobby— er— I mean Robby," she says, blushing and immediately covering her mouth. "Oh my gosh, I'm so sorry – I didn't mean to call you that, I just—"

"It's ok," I reassure her, though it kind of hurt to hear the old nickname as the first thing from her mouth. That's another thing to thank Vic for. I guess a three hundred-and-fifty-pound man standing at five-feet nine-inches makes for an easy target.

"I just—I just saw you there, and that's the first thing that came out. I definitely wasn't planning on saying that," she continues, her eyes wide.

I actually believe her.

"No, it's really okay, Maria," I say. "I go by Robert now, though. When I can."

I only go by Robert because I was trying to get Vic to stop calling me Blobby. I guess I still prefer Robby, but I've been in the habit of correcting him.

"Oh, okay – then, hi, *Robert*," she enunciates slowly. "How are you doing?"

"I'm doing pretty good," I lie. "Still trying to figure out what I want to be when I grow up, I guess."

It's the same thing I always say, because in general a twenty-one-year-old college dropout without a job isn't keeping their schedule open to be available for random heroism.

She smiles, revealing perfect teeth. She has a pretty smile. And man, she really smells good.

"How about you?" I ask after an awkward silence. I don't really know how to do the small talk thing.

"Good, good," she says, far more convincingly than me. "Trying to make sure that my new journalism degree doesn't go to waste."

"Yeah, I saw your posted a—you posted blog on your blog—I mean… I saw you posted a website on your blog—"

I sound like a crazy person. Can someone please just pull a gun on me so I can get back to a situation I can handle?

"Yeah," she gracefully agrees. "I've been trying to keep my website up to date with the articles I've gotten published. Not as frequently as I'd like, but at least it's something, right?"

"Absolutely, it's great," I say. I haven't actually read any of the articles – partly because I've been fairly distracted, but also because seeing her name and picture pop up doesn't make me feel too strong.

You know, emotionally.

She stares at me for a few more awkward seconds, then points to the interior of my apartment. "Can I…," she says as she kind of peers around me.

"Oh, yeah, sorry – of course," I answer, feeling like a moron. I move out of the way and she crosses the threshold. "Come in. Make yourself at home. Can I get you anything? Like a soda—er, a diet soda or something?"

"*Diet* soda?" she asks with an accusing look on her face as she passes by me. "Are you calling me fat, Robert?"

"Oh, crap no, Maria, I'm sorry," I say. I'm an idiot, again. "There's no way I'd call you fa— I mean, look at me," I say motioning towards my huge stomach. "That's the last thing I'd think. I just thought girls only drank diet—"

She grabs my arm and smiles. I hold my breath, as if that would help me more intently feel her skin against mine.

"I'm messing with you, Robby," she laughs. "Do you really remember me as that serious?"

I laugh awkwardly, as if I was in on the joke. Even though I just told her to call me "Robert," it was nice to hear her call me Robby.

Without acknowledging my offer for a drink, she walks through what I suppose would be called my dining room. She lightly sets her purse on the floor and eases into one of two swivel chairs I have in my living room, both of which are facing the TV. There were two simply because Vic would occasionally come over to watch some sports game when he would forget to pay his cable bill. Which is pathetic, considering pretty much everything else in his life was free as a payment from the city for his numerous good deeds.

But it's a good thing he didn't pay the few bills he did have, because having only one chair would make this situation even more awkward.

She turns the chair so that it's facing me. I copy her action, turning my chair as I sit down and look at her.

Stop staring, Robby. You've seen pretty girls before. They're just usually talking to Victor.

"You may be wondering why I'm here," she says mysteriously.

"Oh, yeah," I say, just now fully realizing that there are zero reasons I can come up with that would bring her into my living room. "I guess it's not because you need help with your chemistry homework, right?"

She laughs.

Like, genuinely laughs. I didn't think it was that good of a joke, but it's been a long time since someone was laughing with me rather than at me.

"No," she says, smiling. "No chemistry, although you *were* the only reason I passed that class."

My dad was a chemist, so I guess it came naturally to me. Well, he was actually a geneticist practicing in chemistry and biology, but saying it like that made it a lot harder to explain to people if I ever had a conversation about it. I never really saw a huge upside in being a nerd until Maria asked me to help her with her homework. Of course, it became fairly obvious that she only continued to hang out with me because she knew—or, at least she *thought* she knew—that Vic and I were somehow good friends.

Not like Maria and I had any real *chemistry* together, if you know what I mean.

"So, why are you here?" I ask, hoping that it's not to be interviewed about what I think regarding the passing of my buddy Victor Boone. I'm not sure I could keep a clear head while answering those kinds of questions. Luckily, no one would be interested in reading my point of view.

"Well, Robert," she says, pausing for effect. She leans in as if she were about to tell me a secret. "I'm here because I know that it's you."

CHAPTER THREE

"What?" I say, a bit too defensively. "What do you mean, you know it's me? You know that *what* is me?"

She reaches into her purse, pulling out her phone.

"Honestly, I don't know how in the world I didn't figure it out back then," she says, fairly calmly.

So calmly, in fact, that she's obviously talking about something other than what I assume she could be talking about. If she knew that I was the real superhero and Vic was just my handsome mask, she would definitely not be so composed. I start to relax when she hands me her phone.

"What's this for?" I ask. "You know, besides calling people."

The joke doesn't really go over that well. She snickers a little, probably out of sympathy.

I don't know why I'm trying to be ironic right now — maybe because I'm sweating a bit more than usual. Not only is there a beautiful girl sitting in my apartment, but she's acting like she knows something. I've got too many secrets to not be worried.

"Hit the play button," she says.

I look at her phone and remember the scene immediately. It's the bank. The day that Vic died. I don't need a video to remind me of the incident – it's all etched in my brain quite vividly. I could simply close my eyes and I'd see a better angle than the one on the screen in my hands.

Before I hit play, I look at the paused picture. The phone is still low, most likely to avoid any glances from the gunman. There are hostages taking up most of the bottom of the screen.

I recognize it perfectly, but I need to act like I don't.

"I've seen this on the news," I say. "Isn't this of where Victor dies? I'm not sure I want to watch it again."

"I understand," she responds. "But I really think you should. There's something interesting in it."

Something interesting like my only friend having his brains blown out with a bullet that I didn't stop. I make a noise, as if I'm going to resist, but Maria casually flicks her hand, indicating any of my objections would be dismissed. I don't like where this is going, but I've got nothing to do except tap the play button.

When I do, the camera scans up slightly, revealing Vic holding his hands out, acting like he's controlling my movements. The camera is filming from behind, so it isn't showing his face, but I can visualize him squinting his eyes in concentration, as if his "telekinesis" is taking a large amount of effort. Even though I always hated when he did that, I kind of miss it. I kind of miss all of the terrible things Vic did.

Sounds of a struggle are coming from off camera, which would generally cause someone to change the angle to the action. However, the lens stays on Vic, revealing the man tip-toeing behind him with a gun trained at his head.

Because of the angle, the gunman's head covers the carnage when the gun fires and the bullet goes through Vic's skull. Another high-pitched explosive noise resounds – a noise that I've heard when this video played on TV, but not one that I remember while the incident was actually happening. Less than a half second later, the gunman has disappeared from the screen, and Vic's body falls to the floor. An extremely long twenty seconds pass, and then once everyone realizes what happened, the red-haired hostage runs over to Vic's lifeless shell.

I hand the phone back to Maria.

"I don't know why you'd show this to me," I say. "You know that Vic and I were…friends. And this was on an endless loop for days after it happened."

She takes her phone and taps on the screen a few times.

"I know, I'm sorry," she responds. "I'm not trying to be mean. There's just something that I think you might've missed."

She looks at me for a moment, eyes squinting, obviously trying to read my face. I doubt that I'm revealing anything more than a puzzled look. I'm hoping my nervousness is covered up by a true sense of confusion.

She continues.

"You know that I'm trying to be a journalist, right? Well, something about this scene just didn't sit right with me, so I asked a video editor friend of mine to help me out." She hands the phone back to me after a few finger swipes and points at it. "Play *that* one."

I reluctantly take the device, very unsure of the rabbit hole that she's leading me down. After pressing play, I realize that the video has been slowed down tremendously. I see the gunman's head blocking Vic's, and I hear the low, distorted sound of what I assume is the gunshot.

And then I hear my own voice screaming, "NOOOOOO!!"

Wait – what?

That was the high-pitched explosion of sound I heard earlier. It was *me*.

Then for just one frame, I see an extremely blurry—completely naked—blob of a man.

In the next frame, the gunman and the blob are both gone.

I remember the moment. I remember the chaos inside me that made it hard to stay invisible – that made it hard to stay in control. But obviously I didn't stay in control; I acted without realizing what I was doing. Apparently the same momentary lapse of control applied to my struggle to remain transparent as well.

She captured me in a single frame. I stare at the phone for longer than I realize when Maria's hand covers mine.

"I know," she says, as if she's trying to console me.

I wish I could concentrate on her hand. Or maybe it's good that I can't, because if I thought about it too much I might pee on myself. But in normal circumstances, her soft skin touching mine would be a moment that I would lock away in my mind, a memory always ready to be recalled. I'd slow everything down, taking note of her smell and how she looked at me without disgust. I would drink in the scene, knowing this might be the only time in my life that the beautiful Maria Truman would hold my hand.

But instead, I replay the video.

I can't really see much of anything. I mean, *I* know it's me, but there's no way that she does. It's just a large blur of skin, possibly in the shape of a person. She's got nothing.

"I don't understand," I say, still giving the best confused expression I've got. "What do you know? That your video editor friend isn't very good?"

She smirks at me and raises her eyebrows.

"I had my friend slow it down because of all the weird theories about power leaving through the bullet hole," she says. "It seemed stupid, but I hadn't seen anything more reasonable, so I figured I'd check it out. You might not remember, but I was kind of obsessed with Victor in college."

Wow. You definitely don't need to remind me.

"Yeah, I remember," I mutter, disappointed that's where our conversation is going.

She looks at me with puppy-dog eyes for a split second, as if she's surprised that I would care.

"Well, it might not be what you think—" she tries to continue.

"No, I understand completely," I interrupt. "I mean, who wasn't impressed by the great Victor Boone? Even before he had any super powers he was always surrounded by adoring women. And once he saved that one girl, there was barely a moment when people weren't banging on his door to be close to him."

I pull my hand away from hers, surprised that we were still touching – but also surprised that I barely even noticed it.

"No, that wasn't it," she says as she pulls her hand back as well. "Robby, I wanted to be a *journalist*. I thought that I could get a story on him – one that no one else was getting. Sure, he talked to the press all of the time, but I was always hoping I could get to a different level since we knew each other before he saved that girl. Besides all of that, he was an absolute jerk and I could never stand to be around him."

My ears perk up a little bit.

She thought he was a jerk the whole time? That's not how I remember it. It seemed like she would've jumped at the chance to be one of his many female conquests.

"But you flirted with him – a lot," I say, not quite believing her new story.

She laughs a very cute *don't-you-know-anything-about-women* laugh. Well, no I don't, actually.

"Robby, I was flirting with him just to get the story," she says, as if I should already know it. "That was the only way he would talk to me. Did you not notice that he never did an interview with a male reporter? I flirted with him because I hoped he'd talk to me, especially because he didn't realize I was a journalist. Or, you know. That I was trying to become one."

"That doesn't seem very honest," I say a little sheepishly. I'm actually surprised it came out of my mouth, because—even though the thought was in my head—I had no intention of verbalizing it. I usually wouldn't say something so accusatory out loud, except maybe to Vic during one of our many talks about him being a better role model.

"Yeah," she agrees, looking away. She looks as if she was a little girl who had gotten caught with her hand in a cookie jar. "I guess I hadn't learned much about 'journalistic integrity' at that point," she says with air quotes, "but I don't really believe there is such a thing anymore."

I guess it makes sense. It always made me sad to think she had a thing for Vic when she seemed so wonderful otherwise. I knew nothing ever happened between the two of them, and I was always relieved. She was gorgeous, and I knew I never had a chance with her, but part of me was sick to my stomach at the thought of him even kissing her.

"But as I was saying," she continues. "I was obsessed with Vic in college, always trying to figure out the story. Why hadn't he revealed his powers before that moment? He was so full of himself, so if he'd had the powers before that, I don't think he would've had the patience not to show the world.

"I never got very far with the story, but I've always kept tabs on him. I guess it bothered me that he was a mystery I never solved. So when he was killed I pulled out all of my old notes and pictures.

"Honestly, I wasn't even looking for you in this video," she says, motioning toward the phone that was still in my hand. Crap – I'd hoped we were moving away from me. "But when I saw it, it all made sense."

Still nothing incriminating, but enough of an insinuation to make me nervous. She's on a trail, and I need to get her off of it.

"I'm sorry, Maria," I say, faking innocence. "But you're losing me. I've seen the video a hundred times, and this slow motion version doesn't really show anything else. Except maybe a weird glare or a reflection of light."

Yes. A glare in the shape of a three-hundred-and-fifty-pound screaming naked man.

"Maybe so," she says, pulling some pictures out of her purse. "But it made me curious. I looked at all of the pictures I had of Vic after he did some good deed in the early days. Not the ones where he was interviewed on a talk show or anything, but the ones where I was there within a few minutes of him being heroic. And do you know what I found?"

She hands me the photos and I flip through without actually looking at them. Dear Lord, please don't tell me I'm in all of these photos.

"Large-breasted women hanging on the hero?" I ask sarcastically.

She genuinely laughs again. Is she just humoring me, or am I actually being funny today?

"Of course there are beautiful women around him," she says. "But I'm talking about this."

She takes each photo individually and points at various places in the frame. In every single one of them, I am somewhere in the background, looking on at Vic's celebration, occasionally with my shirt on inside-out or backwards.

I sit in silence for a moment.

"That doesn't mean anything," I say, wishing it were true. "I've spent most of my life in shadows and off to the side of any sort of activity. So you discovered that I was one of Vic's admirers, too. So what?"

My chest tightens a bit. Even faking the thought of being one of Vic's admirers is a bit nauseating. Heck, it was my fault that he had such fanatic groupies, but to toss myself into the same category hurt my tiny ego. I hadn't thrown up since before I was a teenager—my body would no longer allow it to happen because my insides were just as strong as my outsides—but if I could, I imagine I would do it at such a thought.

"It all made sense," she says with confidence, as if she knew everything.

But she can't know everything. She just has a handful of pictures and a blurry video. It's not a stretch for me to deny this stuff.

"Victor Boone was never heroic," she continues. "Before everybody discovered his 'powers,'" she air-quotes again, "he was just a jerk who was full of himself. He was the kind of mean jock who would trip somebody or knock books out of their hands. Then one day he develops fantastic abilities, and instead of just using them for his own benefit, he saved everybody from everything?"

She pauses, letting me marinate on where her theory is going.

"I never believed it. I always knew there was something more, but it took him dying for me to see the connection. To see you. That's you in the slow motion video. And it was you every single time Victor acted like he was saving the day. *You* are the actual superhero."

Still no evidence. I'm clinging to the hope that she's just moving forward on eerily accurate hunches, which—though it makes me uncomfortable—doesn't threaten to actually reveal me to the gigantic, terrifying, bloodthirsty world.

"I'm really sorry to disappoint you, Maria," I start out. Part of me truly is sorry to disappoint her. If I could share my most intimate secrets with anyone, a beautiful-smelling girl like Maria would be at the top of my list. And even though *Beauty and the Beast* was an inspirational film for me in my awkward teenage years, I think if it were real life the Beast's head would've ended up on a stick way before meeting Belle.

My grandma was the only woman that I could've shared any of these secrets with, but I didn't even trust her with them before she died. Vic was the only person who knew who I was, for better or worse. And now he's dead. I hope that's not a pattern.

But that's not even the reason I don't want Maria to know about me – I just don't want *anyone* to know. I'm happy enough to lurk in the shadows, and no one else getting killed because of me is just an extra benefit.

"Superheroes are muscular and good looking," I say. "They're guys like Vic. He won the genetic lottery, with magical modifiers to boot. God kept rolling natural twenties when He was making Vic's character sheet. Besides, if I were to have powers, how would you explain *him* being the one saving everyone?"

She grabs the pictures that I'm no longer looking at—not that I was ever really looking at them—and drops them into her purse. She shoves her hand in the bag and leaves it in there awkwardly.

"I was wondering if you'd deny it," she says blandly, taking a long breath. She obviously doesn't believe me, which is weird considering how little evidence she actually has. She'd have as much a right to claim that a secret service agent was actually the president because he happened to be around every single time a speech was made.

"I did more digging after I started wondering about you," she said, her heart quickly picking up its pace. She fumbles inside her purse for a moment. "I'm absolutely sure it's you, but I really wanted you to admit it voluntarily."

Voluntarily? Flash a blurry naked picture that *might* be me in front of my eyes, and I'm supposed to feel compelled to divulge all my deepest, darkest secrets? If that's how the world actually operates, then our judicial system has things very wrong.

Which makes her next move so unbelievable.

In the time between speaking her final word and her hand leaving the bag, I notice a change in her scent, as if her pores have opened up to release an alarm pheromone.

She pulls out a gun.

I immediately stand and back away. That's what people usually do when someone draws a gun, right? I've seen plenty of people draw guns, and everybody always seems to move away and brace themselves, as if covering their face with their hand would actually stop a bullet. I've never reacted the same way, though, because not only would my hand stop a bullet, but so would my eye or any other inch of my skin. A strand of my hair would probably make it ricochet.

"What are you doing?" I scream in my best "afraid" voice. I never realized how hard it would be to act like I was afraid of this kind of physical harm. If she were to start calling me dirty names and go for emotional pain, I'd be far more equipped to cower in fear.

I didn't have to fake the surprise, though. I've never had a weapon aimed at me by a friend. As much as I get social anxiety, I've never thought about this scenario being a possibility.

She brings the gun up and aims it at me. In a normal situation, I could easily stroll over to her and remove the firearm before she would have the chance to blink. But I'm not invisible, so that would just confirm her suspicions. And I could obviously move away from any speeding bullet heading my way, but the distance between us is way too small for a normal person to avoid being hit.

The most beautiful smelling girl I've ever known is about to kill me – that is, if I were indeed a normal person. But instead, I need to figure out how I can act as terrified as a normal person would be, even though there's no chance I will even feel a pin prick.

"I'm sorry to do it this way," Maria nervously says with the gun trained on me. Her hand is shaking. "But I know I'm right. I've done all kinds of research and I have no doubt that you're the one with all of Victor Boone's powers. So as soon as I shoot you, you won't be able to lie about it to me anymore."

"Maria," I plead, as I've often heard hostages do. "Please don't do this. You could kill me. You're at least going to send me to the hospital."

The worst part about it is that I know there is nothing I can do. Her scent, heartbeat, and pupil dilation are exactly the same as the hundreds of criminals before who were fully prepared to shoot. They'd never let you know it, but most of them were just as nervous as the fragile woman standing in front of me now.

She pulls the trigger, and I have to stand there and take it.

CHAPTER FOUR

I watch the bullet creep through the barrel of the gun, disrupting the air surrounding it, then crawl through the space between the weapon and myself.

I have a million thoughts. A billion. If I avoid getting shot altogether, my speed would confirm her theory. If I allow myself to get shot, maybe I have a slight chance of faking pain and forcing her out of my apartment, voicing a fear that she is, in fact, a psychopathic killer. I hate to make her feel bad, but she *did* just shoot me.

Sheesh – the bullet still hasn't reached me yet. Should I do a quick search of the apartment to try to find anything that would resemble blood? I could figure out where the bullet would impact my body, cover that spot with ketchup or something, and she would even see a small spatter as I grab the bullet that would invariably tear my shirt before it changes direction. Or would it be safer to do that after it connects with me, so that I can fall backwards? If I'm falling, maybe her eyes will get lost in tracking my movement, which might give me a little leeway. That way it wouldn't seem like my body teleports if I don't make it a perfectly smooth motion.

But who am I kidding – ketchup?

She's so entirely convinced of her theory that she's willing to shoot me. She won't be thrown off by something that happens to be red, but shares no other quality with blood.

Ugh. I've got no ideas. I'm going to have to rely on my acting skills. That's not so terrible – I've tried to act like a normal human being since this whole superpower ordeal happened to me, so maybe I can convince her. I mull it over for a while, but eventually just let the bullet career against my chest.

Her eyes close just before it hits me, so I'm free to grab the bullet before it bounces off me and ricochets all over the room. I fall back, purposely breaking a cheap table standing against the wall to add a bit of drama to the situation. I wait at least a second and feign catching my breath.

"Are you insane?!" I scream, mustering as much of a painful moan as I can. I clutch the supposed wound, which definitely would require an ambulance if my skin weren't stronger than steel. I suppose I could act like I'm dialing 911 as I shoo her away.

She opens one eye with the gun still aimed where I was standing a moment ago. She releases the breath that she's been holding. Obviously she isn't one-hundred percent sure of my powers if she's bracing herself the way she is. She doesn't say anything.

"You just shot me in the chest!" I scream again, writhing in pain on the floor. At least, I hope that's what it looks like.

She finally breaks free from her frozen position and rushes over to me. "Let me see," she says.

"You're crazy," I yell as I turn my body away from her. "Are you planning on shooting me again?"

She looks down at the gun in her hand as if she doesn't realize she's still holding it. She drops it on the hardwood floor and moves her hands toward my chest.

"Get away!" I shout. "You just shot me and now you want to patch my wound? Or do you just want to watch me die as closely as possible?" I don't like being so harsh, but I think it's probably merited in this instance.

"Did it really hurt you?" she asks with surprise.

"Of course it hurt me!" I continue in an irate voice, standing up while bracing myself against the wall. I make an effort to stumble on the broken table and the objects that were once sitting on top of it, to let her know how much of an inconvenience this whole thing is.

"Let me see!" she demands again.

"Get out," I counter, pointing my finger towards the door and trying to remember to take gasping breaths. "Get out or I'm calling the police."

She seems nervous and her heart is racing a mile a minute, but she doesn't move.

"Just let me see and I'll go," she says. "If I really did hurt you, I'll do whatever you want."

"Wow, what a deal," I sarcastically yell. "I didn't realize I could enslave people if I simply let them fatally wound me."

I pick up the cordless landline and the dial tone adds to the chaos of noise I'm making by still kicking against the defunct furniture.

"I'm calling right now," I warn as best I can. "You are absolutely going to jail."

The problem is, now that I've picked up the phone, I've painted myself into a corner. I can't call the cops or an ambulance, because any first responder would want to see my non-existent wound. And she's simply standing there, waiting for me to dial.

"I'm serious, Maria. I haven't seen you in years, and the first thing you do is shoot me. You deserve to be in a prison or a mental institution."

"Just let me see it," she says again, putting her hands firmly on my shoulder.

I shove her away, my fingers hovering above the buttons on the phone. She's calling my bluff. Several seconds go by, and I feel like I'm in a middle-school standoff where I'm yelling "nuh-uh" and she's screaming "uh-huh."

I push buttons, but opt for 611 instead. I don't think landlines can access my phone company's customer service with the number, but that's better than an emergency operator. If someone *does* pick up, I just hope they don't actually transfer me to 911.

"Yes, I've just been shot and the perpetrator is still in my apartment," I say into the receiver, even though it would've taken an operator longer to have truly connected on the other side of the line. I'm still trying to make sure I'm breathing hard and acting like it's difficult to talk. It feels completely unnatural to me, and I have no idea what I look like.

No one is on the line – just silence. That's good. I think about the many 911 calls I've heard either because of my keen ear or because of the radio that the police gave Vic. Running through the standard questions in my head, I give my address and my name.

"The assailant is still in the room with me!" I shout.

Maria just looks at me. Her heart is still beating quickly, but she doesn't move. Instead, she squints a little bit when I say words like "perpetrator" and "assailant." I realize those generally aren't the words people use when they're in fear for their lives.

"A crazy chick just shot me and she's gonna shoot me again," I say as exasperated as possible. "She's still got a gun and I'm about to die!"

She doesn't budge, even though her heartbeat and breathing tell me she's terrified.

I have no idea what to do. This is my greatest fear: she has figured out my secret and in less than twenty-four hours, all of the cameras in the city will be at my doorstep. I am no longer invisible.

A short three-tone melody comes through the receiver with the standard "We're sorry, but your call could not be completed as dialed." I glance at her, and she definitely heard it.

I sigh and just stand there long enough for the message to play twice, telling me to try the call again.

"Why did you do that?" I ask, motioning towards the gun as I put the phone back in its charging stand.

She looks at me with those terrible, beautiful green eyes.

"Because I'm sure it's you."

I shake my head as I drop my hand, revealing a slight tear in my shirt where a bullet wound should be. I drop the crumpled projectile from my fingers and it echoes through my head as it makes a metallic thump against the wooden floor.

"But what if I didn't have superpowers?" I ask, defeated.

Her eyes widen. As she takes in the lack of a bloody wound, her mouth drops open. She immediately celebrates by jumping up and down, squealing, "I knew it, I knew it!"

She runs around the room for a moment before hugging me. It's wonderful, but I'm too scared of what it all means to really enjoy it.

"What if I didn't have superpowers?" I ask again. "I'd be dead right now."

She has a huge smile on her face and tries to contain her excitement as she answers me.

"I wasn't going to kill you," she says, playfully smacking my arm. "If worse came to worse, I would've just hurt your shoulder really bad and then drove you to the hospital."

"You shot me in the chest," I exclaim. "You would've hit a lung, and you were really close to hitting my heart!"

"Oh," she says, trying to stop smiling. She only manages to bring it down to a smirk. "I meant to shoot you in the shoulder."

"How many times have you shot that thing?" I ask. "You'd better be glad you were right, because your aim is terrible."

"Never," she responds, having trouble containing herself. "That's the first time."

That makes more sense as to why I couldn't smell the gun before she pulled it out of her purse. She'd never fired it, so I couldn't smell any gunpowder, and any metallic scents would've been explained away by keys and coins. Then again, I was definitely distracted by her perfume.

"Don't ever shoot it again," I demand. "What could I have said to you so that you wouldn't have shot me? Tell you I'm a super hero? What if you were wrong?"

"But I was right," she says, slipping back into her celebratory dance. Even though I'm in a huge predicament, her performance is very cute.

"I'd still call the police for them to take you away," I say, "but I think the only evidence I could give them for your insanity is your dancing. And I'm not sure that's a prosecutable offense."

<**••>

After several minutes of Maria assuring me that she won't tell anyone, she spends several more minutes asking me to do tricks like a newly trained puppy. She thought it was hilarious that I could turn myself invisible, but couldn't do anything to change the transparency of my clothes.

It got a little awkward when she asked the specifics, finding out that Vic had actually been riding a naked man each time "he" was flying around, with only a thin layer of spandex separating us. I had sworn to him that I would never tell anyone that particular detail, but since he was dead I didn't feel the need to protect his secret anymore.

She actually asked me if it was okay if she recorded the conversation, but then her face told me she realized how silly of a question it was, considering it was only moments after she said she wouldn't tell anyone. I never doubted that Vic would keep my identity hidden, because otherwise everyone would discover he was a sham. I have no such confidence with Maria. She has nothing to lose by revealing who I am. I merely have to trust her. And that's not something I'm very good at.

Though it makes me incredibly uncomfortable, I'm relieved to have someone to talk to. The powers came after my parents died, and I never told my grandma about them before she passed away. The only person that ever knew about me was Vic, and he made it abundantly clear that he wasn't the type to have emotional conversations.

Maybe I really can trust Maria. As long as she doesn't try to shoot anyone else.

Currently, we're sitting in the swivel chairs, staring awkwardly at each other. At least, I'm staring awkwardly. She looks more like she's a supermodel ready for me to take her picture, totally at ease with herself. That's something I envied about Victor. Not the chiseled good looks, but the confidence of not worrying about what someone else was thinking.

"So what are you going to do?" she asks.

I'm a little confused because I feel like that's more of a question I need to be asking her. Even though she promised me that my secret's safe with her, she *is* a journalist who has been looking for a way to get her name out there. And this *is* the story that she was obsessed with for years.

"What do you mean *me?*" I respond. "You're the one that holds the cards at this point. You're the one that has to decide what you're going to do."

She shakes her head.

"No," she says adamantly. "I already told you that I won't tell anybody. You don't have to worry about me. What I mean is, what are you going to do about the city?"

I glance outside the window, briefly focusing on the vast landscape of buildings, streets, and bustling activity. I hear a lot of horns, a few screams and a single gunshot before I quickly bring my focus back into the room.

"I don't understand," I say.

"It was never Victor Boone," she says, leaning towards me. "It was always you. He took the credit, but you were the one saving all of those people, keeping the peace out there. The city has fallen apart without you, and it desperately needs you back."

"It doesn't need me," I quickly respond. "I can't control myself. I get people killed. Heck, I kill people. They're much better off without me."

Maria looks at me with a stone cold seriousness, her eyes open wide.

"You didn't kill Vic, and it was completely his choice to put himself in harm's way," she reassures me. "I know that he was stubborn enough to do whatever he wanted, no matter what you told him. It's not like you forced him to put on that suit."

"Maybe," I slightly agree, "but I did kill that robber. The one that shot Vic."

She puts her hand on mine. It's something that seems to have happened a lot in the last hour or so, but it still gives me jitters.

"Robby. How long have you been doing this? Three or Four years?"

I nod. I was eighteen when Victor Boone donned the spandex suit and I'm twenty-one now. I did a few small "heroic" things before that point, but nothing like what we did together, after he unveiled himself.

"I'm not trying to dismiss what happened," she continues, "and like I said – journalists aren't the most reliable when it comes to ethics… But it was an accident. I'm pretty sure any judge or jury would see that as self defense, or at least temporary insanity. You spend so much of your time holding back your powers, and the guy just murdered your best friend right in front of you."

"That doesn't make it okay, Maria."

She doesn't understand. It would be incredibly easy for me to kill people just by bumping into them. Maybe I *am* just a killer, and my natural state is destroying everything I touch. Maybe I could control myself before now, but I'm one step away from being a supervillain. Maybe this is how they always start. Maybe *this* is my origin story, rather than—

"I didn't say it was okay, Robby," Maria says, interrupting my self-loathing thoughts. "I'm just saying that one mistake doesn't mean you should throw away being a hero. A lot of people would've died if you weren't there to save them. A lot of people are dying now."

I shrug. I guess she's right to a certain degree – I can't stand the thought of innocents paying for my crime, but they're the same ones that I could put into danger by trying to be a hero again.

"What do you think about seeing a therapist?" she suggests. "Not to say that I'm not willing to help out – I absolutely am. I just don't know what I can say or do with some of this. They're legally obligated to keep quiet. I just think the city really needs you, so maybe talking with someone like that would get you out there faster. I'm happy to walk through all of this with you, though. From here on out, we're a team."

Great. Just what I need. Another beautiful partner.

CHAPTER FIVE

I'm in the room again.

Fire licks the white walls and the remaining fluorescent bulbs explode in the ceiling, one right after another. Everything is too blurry for me to really concentrate on anything specific. Metal surfaces reflect the dancing light all around the room, and I feel like I'm spinning. I should be hot with all of the flames surrounding me, but for some reason I don't feel any heat at all.

I finally see my dad, though he's barely in focus. He's yelling something – I can't tell what. My ears aren't working right; I just hear a high-pitched ringing.

He grabs me and drags me between the burning surfaces, and before I know it, I'm in the glass cage. I'm staring at him as he slowly mouths the words, *I love you, buddy.*

I jerk forward in bed, sweating even more than I do normally. It's always the same nightmare – the same fire, the same steps dragging across the smooth floor, the same glass cage. When I try to concentrate on remembering it, more and more of it disappears.

I know it actually happened – that it's really just a memory. But the only time my mind can recall any details about it is when I'm asleep. When I'm awake it's just something that I'm supposed to remember but can't. It's like an object that I can see in the periphery of my vision, but as soon as my eyes dart towards its direction it disappears.

It's the last time I saw my parents.

I look over to where the glowing red numbers on my night stand should be and realize that I'm not actually in bed. Rather, I'm hovering a few feet above it. Instinctively, I lower myself onto the mattress and the red digits move into view.

It's 2:14 AM.

I don't need nearly as much sleep as a normal person, but I wish that I could at least *relax* for a whole night. Between the dreams about burning rooms when I'm asleep, and the visions of Vic's forehead exploding when I'm awake, actual rest isn't generally on the menu.

I roll, kicking my feet over the edge of the bed onto the floor. I sit up for a minute, just staring at the dark room subtly illuminated by the glowing red digits. The numbers tell me that almost everyone else in the city is somewhere deep in a dream. I'm alone.

It's when my realities collide, because the truth is I'm always alone. But at least at 2:14 AM – wait, 2:15 AM – I'm not avoiding people in order to be isolated. If it were 2:15 PM, I would be alone because I've holed myself up in my apartment, and because there isn't a single person in the world that even knows or cares that I'm here. As long as my bills are paid, I could sit in here for a decade before a maintenance worker would come in to check on some leaky pipe or something.

I tell myself that it's what I want, but I'm not so good at believing me. When invisibility showed up along with the other powers, I thought it was the greatest perk. Not only could I avoid conversations by ducking around corners like I did in middle school, but there came a welcome day when I could truly not be seen.

The loneliness was even worse that way, though. I couldn't avoid the temptation to see what everyone else thought of me. Eavesdropping on even the people that I thought liked me revealed that they, too, talked about how weird I was. Twenty-one year-old me understands that the secret words of twelve-year-olds shouldn't have a catastrophic affect on someone's self worth. But twelve-year-old me couldn't handle it.

Of course they talked about me. Both of my parents were killed in front of me and I emerged without a scratch. My grandma was way too overprotective and overbearing and wouldn't let me out of her sight. When everyone else was eventually old enough and confident enough to drive, she even got a job as a lunch lady so that I wouldn't have to ride the bus – though her health and vision should have prevented her from having a license.

God knows I had enough money to buy a car. A nice one. The substantial life insurance policies from both of my parents ensured Grandma and I would never need to worry about money as long as I didn't go on some pre-emptive midlife crisis spending spree. But I didn't want people to notice me, and an Aston Martin or Porsche wasn't exactly a means to that end.

Instead, I slipped further into isolation. I eventually convinced her that I could educate myself better than the public school system. She even agreed to legally emancipate me, because her worsening health meant I was the one taking care of her rather than the other way around.

When grandma died two months after my seventeenth birthday, I had no one. I had more than most could dream of—millions of dollars and an ever-growing list of super powers—but I didn't have a single friend. I was completely alone.

I guess that's why I didn't push Victor away. Even though he was terrible and selfish, and only stuck around because of what he could gain from me, at least I had someone I could call a friend. Someone who would stick around no matter how weird I might be.

But now, once again, I am completely alone.

I finally stand up and make my way into the kitchen, not bothering to turn on a light because my low-light vision shows me everything by the faintest glow of the moon coming in through the windows. I turn to my left while still in the living room and notice the broken table.

Wait—

Oh, yeah. Maria. That part wasn't a dream.

Maybe I can try to have another friend, but I'm not sure if I can let her into my thoughts. It's darker in my head than anywhere else in the world. And while I was okay with Victor leeching off of me, I'm not sure what she has to gain from it. Yet.

Sheesh. Maybe she's right... Maybe a therapist isn't such a bad idea. Maybe a professional can help me get through the baggage I keep carrying around about Vic. Maybe they could even help me process my nightmares so I could take a nap without waking up to my own screaming in a sea of perspiration.

I had a therapist after my parents died – Grandma insisted on it. He was actually really cool, but I don't remember telling him much of anything. I figured that even he would laugh at me if I told him about the fact that my skin was so strong that I couldn't pop a pimple, or that scissors would break when trying to cut my hair, or that starving myself for a week wouldn't reduce my weight by a single ounce.

Instead, we talked a lot about me becoming comfortable with who I was. Fat chance. Though he did have good intentions, as far as I could tell.

What was his name? Harris? Hill? It was definitely a one-syllable word that started with an H. He was nice, and if I remember right, he worked with my dad's company on some stuff. Not that I understood any of it at the time – he was just the guy that Grandma took me to see until I could get "better."

I grab one of the two-liter bottles of cherry cola from the fridge and take a few large gulps on the way to my computer. I turn on the screen, flooding white light into the room when it finally wakes up from its own sleep. Once I'm on the internet I search for therapists in the city, then narrow it by where I vaguely remember his office being.

"Joe!" I say out loud.

The image of Joseph Hughes, PhD, PsyD, looks exactly like I remember him; it actually spreads a sense of calm behind my eyes, as if the sight of the man flushed away the pressure my sinus cavity had previously held. For all I know, the picture could've been taken almost a decade ago when I was seeing him regularly, and he refused to update it because of graying hair or a wrinkling face. But, whether or not he still looks the same, maybe I have another friend. After all, he did tell me to call him by his first name, and that made me feel pretty cool as a twelve-year-old.

All right. I guess I'm doing this.

I take a deep breath to brace myself for having to talk to someone on the phone. I would send an email, but paranoia prevents me from wanting to leave an electronic paper trail for just about anything – especially if it could be used to prove my special circumstances.

I pick up the phone, slowly dial the number on the screen, and am immediately met with an answering machine. Of course I would – it's two in the morning.

After I hear the beep, I start mumbling. "Uh… Hi… Uh… This is Robby Willis. I, uh… I used to see Joe – er – Dr. Hughes a long time ago. I'd like to come back in as soon as I can…?"

I rattle off my number and the flexibility of my schedule, which is all day, every day. Then I silently stay on the line a little too long, wondering if I missed any information that I should be giving. After I'm sufficiently awkward, I hang up with a rushed thanks.

I didn't even think about it, but I guess I'm going to be leaving the apartment fully dressed and visible. I should do some laundry.

<**●●●●>

I step out into the moonlight, taking a moment to quiet my senses. I suck in a deep breath, noting all of the differences between my apartment and the air outside. It's not completely different, though I suppose I've gotten used to blocking it out a little better while I'm within my familiar walls.

The smells are more pervasive. The moonlight covers the smallest cracks in the pavement, confirming that this outside world is worn and dangerous. A gentle breeze carries random noises to me: sounds of distant gas engines, hungry animals scrounging through garbage, and electric switches changing traffic lights from red to green and back again.

I glance at the Vs spray-painted on several alleyway walls, wishing Vic's mourners would express themselves in less destructive ways.

Maria told me—or *urged* me, as she put it—to get outside. She was insistent that my few grocery trips were not enough to keep me connected to the city that she swears needs me.

"You've been cooped up in here for too long," she'd said the evening before. "You should remind yourself what's out there. Not as a superhero – just as a normal guy."

That's easy for her to say. But after I refused and whined a plethora of excuses, it became clear that the best thing I could do was comply. However, we didn't lay out the stipulations.

As a result, I'll just take another leisurely invisible stroll through the quiet streets at three o'clock in the morning. She didn't explicitly tell me that I couldn't be transparent, though it's obvious that's what she meant. As it is, the worst thing that could happen is I stumble upon a stray dog who growls and barks at the air that I'm filling. At least I'll be able to tell her truthfully that I did what I said I would do.

My bare feet are silent against the concrete sidewalk, despite the several hundred pounds of force that should be behind them. I've always been self conscious about my weight, so a long time ago I decided to fake the art of walking. Even though I certainly connect with the ground, I defy gravity enough so that I'm about as forceful as a falling flower petal. My body might not look any different, but at least the kids in my middle school stopped saying that my steps shook pictures off of walls. Which, of course, they did.

Ironically, looking at all of my powers, the ones I'm most thankful for are those that allow me to go unnoticed. Most people would think of billions of possibilities with flying, invisibility, and invincibility. But personally, my first thoughts were quiet steps, hiding from everyone, and not feeling a bully's fists when I couldn't avoid them without raising suspicion.

Speaking of bullies, I hear a gruff voice from a few streets over. It's obvious by his slurred words that he's drunk, even before I smell the cheap vodka.

"...you ssstupid bum," the man says. "Jus' stealing from hard working people...like me. With your stupid cardboard... stupid cardboard signs."

I'm there before he finishes his beautiful poetry.

The voice belongs to a man in his mid-thirties who looks like he's had a rough run-in with the rat race. His untucked blue dress shirt is somewhat unbuttoned, and his striped tie is loosened so that it's hanging freely on both sides of his chest. He tightly grips a flask, but considering how much still remains inside of it, it must be his dessert after whatever he'd been drinking at a bar for the previous few hours.

He's standing over a pile of newspaper blankets. Under the rustling periodicals, I can hear a racing heartbeat and uneven breathing. I hear fear.

Maybe the drunk businessman is just having a bad day, I try to convince myself. Perhaps he got laid off, or his girlfriend cheated on him, or some other event that justifies his misery. Maybe he had one drink to unwind and simply got caught up in drowning said sorrow when that glass needed a refill. We all lose control a little sometimes, right?

Heck, I'm no saint – I murdered a man.

But something about alcohol seems to bring out a person's soul. It washes away the filter that most people build up over time, so that when it's in charge it just gives the world a front row seat to who you really are.

And this guy is a bully.

He kicks the homeless man in the head.

I wince along with the victim. I might not be able to feel that kind of physical pain anymore, but my empathy is strong enough, and it makes me angry. It reminds me of the days before my powers, when each fist or foot could bring me to tears – not because I was emotionally crushed.

I could've stopped him. This guy is drunk enough that he might not have even realized an invisible hero intervened. But what if I can't stop *myself?* What if this guy pushes some button inside me and it sets me off again?

He continues with a handful of slurred words that even I can't understand, each taking longer and longer.

"You hear me?" the belligerent man rambles. "I said you're stupid! And worthless. And... and stupid!"

I mean, I don't *think* I would snap, but I can't trust myself. I feel something warm bubbling up in my chest. There's not much worse than a bully picking on someone helpless. Maybe I should just get out of here. Maybe he'll leave on his own.

But the drunk guy pulls his foot back again, preparing for a second kick.

Crap. What should I do? I can go back home and sulk about how I can't change anything without hurting people, knowing that an innocent guy is being beaten because of my inaction. Or I can get involved, knowing that I might lose my cool. And even if this man is a bully, he hasn't yet done anything that is deserving of the full wrath I could unleash.

But as the foot starts swinging towards its target, I realize I can't let him do this.

The warm bubbling in my chest grows, spilling through my ribs and reaching into my arms and legs with its tentacles. It's as if my heart is sending a signal to the rest of my body that *this* man is the reason for all of the hurt in the world. For all of the hurt that I experienced as a kid, and everything since.

I'm on the verge of losing control. I barrel through the air, my eyes fixed on his scuffed, evil dress shoe, knowing I could easily remove the leg from the socket it belongs to. I'm parallel to the ground as the foot moves towards my trap, completely unaware of what is waiting for it.

It connects with the back of my head.

I lie down beside the shaking homeless man, crinkling the newspaper and cardboard that is his bed. The drunk guy is silent for a moment – possibly because he could see that his foot hit a strange immovable space about a foot away from his victim.

"What the..." the unsteady voice says above me.

I don't want to look at him. I can't guarantee that his frustration with not causing pain won't affect me. Instead, I just lie there and listen to the nervous heart of my fellow outcast.

The shoe strikes the back of my body in multiple places, each time garnering an incoherent scream from the drunk man when he realizes he's not hurting the homeless man. He is obviously angry, but like a child having a temper tantrum he seems to exhaust himself.

"Freak," the bully slurs. "Not worth my time anyway."

He stumbles through the alley as if it was his own idea to quit. He mumbles unintelligibly even after he's a block away.

The heartbeat beside me slows down, and the breathing turns into a few fragile sniffs. Maybe Maria is right again.

Maybe there are some people out here who could use a little help. Even if it doesn't come from a guy that looks like Victor.

"You're safe tonight," I whisper as uncreepily as I can.

The homeless man quickly turns his head in my direction, unable to find the source of my voice. He stares for a moment—obviously spooked—then darts his watering eyes around and up toward the sky.

"Thank you, Jesus," he sobs.

I'm sure he wouldn't feel quite as safe if he were to realize the comforting voice came from an invisible naked man lying fairly close beside him. But I decide not to correct his thought process.

He rearranges the papers on his body and falls into a comfortable sleep.

CHAPTER SIX

I open the door before Maria gets a chance to knock, which causes her to jump.

"Oh—sorry," I say.

Between cleaning up my apartment and myself, I'd been focusing a bit too much on listening for her footsteps in the hallway. She was three minutes later than she said she'd be, which felt a bit like an eternity. Or, at least it felt more like *twenty* minutes. I was starting to get afraid that she decided against showing up, and simply sold the story to some major media conglomerate. But she's here.

Waiting is not one of my powers. Unfortunately, I tend to slow time down too often – even if I don't really want to. As a result, I've learned a number of things that can sometimes help me pass the time. Sometimes.

I'd been tidying my apartment out of nervousness, and it stopped smelling like the vanilla and coconut mixture at least an hour ago. I was relieved to smell the source again. Could it be that I now have two weaknesses?

"It's okay," she says, holding her beautiful hand against her visible collarbone in surprise. I try not to stare in that direction. Her heart tells me next time I should wait and let her knock. If there will be a next time. I don't know how long she'll be interested enough to come back. I need to make sure not to blow this.

I move out of the way and she walks across the threshold, heading straight to the swivel chairs. She adjusts the collar of her thin jacket, causing a shift in fabric and her shoulder-length curls. The motion stirs the scent up to me. Luckily, I don't have to sniff her hair awkwardly in order to get the full affect.

"Didn't you break that yesterday?" she asks curiously as she puts her purse on the floor. She motions toward the fully-assembled piece of furniture against the wall.

"Oh – yeah," I say as we both sit down. I consider the morning I've already had.

After the homeless man fell asleep, I hovered above him to confirm that there were no more threats in the area. When I was satisfied with the silence, I ran—er, flew—a couple of errands. First I got a new table from the big box store about 20 miles away. I'm sure someone would be confused if they saw the brown package launch straight up in the air at the backdoor of the store, or drop down again at my apartment. But in my experience, most people don't look up. Especially not before the sun comes up.

A little later, still under the cover of darkness, I took a sandwich and a couple hundred dollars to the lonely drifter underneath the newspapers. I thought about simply leaving it, but I was afraid it would be gone before he woke up. I made subtle bird sounds, but that didn't stir him, so I knocked over a trash can lid. It didn't take long for him to find the loot, and he mumbled another thankful prayer with a mouth full of hoagie.

"I got another table when I was out this morning," I continued, swiveling to look at it. "It's the exact same model. I'm not too fashionable, and you're only the second guest I've had here since—"

"Good, so you got out this morning!" she interrupted with a smile.

"Yeah," I said, still looking at the table with my body turned away from her.

"How did it feel to have people see you out and about?"

Gaahh. I thought I'd be able to follow her literal request without any questions.

"Um, it was early," I stammered, still looking away. "I don't think anyone saw me."

She stood up and struggled to swivel my chair to face her before sitting back down.

"What did you wear?"

Hmmm…

"Uh – a suit?"

Ha! Surely she won't know how to pin me down after that.

"Oh really?" she asks, deadpan. "Can I see it?"

Crap. She's a lot quicker than Victor ever was. Not that he was interested in any of my questions or answers. I'm not thinking very quickly today. Or my blushing cheeks gave me away.

"I don't think you want to. It's… It's my birthday suit."

"Robby!" she says as she feigns anger and smacks my shoulder. "I thought we agreed yesterday that you'd go outside *visible?*"

"Well, we didn't actually specify that part," I mumble as I look away. I'm not really sure why it matters so much that I get outside.

"Well, you're dressed now," she says, grabbing the purse that she put on the floor only a minute or so before. "Let's go."

"What?" I ask. "I did what you said – I got outside."

"Yeah," she answers, "but lurking around invisible isn't exactly what I had in mind. What do you have on your calendar today anyhow?"

I grunt. I guess *she's* the only thing on my schedule, and she's already here.

A few minutes later, we're on the sidewalk. The smells surround me again, competing with the vanilla-coconut mix. I don't like that. My nose is filled with freshly baked pastries, every kind of flower imaginable, and a baby's incredibly dirty diaper.

The sounds of my fat footsteps match the volume of her tiny ones, but the vibrations of the city in my ears are much louder than our shoes. I hear countless car horns, screeching tires, and drivers rolling their windows down to scream and extend fingers. I listen to a shopkeeper spraying the sidewalk with a water hose a few blocks away, trying to clean up a present left behind by someone's very large pet.

Worse than my own senses, though, is the fact that everyone else can observe me with theirs. Other eyes can see me.

She grabs my arm, as if we're entering a fancy dinner party. How am I supposed to focus on the city when all I can do is hope that I don't gross her out by sweating on her? Her grip is soft and invigorating, but somewhat suffocating.

"So, have you thought anymore about a therapist?" she asks, as if everything is normal.

"Uh, yeah," I stammer, swallowing hard and trying to avoid looking at her hand on my flabby bicep. "I've got an appointment later this week."

"Robby, that's great!" she exclaims as she squeezes my arm, looking directly into my eyes. Her green irises catch the sun and they make me lose my breath for a moment.

We take a few more steps. I try to remember the last time I was visible in front of other people. I think I convinced myself that it was only since Vic died that I shut myself up in my apartment, but I realize that no one else had seen me for months before that. Even deliveries from the internet would be left in the empty hallway in front of my door, never requiring a signature.

I was used to patrolling the city, listening and watching for someone in need, but always invisible. Sometimes I would just take care of things on my own, when it didn't require a physical presence. I tripped many a mugger – sometimes multiple times before they gave up; I broke the chain of a family's dog if a burglar was trying to break in their home; I'd give abuse victims a much stronger defensive punch than they'd normally be able to deliver. Those involved would chalk it up to adrenaline or divine intervention.

The only times I would swing by and get Vic was when I would be forced to make my presence known. Bank robberies, police shootouts – any crime that was obscenely public. Vic would sometimes get upset that I interrupted whatever date he was on, or whatever sport he was watching, but he always had the suit on underneath. I'm surprised he ever wore any other clothes on top of it.

But after the chaos had ceased, I'd eat dinner in my apartment in my underwear. Victor had become so famous that I felt like I couldn't show my face, just in case someone could place us together. So even when he wasn't around, I was paranoid about being seen.

Wow – I'm worse than I thought.

"So at least half of what I said yesterday is getting through, then?" she says with a nudge, breaking my thoughts.

"Only what you said at gunpoint," I say.

She laughs.

"Seriously, though," I continue. "I still don't know how you were confident enough that you were willing to kill me to find out."

Her smile disappears and she looks away. Her heart starts to speed up slightly.

"I'm not exactly proud of doing that," she says. "And I don't know what I would've done if I was wrong. But for some reason I knew I was right. I didn't come to your apartment right after having a revelation – I'd been sitting on the hunch for at least a month. I dug up everything I could; at first so I could prove it, and then so I could try to disprove it.

"I was too excited when I originally realized it. Everything I found told me I might be right, so I knew that I was starting to get too biased, gathering evidence for something I wanted to be true. When I looked for anything to tell me I was wrong, I ran into a wall. It was as if you dropped off the face of the earth after college. You don't even have a driver's license. And almost everything I found was related to Vic, like phone calls and stuff."

"What?" I ask, stopping in my tracks. "Did you really pull my phone records?"

Maria looks down, her heart running a marathon while her feet stand still.

"I'm sorry, Robby," she says with regret. "Like I said, I got a bit obsessive."

At first I'm slightly ticked off. But I can sense how scared and nervous she is, and realize that in a strange way it might be the nicest thing someone could have done for me. In a *really* strange way. And I guess I can't stay mad at her for trying to find the truth.

I start walking again.

"That's a little weird," I say, trying not to sound too accusatory.

"Yeah, I know," she nods, her pace matching mine. "I've got friends who are detectives, so it isn't too crazy for me to do that kind of research. But I've never done it on a friend."

I don't know how to respond to that. It's nice to be called a friend, even by someone who apparently stalked me.

"That's how I found your apartment, too," she continues. "You don't have hardly anything in your name. Except for the apartment, your utilities... And your house."

I stop again. Crap, she really did do her research.

"You know about the house?"

"I... I had to be sure," she says. "I went through public records when I found your parents' names, and I couldn't just sit on the information while I was figuring all this stuff out. So, about a week ago I—"

Suddenly, a distant voice cuts through and distracts me from our conversation.

"...*has threatened drastic harm unless his demands are met...*"

"Wait," I say, putting my hand up to cut her off. "Something is wrong."

Not here – a block or two away. Or – no, not even there, but on a television.

"...*taken credit for much of the turmoil in the city over the last several months...*"

The voice is shaky.

"We've got to get to a TV. There's a reporter talking about something very—" I interrupt myself, realizing I don't have much of a story from the words I've heard so far. But it has the news anchor upset, and that isn't a common occurrence. They can talk about car wrecks and mass murders without flinching, often with smiles on their faces. "Well, I don't quite know, but whatever it is, it's important."

Maria looks at me dumbfounded for a moment, possibly wondering if I'm just changing the subject to avoid what she obviously knows is painful.

"*...when our station received the video, about thirty minutes ago...*"

"Who's the reporter?" Maria says as she pulls her phone from her purse. No gun today.

"Gar Wexler, I think."

"*...threatening to attack any station that does not play it at exactly 9:30...*"

She types on her phone and I glance up at a clock hanging in a shop window. 9:29am. It probably doesn't matter which live news feed she brings up – they're all likely to be cueing up the same video.

"*I repeat – the message might be frightening for some of our younger viewers, so please use your judgment if children are present.*"

Maria hands me the phone just as Gar's face disappears and is replaced by a dimly lit blank head. The new face has no descriptive features – smooth skin covers where there should be eyes, nose and lips. The scalp is bald, and no hair is present where eyebrows would usually appear. Ears are replaced by two bulgy stumps. There is absolutely no life in the humanoid object. I assume it's simply a picture of some prop until the jaw extends and words are formed from a flesh-covered mouth.

"Greetings fair city," the head announces in a scratchy, distorted voice that makes me believe that he's smiling despite his monotone delivery. I hear the words echoing through the streets on every radio and TV station pumping through the airways.

"I'd like to introduce you to your new master. You may call me *The Vacant*. And if you don't bow to me, I'll kill everyone you love."

CHAPTER SEVEN

I'm fidgeting in a wood and leather chair, watching each second tick by on the clock in the waiting room of Dr. Hughes' office. There's a married couple in the opposite corner – the man flipping through a magazine and the woman looking at her phone. Both seem to have permanent scowls on their faces, and it's obvious that neither is very excited to be here. The receptionist is chewing and popping extremely loudly on her bubble gum, as if I wasn't already about to go in to see a therapist.

The Vacant's message had the entire city on edge over the last several days, as one could expect, but I haven't yet seen many other changes besides fear. No noticeable rise in crime, no increase in screams late at night. The news stations are actually reporting *less* crime, but Maria found out through a friend that each program's producer was given a very individualized threat involving their family. She didn't yet know which stories were being censored or completely kept from being aired, but it was quite obvious from the anchors' faces that they weren't about to step out of line.

Around 9:35am on the day of the message, I heard an explosion in the distance. I flew as quickly as I could to find a tiny local AM radio station that had been blown to smithereens, as they had opted to ignore the threats and play their regularly scheduled jazz fusion program. The station manager, who was taking a smoke break in the parking lot, had barely survived the blast and is still on life support. His entire family, on the other hand, was found dead in their home that afternoon. Something tells me that single incident would be enough to cause the media industry to never question whatever the faceless head might threaten in the future. If he was so merciless with an *AM station* of all things, he would definitely not spare the more influential.

Maria found out that the police were quietly searching all stations for explosives, speculating they'd all been rigged in case they hadn't aired the message. There was simply not enough time for a maniac to get a bomb to a station that hadn't played the clip only a few minutes earlier. Everyone started assuming that each building was only a button push away from destruction at all times.

The Vacant gave a fairly standard speech, I guess. I've only seen such things in comic books or movies, so I'm wondering if he's simply borrowing theatrics from some of those. Low lighting, weird costume, strained distortion in his voice... Even the "The" in his name felt a little campy. The only way he could have been more predictable is if he called himself *Doctor* Vacant.

The biggest takeaway from his message was that he was the one responsible for the death of Victor Boone, and he'd been orchestrating a number of large-scale crimes in order to do so. He said it matter-of-factly, probably to let everyone know what he's capable of.

Unfortunately, it makes sense. During the bank robbery when Vic was killed, there were too many things that were out of the ordinary: zip-tied hands, none of the thugs running once the beatings began, triggers pulled well after it was obvious they were all going to end up behind bars. They weren't there for the money, they were there to draw Vic—er, me—out. Maybe this guy somehow found out that the great Victor Boone was only human. Or maybe he was simply okay experimenting with numerous henchmen's lives to find out if he had a weakness.

After all, if The Vacant was controlling them from behind a faceless curtain, he didn't have to fear jail time, even if one of the thugs talked. They would sound like babbling idiots and would end up in a chair similar to the one I'm sitting in now. The difference is that they'd be wearing a fancy white coat that made them hug themselves.

"Mr. Willis?" a woman announces after walking through the door that separates the crazies like me from the guys with big desks and expensive degrees. It's fairly obvious from her posture and voice that she doesn't want to be working.

"Yeah," I mutter as I stand, making my way over to her.

"Dr. Hughes will see you now," she says, also smacking on chewing gum. What is it with this office? Have they no sympathy for sensitive ears?

My mind wanders as I walk through the long, bare hallway with doors leading to people whispering their deepest, darkest secrets. Unfortunately, I can hear what every single patient and therapist is saying. That is perhaps one encouragement; there are several people in the clinic that might be even more depressing than I am.

A few of the conversations are of how worried the subjects are about the appearance of The Vacant; how they're quite sure the villain is watching their every move and targeting them specifically. There's even one person who's terrified that she actually *is* The Vacant, but—from the sound of her voice—she has to be at least eighty years old. I'm pretty sure her heart would be too frail to take on the stress of what he's already done. Not to mention the therapist has reminded her of her own name a couple of times.

The Vs spray-painted through the city apparently aren't a tribute to Vic – rather they're a marker of where The Vacant has claimed territory. They're everywhere now.

Maria has been trying to dig up any consistent connections with some of the previous criminal shenanigans. So far, all she has come up with are dead end trails of digital currency and decentralized asset exchanges. But, the fact that almost all of them revealed similar internet-money rabbit trails is enough for her "hunch" meter to rev back up again. At least she's not looking further into *me* this time. I mean, I don't think she is.

She's a much better detective than me, apparently. Not that I've tried to delve too much into that realm. I generally just leave that side of things to the somewhat-capable legal system, and I'd only poke my nose in if things were starting to look like a very guilty person was about to be declared innocent. And even then, I would just nudge actual detectives to the truth.

Vic's death wasn't the only crime scene that had seemed strange. In previous stickups, there were increasing numbers of criminals who made things a bit too easy for me. Henchmen who didn't act as if they were totally committed to their heist, but more as if they were just doing what their boss told them to do. No conviction. I assumed that their boss was whoever was in the room running the operation. I didn't realize it was a lollipop made of skin.

But however the scenarios played out, still my actions were the ones that put Vic in front of the guns. Even if The Vacant was training all of his efforts on the supposed superhero, it was my own insecurity that allowed it to happen.

Heck, I should have known something was up a few months back, when a *hostage* pulled a knife on Victor after we thought the ordeal was over. Vic didn't even know it had happened until I whispered it in his ear, so that he didn't look like an idiot when the girl he tried to make out with unexpectedly flew across the room.

"She was in my blonde spot," he'd explained with a shrug and a goofy grin when we talked about it back at his apartment. "You know my eyes get a little screwy when one of them sexy, golden-haired chicks catches my eye. You can't blame me for not seeing that one coming."

"Okay, but why did she *attack* you?" I'd reasoned with him. "Why did she have a knife in the first place? She was the hostage. All of the gunmen had already been knocked out, and she had absolutely nothing to gain. She had to know that cameras were on her."

"Pfft. Everybody wants a piece of this," Vic said while slowly moving his hand across his chest like a game show model presenting a state-of-the-art vacuum cleaner. "Maybe she just wanted it a little more than most ladies. Who am I to judge a Victor Boone fetish?"

The conversation wasn't very fruitful.

The supposed hostage ended up committing suicide in a hospital room only two days later. I had assumed she'd killed herself because she regretted the attack, or at least because she knew that she'd always be known as the crazy woman who tried to kill a superhero who "saved" her. After that point, there were rumblings that she was an accomplice from the beginning, but nothing was ever confirmed by the rest of the imprisoned thugs. Something tells me Maria will find a money trail leading to her as well – or to her family, more likely.

The gum-chewing assistant who is guiding me through the hallway stops at a door and says, "Right this way." She opens it then motions me through.

I enter the dimly lit room, flanked by books and framed degrees on all sides. White noise is playing softly from a sound machine near the door, but it doesn't drown out any of the other frequencies in my head. The furniture is almost the same as it was ten years ago – a thick mahogany desk, multiple leather chairs, plus an updated plush couch. The only other difference is the amount of white in Dr. Hughes' hair and beard.

"Robby!" the doctor announces as he stands from behind his desk and makes his way toward me. "Great to see you again!"

I reach out for a handshake, but he swings his arms open and hugs me. Not the typical greeting from a therapist, I assume. But I don't have experiences with any other such professionals to base it on.

"Hi, Dr. Hughes," I say, slightly uncomfortable from being hugged. But at the same time, it *is* actually comforting. I hadn't smelled the blend of Old Spice and old books in a long time. It reminds me of my dad. Just *seeing* him reminds me of my dad.

"Goodness, no," he reprimands me as he leans back, still keeping his palm on my shoulder. "It is, and always will be, *Joe* to you."

"Uh... Okay," I mumble. "Good to see you too, Joe."

I suppose a part of me wants to stay a little detached. But another part of me would prefer if the embrace were to continue. The familiarity of the room is already making me feel more vulnerable than I expected.

"Please, please – sit down," Joe says as he motions towards the couch and takes a step to the nearby chair. "We replaced the sofa since you were here last. I remember you weren't a fan of the other one."

I don't know how he remembers that, but he's right – the last couch never felt too supportive. Especially considering all of the furniture I'd broken while trying to come to grips with my weight, as well as my tendency to sit down with the force of a comet.

"Yeah," I verbally notice. "It looks like a nice one."

He smiles quietly as both of us take our seated positions. I observe a blank yellow legal pad sitting on the table next to his chair, with a manila folder poking out underneath containing some decade-old handwritten papers. The folder is labeled *Willis, Robby*. I don't quite remember how all of this is supposed to go, but I *am* relieved the couch is comfy.

"It's been a long time," Joe says, as if we're just going to make some small talk. "Almost ten years, right?"

"Yeah."

"Well, you've grown into a fine young man," he continues. "You have a lot of your father in you."

"Thanks," I respond. It's nice to hear, even though I don't really believe him, especially with my unshaven face and disheveled hair. My dad was clean cut, as if he were always ready to meet the pope or something. *I* avoid grocery store managers. And it doesn't help that I have to use a miniature chainsaw to trim my locks. I go through more diamond tipped saw blades than any professional lumberjack just to look presentable. Those things aren't cheap.

After a comfortable beat of silence, Joe removes a pen from his breast pocket and, placing it on the notepad, says, "So what brings you to my office today?"

Sheesh, what a loaded question. What do I lead off with? I have a hard time leaving my apartment? The city is being terrorized by a new supervillain, and I'm probably the only one that can stop him? But I'm afraid that I can't control myself and might get a lot of people killed? Because I'm the one responsible for Victor Boone's death? Oh, and I'm a superhero?

"Uh," I stutter. "I guess…just because life is… Weird?"

Joe smirks.

"I would agree with you on that," he responds. "Care to elaborate on how life is weird for you?"

I want him to fix whatever's broken without having to show it to him. My mind is like a rat in a maze, trying to figure out how to find the cheese without actually having to run through every twist and turn to do so. There's no easy way to get into it, and I don't have a clue on how to start.

I stare blankly into space for a moment, wondering how in the heck I couldn't have thought about this answer before I got into the room. I mean, sure, I've been distracted, but it's a simple question. One that I knew I would have to face when I made the appointment.

"Well," I finally say, as if starting to speak will make the rest of the words follow. But they don't.

After some silence, Joe asks, "Is it about your parents? Or your grandmother?"

I shrug.

"Not really," I mumble, starting to analyze myself. "Or maybe. I don't know."

Joe furrows his brow in confusion.

"Unfortunately, I can only ask questions," he says, switching his expression to an understanding smile. "Mind reading is not a power I possess."

I chuckle a bit. A power I don't possess, either. And recalling my junior high eavesdropping days, not one that I'd want.

"Why don't you start with now," he continues. "What made you decide to call?"

"A girl, I guess."

Joe's smile widens, exposing the whites of some of his teeth. "I like where this is going," he says through the grin.

"It's not like that," I say, hoping to cut off whatever idea might be forming in his head. "She... she found out something about me, and she's trying to help."

"Oh?" he says, his smile dampened. "What did she find out about you?"

I guess the answer to that question is where we're going to end up eventually, but I'm not ready for it yet. And even though I really like Joe, and I think I can probably trust him, I feel like having one person discover my secret in a week is already too many.

"She was a friend in college," I continue, slightly changing the subject. "Er, she was kind of a friend. More like she was a girl I knew. We didn't talk very much, except I would help her and another guy with their homework before—"

Crap, it all seems to trail back to the big secret.

"Anyhow, things got really weird, because I thought maybe she was using me to hang around him. She told me that wasn't the case, but it's still hard to believe."

I pause, taking a moment to figure out what I'm trying to say.

"I still like where this is going, Robby," Joe says through his returning grin. "It sounds an awful lot like it *is* what I was thinking."

"No," I shake my head, figuring he's expecting for me to ask his advice on proposals or something. "I hadn't seen her for a few years, but she recently showed up because the guy... The other guy died."

"Oh – I'm sorry, Robby," Joe says as his smile drops. "It's definitely hard to lose a friend. Especially with how many loved ones you've already lost."

Yeah. But even *more* especially if I'm the reason this one was lost.

After another pause in the conversation, Joe says, "and this friend that passed – he's the reason you're here? Because of his death?"

"Yeah, kind of," I stumble. "Not completely."

Joe nodded, lifting his confused eyebrows as if to say "Continue."

"The other guy knew something about me that I've kept a secret. But after he died, she found out. And she felt like maybe I should talk to someone about it."

"Hmm," Joe says as he scribbles on his paper. "Because *you* don't want to talk to *her* about it, or because *she* doesn't want to talk to *you* about it?" He focuses a little too heavily on the pronouns littered throughout his sentence.

"Well," I start again. "It's not really a normal thing. I've already talked to her a little bit about it, but she doesn't think she can help me in the way I need. And yeah – I guess I don't want to tell her everything about it."

After another moment he says, "So you're here to talk to me about this thing, yes?"

I nod, but don't say anything else.

"Okay," he says, putting the pen down again. "I can tell that whatever this secret is, it's causing you a lot of stress in trying to talk about it. Remember that I'm only here to help. I'm not going to force you to reveal something you're not prepared to. But you came to me, so I will to do my best to pry a bit about it."

"You're not allowed to tell anybody what I say here, right?" I somewhat abruptly ask.

He barely flinches. It doesn't surprise Dr. Hughes as much as I thought it would. Actually, I don't think the words surprise him at all, but maybe just how quickly I spit them out, and the fact that I used absolutely no transition to it.

"That's correct," he says. "Anything we say here is completely confidential. Unless someone is abusing you, or if you've made a plan to hurt yourself, or if you're planning on hurting someone else. In those circumstances, the law requires that I speak to someone about it. Besides that, nothing you say will be repeated or passed on to anyone else."

I nod, but still don't speak. I stare at a clock on the wall as fifteen seconds tick by incredibly slowly.

"Is it one of those things, Robby?" Joe eventually asks, his eyes widening just barely. "Are you planning on hurting yourself?"

"No," I say, shaking my head, restraining a laugh. Even if I wanted to hurt myself—and there have been times—there's no way I could. Unless, of course, I would consider electrocution. However, that would just be hurting for the sake of pain, with no other result. That doesn't sound like a good choice.

"Is someone hurting *you*, then?" Joe continues to prod.

"No," I say. Still physically impossible, and Maria is now the only other person who knows that I exist and could emotionally hurt me. And so far she's safe. I think. She did shoot me.

"Robby," Joe says, leaning in a bit. "Are you planning on hurting someone else?"

"No," I say, a little less confident. "I mean— I'm definitely not planning it. I guess that's part of the problem. I don't want anyone to get hurt—I mean *really* hurt—but I feel like that's all that ever happens when I'm around."

"Is there someone in particular that you're afraid of hurting, Robby?" His pen is perched on the paper, ready to capture whatever words I use, which kind of sets me on edge. I'm afraid if I say anything with the wrong inflection, I could end up with a million eyes on me rather than just his and Maria's.

"No," I insist. "I'm avoiding anything that might get someone hurt. I don't really even leave my apartment. There's no one in particular – I just feel like I need to protect everyone from me. I…"

I trail off and pause again. I don't know if I'm making any sense.

"I'm dangerous," I finally say, feeling as if the word is a little anticlimactic.

Joe scribbles something, and it makes me paranoid. I can't really read his writing, even when it's *not* upside down.

"Robby," he says, laying the pen back down on the paper. "It's not your fault."

"What?" I ask, wondering what in the world he knows. How could he know anything? Surely Maria didn't tell him before I got here – though I guess that *would* make things slightly easier.

"Your parents' deaths were not your fault," he says. "Neither was your grandmother's."

"What?" I ask again, a bit bewildered at the suggestion. I fight the urge to say *duh*. "I know that."

How could they be my fault? My parents were killed in a fire trying to save me when I was a kid, and my grandma died from a heart attack. I did everything I could to keep my grandma alive, concentrating on listening to her heart beat every moment that I was around her. Eventually pills and quick reflexes couldn't help her cheat death. *Of course* they weren't my fault.

Dr. Hughes continues.

"And I'm fairly confident that your other friend's death is not your fault, either."

I look down, staring at the floor. The pattern in the carpet is most likely there to hide crumbs and stains, but it's not able to hide them from me. I'd rather ponder how long it has been since he professionally shampooed the floor than talk about how I'm the reason Vic died. And I'd definitely prefer not to talk about the gunman that I killed.

"Do you think you caused your friend's death?" Joe asks, lowering his head to see if he can catch my eyes.

"Yes," I say.

"Why do you think that?"

I guess I'll have to wait to count the floor crumbs later.

"Because it's true," I answer.

Joe leans down further until I can see his pupils looking at mine.

"What reason could you possibly have to think your friend died because of you?" he asks.

Here goes.

"My friend that died is Victor Boone," I say after a long pause. "And the reason I got him killed is because *I'm* Victor Boone."

CHAPTER EIGHT

Well, that's not what I meant to say. Now he's sure to think I'm insane.

"Victor Boone is dead because you are Victor Boone?" Joe asks, his face emotionless and his voice calm. I assume it's a skill he's learned from decades of listening to crazy people babble on about similar things. I'm quite amazed at his reaction – somehow he makes me feel comfortable even though I said something completely nuts.

"Wait – that came out wrong," I say.

"No, it's okay," Joe says, picking up his pen and scribbling on his paper again. "Did Victor Boone jump into your body *after* he died? Are you saying Robby is actually no longer here?"

Ugh. He thinks I'm absolutely bonkers – that I'm one of the crazy conspiracy theorists. But he's so nice about it.

"I'm sorry, I'm Robby," I try to recover. "I'm not Vic."

"Hmm," Joe says with a thoughtful frown. "You don't have to lie to make me happy, you know. You can be completely honest in here and I won't judge you."

"Joe," I say as calmly as I can, even though my finely-tuned embarrassment meter is off the charts. It's like a spider sense, except it's only good for making me freeze in my tracks and then trip over myself. "I'm Robby. I'm not Vic. That came out completely wrong."

"Okay," he says, poised to write whatever I say next. "What did you mean?"

I take a deep breath, preparing myself to say any number of things that might sound equally insane.

"Victor Boone was my friend. Er, sort of."

Scribble, scribble.

"He was the guy I was referring to when I was talking about the girl – Maria," I specify, not knowing how to recover from crazy town. "After he died, she searched me out. We reconnected just a few days ago."

"You, Maria, and Victor were friends in college," he said, still scribbling. "Gotcha."

"Dr. Hughes – would you mind maybe not writing anything for a minute?"

His pen stops mid-word and he looks at me. "Sure," he says with a somewhat patronizing smile, then sets the writing utensil down.

"I'm not Victor Boone," I say again, "but I'm the one with superpowers."

His eyes dart to the pen and paper, his finger fidgeting once, but he restrains his movement. He looks at me again, his face completely unchanged.

"I'm very glad your friend Maria asked you to come speak with me," he says very casually. "I would love to hear all about it."

I let out a sigh.

"Vic, Maria and I had a freshman biology class together," I say. "He sat behind me one day, making fun of my haircut and my weight, and I just tried to ignore him. Maria got up, sat next to me and told him to shut up."

As I talk to Dr. Hughes, my mind drifts back to the one-hundred-person lecture hall. I would get to each of my classes early and leave late so that I could wedge myself in and out of chairs without anyone watching, because they were the kinds with the desk attached on the right side. Whoever designed them did not think of them being used by students of my size. I would usually be sitting in the room completely alone for several minutes, near the back wall. I don't know why I didn't simply sit in the back row so that no one could sit behind me, but I honestly thought that being picked on was a high school thing, and that we'd all matured past it. I figured I was just being paranoid.

But Victor hadn't left high school yet, even though he was a junior in college. Sure, he traded his high school letter jacket for the one from the university's football team, I suppose needing to announce to everyone that he was an athlete without using his words. I'd seen him other times – not just in that class, but all over campus. Girls looked at him in ways that they never looked at me. He had no problems with all of the eyes on him, and his actions were larger than life so that he could draw even more attention. I was envious. He seemed to have everything I wished I had – namely, confidence.

So when he sat behind me that day, complaining of smelling rotten garbage, I just froze with tears welling up. Because of my heightened senses, I was extremely nervous that everyone else could smell me like I could smell myself. I took laborious showers to get rid of any possible stench. I probably used deodorant a bit too much, because I could never cover my own odor. In junior high and high school, I'd made friends with several of the adults—teachers, guidance counselors, janitors, lunch staff—whom I would ask to let me know if they ever thought I smelled bad. No one ever told me I did, but I just figured they were being nice and didn't want to hurt my feelings. Looking back, everyone had the same smell I had, but they couldn't notice it. My own smell was just *worse* somehow.

It wasn't until Victor threw a pencil at me that anyone else in the lecture hall noticed. It didn't hurt when it hit me, but it did surprise me. As a result, my body stiffened, and the desk attached to the chair buckled. The metal rod that connected it to the rest of the piece of furniture broke at the welded joint, and he and his friends broke out in hysterical laughter.

I didn't know what to do. I wanted to stand up, grab him by his pompous letter jacket and throw him across the room. But I decided to do nothing. I'd endured far worse in previous classrooms, and I counted on the fact that I only had a minute or so before the professor would arrive to start the lecture.

But that's when I noticed the scent. Her scent. Vanilla, coconut and a dash of fresh cotton. I'd smelled it a hundred times before from across the room. If I was outside, I'd focus on it and find her in a crowd. I'd follow her from far off until she would walk into a building. I'd watch her laugh with her beautiful friends in the large atrium dining room from a balcony above, eating by myself.

But this time, her scent was moving towards me. I didn't look up. This wasn't the time I wanted her to notice me, when I was in my most fragile state. Bullied on the outside, but boiling on the inside, doing everything I could to not go into a rage. But the smell wafted closer and closer, until finally a voice broke through the cloud.

"Leave him alone, you losers," she yelled with authority. "Or I'll fill the school paper up with the lists of STDs you most likely have. You won't get another date until after you graduate."

There were other words exchanged, but I don't remember them. It was the first time anyone had stood up for me like that, and even though her lips mouthed some incredibly off-color words, she was still the most beautiful thing I'd ever seen. Her dark hair swayed as she shook her maroon painted fingernail at the jerks.

She asked me to come sit with her on the other side of the room, and I obliged. I didn't completely want to—it required me trying to sandwich myself into another desk-chair combo closer to the front of the classroom—but the alternative was worse. And I wasn't about to tell the beautiful creature no.

She sat next to me for the rest of the semester. A horrible moment that I thought was going to define the rest of my college career turned into something nice. He was still the jerk in my periphery, but he was no longer directing any of his ill will towards me. And that one-time experience led to Maria and me sharing small talk up to three times a week.

However, one day towards the end of the semester she didn't show up. I was disappointed, though I assumed she was sick because she'd been a little under the weather during the previous lecture. I'd relaxed in the class, so I was surprised when I smelled a letter jacket nearing me after the teacher was done and almost everyone had already shuffled out.

"Hey, uh, big guy," his throaty voice said, as if he wanted to whisper, but didn't want to act like he was capable of being vulnerable. I let out a breath, afraid that not having my sweet-smelling shield meant I was going to have another run in with this jerk.

I could tell he was by himself, and that he was even a little nervous. I looked up at him as I slipped my textbook into my backpack and didn't say anything.

"Uh," he stammered, then paused. "No hard feelings for what happened a long time ago, right?"

A long time ago, eh? I could still feel the pencil bouncing off my back. The broken desk had been replaced, but the sound of the weld breaking ricocheted inside my brain.

I didn't say anything in response. I was doing everything I could to not let any of my thoughts turn into actions.

"You're real smart with this science stuff, right?" he asked, ever so smoothly changing the subject.

I nodded as I zipped up my backpack.

"Coach said I'm gonna get kicked off the team if I fail this class," he said, a little under his breath, while he looked around the room. "And that's the road I'm on right now."

"You're a junior, aren't you?" I asked, trying to hide the snicker that was obvious in my voice. "You're failing freshman biology?"

He aggressively moved up close to me and said, "Hey, what're you trying to say, nerd?"

I'm sure almost anyone else in my circumstance and body type would have cowered at such an advance, but physical pain wasn't something I was afraid of. We were alone, and I didn't want him to think he could start the bullying again. As long as he didn't make fun of the way I looked or smelled, my composure was not going to change.

"Sorry," he said as he backed off and glanced around the room again. He seemed surprised that I stood my ground. "Right – sounds pretty bad, I know. But my mind is on more important stuff, you know? I know I ain't gonna be a *scientist* or something – the only way I'm gonna make it in life is if I prove it out on the football field. But if I don't get caught up in here, I'm gonna end up selling used cars like my idiot old man."

Makes sense. I should've realized he probably had some daddy issues for him to act like he did. All of my time with Dr. Hughes as a teen taught me that.

"And you need my help?" I asked.

I could tell Victor was not the kind of guy that generally asked for assistance – especially from a nerd such as myself.

"Man, maybe I could pay you to help me study for the final? I've got to pass it." His voice told me that I was probably his last hope.

"No money," I said. I had all of it that I'd need. "But you have to promise me something. No more bullying."

"Sure, man – you help me, and I won't make fun of you anymore. I mean, I haven't for a long time, right?"

"You don't understand," I countered. "No more bullying anyone. Not just me. No more jokes at other people's expense. No more throwing stuff at other people. None of that."

"Pssh," he said, discounting my words. "I don't do any of that."

I rattled off a handful of times in the last week where I saw him do exactly those things. Vic chuckled a few *huh huhs* with each example I gave, apparently proud of himself.

"Fine, man, fine," he agreed with a smirk after I finished my list. I doubted my decree would stand for very long. He concluded with, "You help me, and I'll be a pushover."

"Not the same thing, but okay," I said, hoping that I might get a chance to learn why he was so self-assured, as well as maybe teach him a little humility.

I spent several evenings with him over the next two weeks, and at the end of the semester he barely edged by with a D. It wouldn't get him on any honors' lists, but it was good enough to keep him on the team. Our time together didn't really blossom into what I'd hoped it might—a jock learning compassion and an insecure nerd learning confidence—but I did notice that he *tried* to lessen his bullying. At least when I was around.

I thought our deal was complete until we ended up in the same science class again the next semester. Chemistry this time. I'd terrifyingly asked Maria if I could schedule the same class period as her, and she actually agreed. I didn't know that Vic would show up as well. He didn't make fun of me, but we weren't exactly on the road to becoming best friends.

The three of us were lab partners, which generally amounted to Maria and me doing the work and trying to explain it to Vic, who obviously felt that his mind had better places to be. Towards the end of the semester, he approached me for another study session, citing the same if-I-fail-the-coach-will-drop-me predicament. I wondered if he had a willing nerd in all of his classes when finals neared.

One night, after attempting to tutor him for a really long time, we were walking from the school's library to the parking lot. We weren't talking much, which was fine with me because I was far more focused on a party that seemed to have broken out on a dorm's roof. The first couple of days of final exams had been completed, and celebrations were springing up fairly often – but this one seemed a bit more drunk and obnoxious than others.

Music was blaring from the top of the six-story building even though the area was definitely off limits. I couldn't see what was going on, but I heard at least twenty quick heartbeats and bodies moving to the frenetic pace of the song. They were drawing way too much attention to themselves, and I could smell several different kinds of alcohol and the vomit of at least two people whose breaths were slow. Most likely they had passed out and were sleeping in a corner.

We were at least a hundred feet away when a girl's head peeked over the roof's ledge, silhouetted by streetlights in the parking lot past the building. She struggled to pull herself up onto the thin edge, stood, then raised her plastic cup and screamed over the noise. None of her garbled words made any sense, but the small crowd cheered as she swayed out of time with the music.

Her body rocked back and forth, and I knew what was going to happen before it did. I quickened my steps, hoping I could get there without using any of my abnormal abilities while Victor was beside me. But she didn't wait for my human pace.

She dropped her cup, and the rest of her body followed suit, pouring over the ledge toward the sidewalk below.

I did it without thinking. I picked up speed and launched myself into the air, aiming at her flailing body. It wasn't enough to simply catch her when she hit the ground – at six stories up, a fall would still break her bones and possibly kill her if she were to come in contact with well-meaning hands or rock hard flab. In no time I had my arms around her, defying gravity by slowing her speed towards the pavement.

We approached the sidewalk and I softly laid her body on the ground, looking at her face for the first time. I just knew that she'd be staring at me with eyes open wide, and would immediately draw attention to what had just happened. And a second or two after that, numerous eyes would be peering over the roof's ledge, followed by cameras and crowds and no personal space ever again. But as I braced myself for the inevitable, I realized an important detail.

Her eyes were closed. She was drooling. She had passed out, and she had no idea what happened. And even better, the amount of alcohol I could smell on her breath told me that if she saw anything, it would be easily explained away.

Ahh. Privacy remained. I hadn't had a chance to turn invisible, but not being seen was just the same. I was able to do a heroic act in plain view, fully clothed, and still I'd be able to take my last exam tomorrow with none the wiser.

Until I realized Victor was running towards me.

"Dude!" he yelled, pointing at the girl. "Dude!"

His eloquent speech continued as he pointed at the roof and back down to me. "Dude!"

I stood and shushed him, but it didn't stop him from yelling at the top of his lungs.

"How did you… She was… And you… Dude!"

I could hear shuffling feet and worried voices from the roof, making their way to the edge to find out the fate of their fellow partygoer. And I couldn't simply disappear before any of their eyes peered over the roof's ledge because my science-inept cohort was staring at me.

"We've got to go," I said, turning to briskly walk away – quickly, but not superhero fast.

"No way, man!" Vic yelled. "She was gonna bite it! How'd you do that?"

"I didn't," I called back. "I didn't do anything. Let's go."

"Dude!" he repeated. "I saw it – you can fly or something!"

"Victor – shut up. We've got to go. I didn't do anything – maybe you did it."

I turned the corner, just enough out of the way that eyes peering from the roof wouldn't see me in a glance across the ground. I looked back, shielding myself with the building, and saw Victor cradling the girl's head as the commotion overhead spilled over the ledge.

"Wha... What happened?" the almost-victim groggily asked.

"Don't worry – I saved you," Victor answered confidently.

I open my eyes and see Dr. Hughes staring at me, his hand scratching his bearded chin.

"Yes," he agrees with me. "I remember the news stories about the girl. It was the first thing that Victor Boone did publicly, even though he didn't claim to be a superhero until months later."

"Yeah, that's because Vic didn't know what happened," I confirm. "People talk about how humble he was for not revealing his powers at first, but it's because he wanted to take credit and didn't know if I really had powers, or if it was some kind of one-time freak accident."

"Interesting," he says, nodding his head. "I don't remember your name in the articles – I'm sure I would've noticed it."

"I didn't want my name in them," I respond. "I stayed a good distance away, watching Vic recount to reporters and admirers how he saved her."

"But you saved her," Joe corrects me.

"Yeah. And Vic followed me around for weeks asking me questions, finally trying to physically hurt me until he was satisfied that I couldn't *get* hurt. He convinced me we could help all kinds of people before he even knew I could turn invisible."

Dr. Hughes tilts his head and asks, "You can turn invisible?"

He still thinks I'm crazy. He thinks I just read the Victor Boone articles, and somehow inserted myself into his shoes.

"You don't believe me, do you?" I ask.

"Robby," he says, pausing for a moment. "I fully believe that your reality is very real to you, and—"

Sigh. First, a girl believes I have superpowers when I don't want her to. Now, a guy doesn't believe when I *do* want him to. I decide the evidence that was good enough for Maria is probably good enough for Dr. Hughes. Before he has a chance to empathize and give me a logical explanation about how he knows I'm wrong but wants me to feel like he understands and is on my side, I take his pen and stab myself in the eye.

CHAPTER NINE

"What's your favorite color?" Maria asks with pencil and paper in hand, sitting on one of the swivel chairs in my living room.

"Uh, I don't know – yellow, I guess?"

My session with Dr. Hughes felt like it ended not long after my self-inflicted violence, though we ran over the allotted time by at least thirty minutes. He was thoroughly convinced, as it was the apparently expensive pen that broke rather than my eye. His assistant eventually knocked on the door because another patient had been waiting, and we had gotten caught up in the same kind of questions Maria asked when she confirmed my powers.

"And your shoe size?" Maria continues.

"Ten," I answer, starting to get confused. "You're not going to buy me yellow shoes, are you?"

"No," she says, smiling.

Apparently my apartment is her new home base – the place where she now does most of her research into The Vacant's very covered-up actions. She never really asked, and I definitely wouldn't have refused if she did. After my conversation with Joe, I was starting to wonder if she merely felt like I needed to be protected again, like she did back in freshman biology. But I'm okay with that.

Today's activities include my searching on the internet for a few things that she requested, and her scribbling on the notepad, a lot like my session with Joe.

"What size shirt do you wear?"

"What are you doing?" I ask, narrowing my eyes as I move toward her. She pulls the notebook towards her chest in response.

"Nothing!" she says with a slight giggle.

I reach out for the notebook and she spins around, keeping it just out of my grasp.

"You know I can just use my X-ray vision to look through you and read whatever it is," I bluff.

"What?" she demands as she spins around, a look of embarrassment on her face as if I just walked in on her using the bathroom. "You never told me you have X-ray vision."

I snatch the notebook out of her hand, without any need for super speed or strength.

"I don't."

"Hey!" she yells as she grabs for the notebook. I float into the air with the papers just out of her reach. "I'm not finished with it yet!"

I look down at the object in my hands and my heart drops. It's a bad pencil sketch of me – or at least it's supposed to be. She kindly trimmed my gut and hair. Cartoon me is wearing a spandex suit, complete with cape and boots, and a characterized version of the letters "VB" is emblazoned across my chest. It's the same logo Vic had worn for the past couple years.

I'm not sure what to say. I'm hurt at the thought that she'd want me to slap on Vic's logo as if I were taking up *his* mantle. And terrified that she'd expect me to act anything like him, wearing a flashy suit and taking credit.

There are various arrows pointing to articles of clothing: yellow suit, size ten boots. I don't read the rest of it before I feel a disappointed frown take over my face. I toss the notebook back to her without saying anything. I float towards my bedroom, struggling with the thought of asking her to leave so that I can sulk, but opt instead to simply separate the space between us with a flimsy door.

"Robby," she says with a playful whine as I shut the door. It doesn't do much to dampen her voice even if I didn't have impressive aural prowess.

I don't lock it, so she just swings it open wide, completely disrespecting my private space. I never had to lock it when Vic had offended me and I retreated for solace. He would just turn up the volume, saying he couldn't hear the TV over my 'estroganoff.' I never did teach him the word *estrogen* because his not knowing the correct word had slightly comforted me. He would have never used it for a positive reason anyhow.

"Robby," she repeats, almost all of her playfulness gone. "I was just messing with some ideas."

"Yeah – ideas of me on TV cameras and shaking politicians' hands," I counter, balling myself up into the corner of the ceiling. "I'm not Victor."

She lets out a loud breath.

"Robby, quit being a baby," she says a bit more curtly than I expect. "Save the fetal position for the therapist and get down here."

She starts moving a piece of furniture across the floor towards me, but I keep my gaze at the wall.

"You can stop a bullet with your skin," she says, scratching my hardwood. "You can take a crowbar to the face. You can dull knives with your hair. But thinking about talking to other humans makes you wet your pants?"

"I didn't wet my pants," I exclaim as I quickly turn around in mid-air.

I turn just in time to see her jump from the surface of the newly positioned bedside table to grab my leg.

"Get down here and I'll show you what real torture is," she says as she tries to move me by bracing her feet against the wall.

"Oh great," I mumble, unaffected. "What weapon do you have in your purse today?"

"Nope – no weapon," she sighs as she gives up and softly bounces onto the bed. "You're going to help me run an errand, or I'm alerting the media."

"What errand could possibly be more torturous than reporters setting up shop outside my door?"

She straightens her hair and gives me a prissy smirk.

"We're going to the DMV."

I've done everything I could to maintain my belief that civil servants are selfless and helpful. But I'd never been to the Department of Motor Vehicles.

There were at least forty people in front of us in line, and only one city worker sat at her station behind the glass. I could hear three other employees laughing loudly and munching on corn chips in the break room. At first I tried to give them the benefit of the doubt – that they'd all accidentally taken a short break at the same time, and didn't think it would be productive for any of them to clock back in when it would only take a few minutes to rest their feet.

But an hour later, much of their conversation was about how the new girl—Gina, the only one at her post—needed to "learn how things really work around here." Apparently, how things work is that the new girl gets to talk to angry citizens while they leisurely enjoy their corn chips.

Not that *I* had anywhere else to be, but everyone else did.

"How have you survived this long without a driver's license?" Maria asks, passing the time by trying to find more topics of conversation; at least, topics that don't involve letting people around us know that I have superpowers.

For some reason, while we're here for Maria to renew her license, she's trying to convince me to take the test so I can get mine. Even though I have absolutely no desire or need to get behind the wheel of a car.

"I had one in high school, when my grandma started getting bad," I answer. "But I haven't needed one since she died."

She's not satisfied.

"You have to go out of your way not to need one," she responds. "How did you get your apartment, or set up your utilities, or get a credit card?"

"You'd be surprised at how few questions are asked of you when you pay with cash," I say. "And I buy prepaid cards, which work everywhere a regular credit card does, but I pretty much just use them to buy stuff online. And we have enough taxis, buses, and subways for me to get around when I'm with someone."

Not that I'm ever with someone.

"But *why*," she says skeptically. "Is somebody after you or something?"

"No. I mean…" I trail off, lowering my voice. "Not that I know of. But that's probably because I've been so careful about staying hidden. If there was more of a public record of me, anyone could find me."

"But no one's looking," Maria says with a confused smile. "Even though I was looking, it took me a while. And if I didn't already know what I was looking for, it wouldn't have done any good."

"But someone could be looking," I say. I don't know why, I've just always felt like I was in somebody's crosshairs, though I've never had any evidence to suggest that it's true. Even Vic had a fairly uneventful life – probably because everyone thought he was invincible. His family enjoyed extra federal protection even though he rarely spoke to them, and no one else seemed to be close enough to him for him to worry. I had even less to be concerned about.

"Speaking of looking into your records, what's the deal with your house?"

My eyes dart around the room, as if that will help me figure out how to change the subject.

"Augusta?" I ask, looking at the license in her hand. "Augusta Maria Truman?"

She looks taken aback for a split second, then notices the laminated card she's holding.

"Oh, yeah…" she says a bit sheepishly.

"That sounds like an awfully fancy name for a girl whose parents are a mechanic and a waitress."

She looks surprised again, probably not realizing she told me all about her family when we were in college. I remember every detail. I avoided talking about mine at all costs.

"My mom was obsessed with the Sound of Music," she says, embarrassed. "Apparently, Maria Augusta von Trapp died like ten years before I was born, and my parents decided to curse me for the rest of my life as a memorial."

"Why not just name you Maria Augusta, then?" I ask. "Why flip it around?"

"They were worried that *everyone* was going to name their daughter Maria at the time, and it wasn't unique enough. They called me Augusta all the way through middle school, no matter how much I complained that it made me sound incredibly stuck up. At one point I realized I could make the decision for myself and started correcting teachers that my name was Maria. It didn't take long for everyone to fall in line. My parents still call me that sometimes. And I still hate it."

"I like it," I say. "It's pretty, so it matches—"

I stop the words before I make a complete fool of myself. You'd assume that my mouth would be able to wait for my superfast thought process to save me from stupid moments like this, but that's not the case.

"I like it," I squeak out again to stop the sentence as she smiles, exposing her teeth.

I spend the next several minutes asking her questions about her family that I already know the answers to.

We're only two people away from being called to the front—the other employees finally decide to end their definitely-longer-than-regulation breaks—and I start to hear a commotion outside. We're next door to City Hall, and the standard sounds of busy bodies were giving way to something else entirely. Yelling, screaming, crying, and feet dragging against carpet.

"What is it?" Maria asks, looking me up and down. Apparently I've stiffened my body like a hunting dog who has caught a scent.

"The Vacant," I whisper halfheartedly. I'm not completely confident that he's there, or if it's just another recording. But something's definitely going on.

"You should go," she says as if it's the obvious thing. I guess it *is* obviously what I should do, but the voices in my head tell me otherwise.

"What if I can't control myself?" I ask out loud. Other competing thoughts scream out *You're going to kill someone else*, and *No one is safe around you*.

"Shut up and go," Maria says quietly, having none of my reservations. "This guy is dangerous, and you're the only one who can stop him from hurting more people."

I think about resisting for a moment, but between Maria's tendency to convince me and the hustle and bustle next door, I realize I would regret not moving. I head to the bathroom as nonchalantly as I can, then strip down to nothing once I'm in the handicap stall. I stuff my clothes into the trashcan so that they don't cause any further suspicion. That's another reason I don't have any forms of identification on me; if my wallet were to appear with a pile of mysterious clothes in a dumpster, I'm sure someone would want to know why.

By the time I'm invisibly hovering above City Hall, several police cars are double-parked on the street, which is not completely abnormal. From the outside everything seems like business as usual, but inside I can hear something else entirely.

"This is a lesson to all would-be heroes," The Vacant's flat, gravelly voice calmly states. I dart through the hallways, up stairwells, over metal detectors, and beside citizens who are completely unaware of the trouble, trying to get to the room from where the voice is emanating. "Your respected councilman refused to obey me. He says he has no family, so I have nothing to take from him. That he'd rather die than accept payments for his loyalty."

I find the scene in one of the smaller court rooms with The Vacant in the center. His skin-wrapped head is as strange in person as it was on the video. I don't immediately sense any unique smells or sounds; in fact, his heart rate is incredibly steady, as if he's resting. The blood pumps through his veins with the consistency of an endurance runner. I'll try to be on the look out for joggers with flesh-balloons for heads from here on out.

Besides his head, The Vacant looks as non-descript as he could possibly be. A form-fitting suit that isn't too trendy, dress shoes that could have come from an upscale clothier or a thrift store, and a solid black tie. If he didn't have epidermis for eyes, no one would have taken notice of him walking into the front door. Which means he came in a back way, or he's wearing a disguise that he put on after he got into the building.

Wait – who am I kidding? Of course the literal skin-head getup is a disguise. Besides the practical questions of eating, drinking, and sucking in oxygen, if there was ever a baby born in that condition it would've been on every news outlet in the world.

Kneeling on the ground next to him is a man in a white dress shirt, and a family of four is standing in a line about two feet in front of both. All five of the hostages are bound at the wrists and the two children in the family are sobbing, asking questions no child should have to ask.

There are maybe ten masked gunmen littered around the room, some with their firearms pointed at the family of four, and the rest looking very imposing with the other random people in the room. It reminds me of when Vic died – too many bullets in close proximity. If I make a move, I'm going to need a plan. Otherwise, there will be a lot of spilled blood. And this carpet isn't the kind that will hide red stains.

"What Councilman Alvarez doesn't understand is that we're all connected in some way. For instance, the family in front of me is the Huberts." The Vacant casually waves a gloved hand in their direction. "They live next door to the councilman. For all I know, they've never even met – but I'm sure he's not happy that they're going to be executed because of him. Not that he'll grieve for long, because he'll only live long enough to watch them die."

Councilman Alvarez interrupts the speech with the word "*No*" over and over again, spouting off words about how he'll do whatever The Vacant wants. The Huberts do some quiet begging as well. The Vacant bends over and puts a single gloved finger over Alvarez's mouth, as if to shush a child. The action is gentle, confirming that he is very calm and in control.

"Councilman," the distorted voice continues, "there's nothing you can do. Do you think I'll release them if you give in to me now? Or that I'd be satisfied with killing you alone?"

The sobbing and pleading from the adults lessens, as if they know it's useless. As if they're trying to calculate another way to reason with a madman.

"If I did that," The Vacant says as his fleshy head scans the room, "everyone in the city would see me as merciful. And I'm *not* merciful. This is being recorded, so everyone will see that to defy me doesn't only mean a definite death for themselves, but for anyone else they're connected to. I require unquestioning loyalty, without a moment of hesitation."

With that, he flicked his finger towards the man whose gun pointed at the broad-shouldered Mr. Hubert. As if The Vacant's own finger was on the trigger, the gun's firing pin connects with the bullet.

Crap. I guess the plan is just to be fast and hope that it works out this time.

I dart towards the gun, grabbing it soon enough to send the bullet in the direction of an unoccupied row of thick chairs. I connect the butt of the gun into the thug's jaw and he flies into the masked man standing next to him, causing both of them to break through a wooden barrier that usually separated crowd from criminal.

I listen hard for more triggers, but fly straight to the next gun down the Hubert line. My only hope is to incapacitate all of the criminals before any of them knows what's going on, which is pretty much impossible. I don't have the luxury of keeping my fists completely restrained, so I pray that no one winds up dead – but someone will definitely wind up dead if I stop to think.

The third gunman, most likely surprised, has moved his gun from a Hubert head toward my general area. If they would all do that, it would make everything much easier. The gun doesn't have time to fire, and a swift kick to the face renders him unconscious. Or – I'm not sure if it was the kick itself that knocks him out, or because his head breaks through a layer of drywall.

Before I fly into the last Hubert assassin's body, I hear a confused cry of "Victor Boone!?" As the thug sails through the air, the shout echoes in the room.

"Victor Boone will save us!" at least two bystanders say.

I don't know why, but this frustrates me. It's been months since Vic died. And it was never even *Victor Boone* who saved them to begin with. This never really bothered me that much before, but now that I'm coming to grips with living without him, I don't want to resurrect his memory.

While I'm tossing bully bodies to and fro, I notice a blue fog swirling around the room. People start dropping— bystanders, hostages, and even gunmen—without my intervention. I feel like I'm falling. I turn back towards The Vacant as I hear the hammer of a gun in his hand.

The scene is exactly like Vic's murder. The bullet goes through Councilman Alvarez's skull, but this time, I can't move. I might've had enough time to get to the bullet before it left the chamber, since all of the masked men seem to be out of commission, but something holds me back. I watch The Vacant run away as the councilman's blood spills across the floor.

I try to move towards him. Not to exact revenge on The Vacant like I did with Victor's killer; even though I can't stand murder, I didn't know Alvarez and my emotions are still in check. I just try to *move*. I didn't realize it before, but I'm barely standing, rather than flying. I brace myself on a chair, hoping some part of me can drag myself towards the councilman as if that will help anything.

Instead of inching forward, I look down and notice that there's a strange blur filling the space that I'm standing in. The blur is different from the blue fog in the room – this looks like skin and hair and flab.

Oh dear God. I'm turning visible.

I do everything I can to get out of the room, but instead just collapse onto the ground.

CHAPTER TEN

More fire.

Flames, exploding bulbs, dancing light against metal surfaces. It's blurry, but I can see my father rushing me between tables and cabinets. There are several beakers and test tubes which contain boiling liquids. I don't think they're supposed to be boiling – I see liquids in those glass containers all the time, and they're never bubbling like that.

Papers are turning to ash, electrical wires are all sparks, and tiny explosions appear around the room. My dad's computer screens are shattered – not by force, but by heat. I don't feel hot, but at the same time my brain is telling me that, in fact, I am burning alive.

Why am I here?

My dad pulls me through the maze, and I try to resist. There's somewhere I'm supposed to be. I feel like I was somewhere else a moment ago. Like I was somewhere important.

My resistance isn't doing anything. I'm moving through the room like a chunky ragdoll with a leash connected to my dad. His lab coat is on fire. I try to tell him, but nothing comes out.

I know there's somewhere I'm supposed to be. Doesn't he know that? Why is he dragging me?

Oh – the glass cage. I remember that, but I don't know why. I'm inside before I can piece everything together, and he mouths *I love you, buddy.*

I'm banging on the glass. I don't even know how he got me inside of it – I've never seen it opened before now. He needs to let me know. I think I'm supposed to help, but I don't remember how or why, or what in the world is going on.

My dad hits a big red button at the corner of the glass cage, and it opens something above me. I think maybe it's air – maybe he's venting outside air in to keep me from breathing in all the smoke from the room.

But no – it's not clean air. It's a different kind of smoke. It's a hot, moist fog. It fills up the cage and I can't help but suck it in like I'm a drowning victim.

Everything hurts.

"Robby!"

Mom? Is that you? I can't see you.

"Robby!"

Oh, wow, my head hurts. I haven't felt pain like this in years. I haven't felt *any* pain in years.

"Robby, are you ok?"

Everything is black except for a horizontal streak of light breaking the center of my vision.

"Robby, can you hear me?"

Yeah, I can hear you, I just can't see you.

Instead of saying anything, I hear a moan come from my throat.

"Robby, wake up *now*!"

The bright slits in my eyes expand, and my blurry vision reveals the outline of someone hovering above me. I think I recognize that fuzzy looking woman.

I moan again and realize I'm being shaken by small hands.

"Robby, please tell me you can hear me!"

Maria comes into focus, and I start drowsily moving my head around. My hands come up to my head, first rubbing my eyes and then holding my pounding skull.

"Robby, we have to get out of here. *Now*!"

Wait – how do I have a headache?

"Calm down, just a second," I say, sounding a bit drunk.

"You might not have a second," Maria says frantically, trying to pull my hand away from my head.

"Maria, my head is killing me. Just give me a second and I'll get up."

She tugs harder.

"Robby, look around."

I look at her, then to my left. I see chairs and a few lifeless bodies. That's strange – why are there people on the ground? Why am I on the ground?

"Why are people…" It's harder to talk than it should be.

"Don't worry about the people, Robby. Look down."

I struggle to look down, but I can't see anything because my fat gut is in the way. I hate my body. It's difficult to work out when I can pick up a truck without straining, but no matter what I've done I haven't been able to lose a single pound. You know it's bad when you go the bathroom and you can't even see—

I jerk forward.

Somehow I've sobered up one hundred percent and realize that I'm sitting in the middle of a court room with bodies strewn about.

Visible.

Naked.

And Maria is kneeling right next to me.

"Oh, God," I say. "Oh, my sweet Lord."

She is right next to my naked body. I'm going to have a heart attack.

"No one else is here yet," she says, as if to reassure me. "Or, at least everyone nearby is knocked out. Everyone for at least two floors of the building. No one has seen you."

Maybe that's true, but *she* has seen me. This is one of my worst nightmares. Let me go back to the burning room.

"Can you turn invisible?" she pleads. "I walked through the halls for twenty minutes trying to find you, and they're filled with unconscious people. I don't know how long before they come to. They can't find you like this."

Believe me, I agree with her. But what about *her* finding me like this?

I'll die of embarrassment later. For the time being I concentrate a little harder than I usually have to and watch my arm go from thick and flabby to transparent.

"I need to get back to my apartment," I say. "It's taking too much effort for me to stay invisible."

"I'll meet you there," she responds quickly, standing up.

While I'd prefer to be alone for a while—perhaps for the next several years—I know I'll probably need her. We need to figure out what happened.

"Wait," I say. "Before you go, grab something. A cloth or something porous, or anything that has a layer of blue film on it. The Vacant released a gas that knocked everyone out – including me. We need to find out what it was."

"On it," she says, already scanning the room.

I think that's what happened, anyway. I barely remember him running when he shot a man.

I look over at the dead councilman. I can't think about him right now. I can't think about how it's my fault that he's lying there with a bullet hole in his head.

"Maria," I say, still gathering my wits about me.

"Yeah," she answers, looking around for the right evidence.

"Call the police."

"But I need to get back to help you—"

"Not yet," I cut her off, looking at two cameras in the corners of the ceiling. "You'll show up on the surveillance cameras. I might, too, but I'm hoping that the angles won't show me. I think I was only visible for just a moment, and I was surrounded by chairs. We'll worry about trying to edit me out later if it did catch me, but for now, you don't want to get caught leaving the area. Be a journalist who stumbled on the scene."

Maria pulls out her cell phone and dials 911.

"Are you going to be okay getting back?" she asks when she hits the last button.

"This is the first headache I've had in ten years," I answer, thinking way more about what she saw than how I feel. "But I'll try to manage."

"Not a single camera was recording all day long."

I can hear Maria pacing through my apartment, but my eyes have been closed since I got back. The only time I'd opened them was to confirm that it was indeed her opening the door and rushing in. I had clothes on, but I still pulled a blanket around me as she appeared. Not because I was cold, but because I needed another layer to separate her eyes from my body.

"It took the cops surprisingly long to get there, considering the police station is just a couple of blocks away, but it's probably because so many of them had blacked out in City Hall."

Maria had only been at my apartment for a few minutes, because for the rest of the afternoon she'd been talking to the cops and editors at three newspapers. Apparently, none of the papers were willing to print anything about the event.

The blue gas was powerful, for sure. I was the last one to fall asleep, but still the first one to wake up. Three hours later, the other victims still hadn't woken up.

"Do you remember how many people with masks were in the room?" she asks, talking *to* me for the first time since she arrived, rather than just *at* me.

"Uh?" I muttered. "I don't know... Ten or so?"

"Twelve," she fired back at me. "There were twelve people with masks in the room."

"Okay – twelve," I defensively respond, still hoping my head will stop pounding. "Why did you ask me if you already knew the answer?"

"Because," she says slowly, "there were twelve people with masks *still* in the room when the police got there."

"The Vacant left all of them behind without a thought," I wondered aloud.

"Exactly. Apparently this guy doesn't care much for his hired help. I don't know why they follow his orders."

"I know why," I interject. "That's why he was there to begin with. He doesn't just kill people who don't follow orders – he murders anyone they might be connected to."

"So the councilman was killed to scare someone else?"

"No, the councilman was the one who wouldn't get in line," I say. "I think The Vacant made sure to kill him before he left so that the message was still obvious. But there was a family there – the Huberts. Are they okay?"

I peek my eyes open just long enough to see Maria nod.

"Yeah," she answers. "They were laying in a line with their hands tied up. The councilman was the only other person who was bound. I assume The Vacant released the gas when you saved all of them, right?"

"I didn't save *all* of them," I correct her.

"Robby, you saved *all* of the Huberts." She puts her hand on my shoulder. "Even with super powers, there were twelve thugs and a maniacal weirdo in there. The Vacant is the one that pulled the trigger on Alvarez."

I just sigh in response.

"I should call my contact at the police station to give him this info," she says as she pulls out her phone.

"No," I say, opening my eyes. I grab her hand before she dials a number. "First of all, where did you get that information? None of the others are awake yet, right? They'll know you talked to someone who was there, which would either be The Vacant or an invisible hero."

"Right," she says as she nods and drops her phone in her purse. "Sorry – I wasn't thinking."

"It's ok," I reassure her. "But second, The Vacant is obviously insistent on having everyone in his pocket. *Maybe* there are still some people at the police station that you can trust, but let's assume there aren't. From here on out, you should probably only give information to the police or newspapers anonymously."

"That's probably true," she agrees, "but it's not like any of the papers or news crews are going to listen anyway. They're refusing to post any actual news."

"They're scared, Maria," I say. "This psychopath doesn't mess around. They probably can't post anything about The Vacant that isn't sent directly from him. At least not without fear of losing someone."

She lets out a *harrumph* and then silently pulls her phone back out. She frowns as she makes swiping motions every few seconds, most likely reading news stories or checking social media. She's probably frustrated at the media because she can't stand the thought of someone doing nothing when they have the power to fix something. I wonder what she really thinks of me, considering I have far more power than news editors.

After keeping my eyes open for a few minutes, the headache has passed enough for me to assume I'm not going to die from it. I'm not sure of the prognosis on my embarrassment, but she hasn't said anything and I'm definitely not going to bring it up.

"Robby," she says suddenly, standing, still looking at her phone. "They're starting to wake up."

"That's great," I say, nervous at her stiff posture. "Are they okay?"

"Victor Boone is trending."

"What?"

"Hashtag *VictorBooneWillSaveUs* is the number one topic on multiple social media sites."

Her answer only adds questions.

"I didn't mean 'What?' as in I couldn't hear what you said," I clarify. "I meant it as in, 'What in the world are you talking about?'"

"I know," she says. "I'm reading through them trying to figure out what's going on. Most of them are saying that Victor is back and he's the reason that the Huberts are still alive."

"But Vic is dead!" I shout, standing. My head recoils from my own voice, and my eyes squint with the reminder that I have a headache.

"I know that," she says, still staring at her phone's screen. "But so far, all of the people who were in the court room are waking up and confirming that a 'Victor Boone like' presence seemed to knock out the gunmen."

"They're insane," I dismissively declare, even though I know it's not true.

"No, they're not," she defends. "The 'presence' that saved everyone while Victor Boone was alive is exactly the same one that was in the room. Even though they're wrong, they're right."

Now it's my turn to release a frustrated *harrumph*. I'm not sure why it's getting to me, but now that I'm trying to wrestle with the idea of getting out there to save people again, I don't want Vic to get the credit. I mean, *I* don't want the credit – I just don't want him to get it. I don't want people putting their hope in a singular human that could easily let them down. Mostly because that human is me, and I'm going to let them down again. I just know it.

"Robby," she says, finally looking up at me. "This is good. The Vacant is going to know that he needs to watch his back. Maybe he'll quit, knowing someone might stop him."

I move to the window and look at hundreds of people milling about the sidewalks, completely unaware of me. The way I like it.

"He won't quit," I sigh. "Not until Victor Boone *really* shows up."

CHAPTER ELEVEN

"It was you, wasn't it?"

Dr. Hughes' pen stays in his breast pocket for this appointment, and there's no notepad nearby. He's sitting on the edge of his chair, a bit more eager than I'd seen him before.

I think he's *excited.*

"Yeah," I mumble, looking down at the carpet.

"Aren't you happy to have helped people again?"

"But I didn't help Councilman Alvarez," I complain. "He died just like Vic."

"Robby, the councilman's death was definitely not your fault. In fact, the way it's been told to me is that there would've been at least four more deaths had you not arrived in time. At least."

"Maybe," I depressingly say. "But that doesn't change the fact that a man was killed in front of me, and I couldn't stop it. The body count may be less, but it wasn't zero. That part is no different than if I hadn't been there at all."

Dr. Hughes eyes me for a moment.

"Robby, obviously yours is a very unique situation," he says. "And there's something I've said to clients who are police officers or doctors and such – something that still applies to you."

He pauses for effect, as if to make sure he has my attention.

"You must understand, even with your abilities," he begins, taking another breath. "You are but one man. You can do great things with your powers. But you can't save *everyone*."

He keeps taking pauses. I'm not sure if he's thinking, or if he's expecting me to talk, but it feels awkward.

"All of us will die at some point," he continues. "Even you, I assume. I don't think you're immortal, are you?"

I shrug. I highly doubt that.

"Well, some people die from old age and sickness – you can't prevent that."

I nod. Grandma.

"Others die by accident – you can't always prevent that, either."

I nod again, though it's less of an absolute truth. I can't save people from a fatal accident if I'm not anywhere near them, but if I'm close by I can.

Or, at least, sometimes I can. I couldn't save my parents. Though I don't remember having any powers until after that point. Maybe there are some accidents that I just can't outwit.

"And others still," he continues, "die at the hands of someone else. You can't always prevent that."

I don't nod.

Victor. Councilman Alvarez. Think about those moments, it was completely within my power to stop their deaths, but I wasn't focused enough.

"Robby, do you agree that you can't always prevent that?"

I still don't nod.

"Hmm," he says, stroking his chin. "Do you mind if I give you a scenario?"

I shrug again.

"Okay," he starts, leaning back in his chair. "Let's say you're back in college."

It's easy to put my head back into that phase of my life, because I never graduated due to Victor's antics. I thought it was bad enough when he made fun of me from the back of the classroom, but after he took credit for several more of my heroic moments, he wouldn't leave me alone. Sometimes he would waltz into one of my classes in the middle of a lecture just to let me know who was really in control of my schedule.

Any time that happened, you'd think the professor would push him out the door and complain of such a rude interruption. Instead, they would roll out the red carpet like he was a rap mogul or Hollywood heavyweight. The entire room would murmur and pull out their camera phones, then Vic would pose for selfies and answer questions about what it was like to be a bona fide hero.

"What can I say?" is how he'd usually start. "When you look into the eyes of some chick who was gonna die, and you grabbed her when she was, like, just inches from getting hit by a train or something... You know... It's pretty great."

He'd often string his speeches with four-letter words, and I would tell him over and over to censor himself. To which he would always call me a pushover. That was his favorite word to describe someone who had a moral conviction above his.

College was officially over, though, when he was kicked off the football team soon after he made his superherodom public.

"Coach said I can't play because I've got powers!" he screamed at me, as if it was my fault. "Said it isn't fair to the 'integrity of the sport.'"

He put air quotes around it, so that I could be positive that he never cared about a game's integrity. Rules never really applied to him before, and he hated that they might be applied to him after he saved so many "hot chicks."

We saved a lot of men, too. In fact, we saved people in every kind of category: young and old, male and female, skinny and not-so-skinny... But Victor really only cared about the *chicks.*

"It makes sense," I'd told him about getting kicked off the team. "If you're flying around, picking up cars with your mind, and deflecting bullets without bruises, it's *not* fair. Everybody else is normal, and super powers give you an advantage that was never intended in a game like that."

"But I don't have powers, asshole," Vic jabbed. "You're the douche with the powers."

"Vic – no cussing. Even at me," I pleaded for the millionth time. "And the rest of the world doesn't know that you're not the one with powers. I'll bet if you came clean, and told them there's nothing super about you, then they'd eventually let you back on the team."

"What, do you want all the credit now?" he yelled, as if it would've been selfish if I actually did want the credit that he was taking. As if it was never mine to begin with, but always his spotlight to bask in.

Part of me knew that I could expose him. But it would mean that the attention would be directed to me. The only way people would believe that he wasn't super would be to give them the whole truth. And even if I didn't tell it, Vic would spill the beans. If he couldn't have the fame and glory, then he would take away my privacy just to spite me.

Right after he got kicked off the team, he didn't see the point in going to class anymore. At first his professors didn't mind; in fact, they were completely sensitive to the thought that a superhero wouldn't have time to show up to every lecture when the city constantly needed him.

My professors weren't so understanding. I'd never made a grade below a B prior to the whole fiasco, but I was logging a lot of zeros and incompletes. For my third and, unfortunately, final semester in school, I had a 1.4 grade point average.

But the grace from the professors wasn't enough to get Vic to the gown and tassel even though he lacked just a handful of classes. He didn't see the point of learning. The only reason he was in college to begin with was football. Now that it was gone, he'd already decided his career would be acting like a superhero.

I didn't bother to go to most of my last final exams either, because I knew I'd fail either way.

Unfortunately, Dr. Hughes is still speaking and I hadn't heard a word of what he said.

"What do you do?" he questions.

"Sorry, Joe, I spaced out a bit," I confess. "Can you repeat that?"

"Sure," Dr. Hughes smiles. "Pretend you're back in college and you have only two classes left to graduate. Unfortunately, both classes are scheduled at the exact same time. It's impossible to take both of them. What do you do?"

"I'd talk to the dean or something," I say.

"No," Joe casually answers, shaking his head. "The dean confirms my story. You can't take both."

Hmmm. This is a weird scenario. Why would a college require both classes to graduate, but make them conflict with each other? Surely that's not reasonable.

"What are the classes?" I ask.

"Doesn't matter," he dismisses. "They're both required."

"Can I take a test for one of them, so that I can study on my own?"

"No," he says casually again. "All options in your mind about somehow taking them at the same time are gone. Given this information, knowing that nothing else is possible, what do you do?"

This is silly. What does this have to do with fixing whatever's broken in me?

"I guess I'd have to take one, then wait until the other is offered again."

Joe's eyes light up.

"Exactly!"

I think I've missed the point, because his body language is telling me that the lesson has been learned.

"Don't you see, Robby?" He leans in, squinting his eyes, as if he can see the moral of the story reflected in my head. "If you choose one, you simply *can't* choose the other at the same time."

I know I'm giving him a *thank-you-Captain-Obvious* look, because that's the only thought in my head. He pretty much repeated back exactly what I just told him.

"There are a multitude of other situations where this same thought applies, and I know it makes perfect sense to you," he says. "You can't always have everything at the same time. And for most of us, it just means we miss out on that class, or we have to choose between restaurants or movies or what have you. Most human beings don't have the pressure of having lives hang on their split second decisions and actions."

Okay, I get it. Mostly. But waiting an extra semester to graduate because a class isn't offered is not the same as watching someone die because I'm too slow.

"You know," Joe continues, "there was one option that you didn't mention."

"You said all other options were off the table," I protest. "You literally said nothing else was possible."

Joe leans back again.

"It's the option you've been choosing for months, though," he says, "so I'm surprised you didn't say it."

I've definitely not been considering my college options in the last few months.

"What option is that?" I finally ask after a long pause.

"Giving up," he answers flatly. "The only other option is that you *don't* make a choice. You quit school with only two classes left, because you're too afraid of making the wrong choice."

"I didn't quit school because of not being able to schedule my classes," I say with a little bit of frustration and defeat.

"I know," Joe softly counters. "I understand why you quit school; that was a poor example. I agree that the work you were doing was much more important than earning a degree. But what I mean is that for months—ever since Victor was murdered—you've been refusing to make a choice of who to save. You haven't saved anyone because you were afraid you wouldn't save *everyone*."

I want to argue. I want to tell him my reasons were far more noble than simply a way to avoid making a bad decision. I want to scream about how dangerous I am, and how no one—not even him—is safe around me. That I was holing myself up in my apartment to protect everyone.

But I'm not sure it's true.

"Robby, can you say it out loud? Can you say 'I can't save everyone, and that's okay'?"

I hesitate until Dr. Hughes urges me again.

"I can't save everyone," I finally mutter.

"And?"

I don't think I really believe the second part.

"And that's okay," I say just above a whisper. I sound like a little boy who is forced to apologize for punching his little brother, even though he still thinks he was justified in doing so.

Joe makes me say it over and over, as if my ears hearing it from my own mouth will make it more relevant, more true.

I'm nervous that it'll go on forever, because he gave me two of his appointment slots to fill. But after chanting for a bit longer, he seems satisfied that I'm saturated with self-acceptance.

Maria and I slink through dark halls of our old university's science building. It's oddly familiar, and I'm hoping it houses the equipment that we need to determine just what The Vacant's blue fog is made of.

We're dressed in normal clothes, even though I presented the idea of an outfit of all black multiple times. I'd seen it on a number of TV shows – people without invisibility apparently felt like shadowy fashion was a good deal of camouflage. That's just what you do when you break into a building.

I've never done this sort of thing without being invisible before. I'd never had the fear of getting caught by security guards or cameras, so I could be as flippant in my actions as I wanted. I never worried about the glow of exit lights scanning across my face to any potential witnesses.

But I had a partner and a piece of cloth. Any security footage would show a floating remnant of Councilman Alvarez's clothing through opening doors and beside magically flipping light switches. Floating objects are not such a big deal—I occasionally carry them when no one is around—but

Maria insisted on coming, and I don't know how to sway her when she's already made her mind up.

Thus, our normal clothes.

She'd said that only criminals wear sneaky-looking garb. That if anyone stops us, we're to just act like we're supposed to be there.

"I've only been stopped a handful of times," she'd said, when telling me the plan. "And when I am, confidence gets people off my back. Or if they don't believe me I just act like I'm dumb and they still let me off."

Apparently she's gotten into numerous crime scenes, rock concerts, and private events with open bars practicing the technique. The problem is, I can't act confident even if I really am confident. I'll be the dumb one, and I'll let her feign authority with any actual authority figure.

The door to the advanced chemistry lab is bolted, of course, but it's no match for Maria's powers. She's apparently really good at picking locks.

Once we're inside I take a short flight to position a security camera towards a dry-erase board, which we will both avoid for the rest of the night.

"All right, what now?" Maria asks with her hands on her hips and a smirk on her face. I think she's proud of getting to show off her skills.

"Well," I sigh. "Now we cut the clothing into multiple pieces so that we can try different tests. We should save one as a control, just in case."

Maria stole Alvarez's suit jacket. I'm sure they noticed it was missing, but we hadn't heard anything about it yet. It was a little more brazen than I'd expected, but it was covered in a blue powder more so than anything else in the room, which tells me it was near the origin of the thick fog. If The Vacant was able to stand right beside the source, then it also tells me his mask has a built in filter—which seems unlikely considering how thin it must be—or he's immune to it.

I've never practiced Mithridatism before, but if I have to breathe in the fog until I'm not affected by it, it's a small price to pay to stop this jerk. But first I have to know what the stuff is.

Hmm... I wonder if I could do the same with electricity?

But currently, I'm in over my head. I watched my dad do this sort of thing every day while I was growing up, but he's been gone for more than ten years. The only practical experience I'd had since then was several years ago in the lab down the hall from this one, with Maria and Vic as my partners. Doing it without Vic this time meant we could be a lot more efficient.

I'd also read a number of things online in the last day or two, hoping to luck out.

"Well, let's do it then, yeah?" Maria stares at me with an expectant look.

"Do what?"

She grabs the cloth from my hands.

"Cut it up into smaller pieces," she answers, giving me my own direction. "Like you just said."

"Right," I say, looking around until I find a pair of scissors. "Maybe I should be the one cutting it up. I don't want you breathing it in and getting knocked out."

She raises one eyebrow. "I pulled this jacket off of a dead body and crammed it into my purse in a room that had a thin layer of the stuff all over everything. Something tells me that I would've already been affected if it's still potent."

She grabs the scissors from me. So much for being the strong one in the partnership.

"Besides," she continues. "If I get knocked out, you can toss me over your shoulder and get me out of here with no trouble. I'm not so sure I can do the same for you."

For a split second I wonder if she's calling me fat, but in no time I realize how impractical it would be for a slim girl like her to carry even a normal-sized person several miles.

"Wait," I say. "Gloves, goggles, masks. There's no sense in us *trying* to black out."

We rummage through the drawers and closets until we find the right gear. We tie rubber aprons on each other to make us look official and ridiculous.

After we play dress up, we cut the cloth and lay the strips across the table.

"And what now?" Maria asks again, muffled through the respirator covering her mouth.

This was a bad idea. I should have read more to prepare myself, but for some reason I thought that everything would come back to me, much like riding a bike. Though I haven't ridden a bike in years, so I'm not even sure if that adage is true.

"Take one of the strips and try to scrape off as much of the powder as possible. Let's see how much we can isolate. It'll be a lot easier to work with the residue alone so the cloth itself doesn't affect the test results."

We gather a couple test tubes full of the powder – way more than I assumed we would. If I'd known we'd get this much of the stuff, we wouldn't have needed to cut the jacket up. Gah – Maria's going to for sure know I have no idea what I'm doing.

We go to work with chemicals and litmus papers; water, vinegar, iodine, and phenolphthalein are slipped into eyedroppers, as well as just about anything else I remember from experiments in classes and books. We make numerous observations, watching the blue powder change colors or bubble depending on the chemical or litmus strips, writing each reaction down.

And a few hours later, I have to admit that I'm grasping at straws without a professor or my dad nearby to ask for guidance. And I'm pretty sure Maria knows it.

"We need help," I finally admit as I take off my goggles.

She nods.

"Have we learned anything from all of these tests?" she asks, scrunching her face a bit as she removes her mask.

"Oh yeah," I confirm. "We've learned a lot. If it were baking soda or citric acid or something simple, we would've known it pretty quickly. We know a ton of things that it *isn't* – I just don't know what it's all adding up to, or what to compare it to."

I point at the papers that I'd printed out from the internet earlier in the day. It was probably a complete waste of time, because the powders on the sheets were mostly household chemicals. We could've eliminated them from the possibilities just based on the fact that it knocked me out, and no kitchen cleaner has such power.

"Then what next?" Maria asks. "We can't just give up and hope The Vacant doesn't use it again. It might not be fatal, but it takes you out of the game pretty easily."

After staring at the lab equipment in hopelessness for a moment, a light bulb goes off in my head. I have no idea why I thought my dad was the only chemist I knew that could've helped me, when he's not the only one who explained his experiments to me when I stood nearby as a kid.

"Let's clean up," I say, now on a clear mission. "We're going to find Winston Bradford."

"Who?" she asks, confused.

"My dad's old lab partner."

CHAPTER TWELVE

Dr. Bradford is not an easy man to track down. Even with Maria on the scent, his trail seems to go cold.

"Says here the company your dad worked for went bankrupt about seven years ago," Maria says while squinting at small text on my computer screen. "Apparently someone was doing tests on humans without getting permission from the FDA."

"That doesn't completely surprise me," I say, "considering I heard my dad complain about the bureaucratic red tape he had to go through to move forward on any of his experiments."

I don't remember it too clearly, but I know that my dad was working on some sort of genetic correction drug. Something that would cure a whole slew of diseases.

"My dad was always bringing random animals home," I continue. "He said he wanted to observe them around the clock."

Personally, I felt like I had my own miniature petting zoo in his basement lab. Everything from mice to rabbits to the occasional monkey. There were certain animals I wasn't allowed to touch based on what tests he was running.

"Your dad's company and the last company that Dr. Bradford worked for have a common billionaire investor," Maria says, her finger sliding down her scribbled notepad. "Does the name Nelson Slate ring any bells?"

"I don't think so – should it?"

Maria laughs, accidentally snorting a bit.

"Yeah, it should," she says with a smile. "He's a jerk. Think Victor as a middle-aged man with tons of money."

"How do you know him?" I ask.

"I read the news, for one," she replies. "And a friend of mine had an internship with his publicist, Trace Guffman, during her last semester. Apparently Trace makes him invest in companies that are 'doing good' because he refuses to give to charity. She thinks it helps his image, since everything else he does is unapologetically selfish."

"What does he have to do with Dr. Bradford now?" I ask.

"The last company that I can find looks more like a partnership between the two of them. Slate was the only investor and our doctor friend was the only employee. The company went bankrupt a bit over a year ago, and I can't find anything else on him online."

"On Dr. Bradford or Nelson Slate?"

"Bradford," Maria clarifies. "Nelson Slate is everywhere. At least, everywhere that there are a bunch of rich and powerful people gathered together. Actually, he's attending a black-tie affair tomorrow night."

She says it with a bit too much enthusiasm.

Crap. She can't expect me to slip into an extra-extra-large tuxedo and nonchalantly bump into him at some beautiful-people gala to pump him for information. I'd fit in just about as well as an elephant in an office building.

"I'm sure you'll find more info on Dr. Bradford," I encourage. "Like you said, you found me, and I don't even have a driver's license."

Maria huffs, as if I doubt her detective skills. She spins around in her chair to face me.

"I just spent the last six hours scouring the web and calling in favors, and you think I'm giving up too early?"

"No, sorry," I apologize quickly. "I'm just trying to be hopeful. There's no way I could be slick enough to look like I belong in a crowd like that in order talk to Nelson."

Maria's furrowed brow eases and she smiles. She's beautiful, and even more so when her teeth are exposed.

"Oh," she says. "I wasn't expecting you to lie your way into something like that. I could tell you were at your capacity when you tried to justify your presence to the coat rack in the lobby of the chemistry building."

"I thought it was a security guard," I defend.

"The only guards at the school drive golf carts around the campus and take donut-induced naps when the clock strikes nine-thirty. Just admit it – you were scared."

Hearing her say it makes me feel silly. Why would an invulnerable man who can turn invisible and fly away be scared of being seen?

I try to recover. "I didn't want you to get caught."

"Thanks," she laughs. "You can attend this party, too – but for the first time, I require that you *are* invisible to do so."

"What if The Vacant shows up and gases everyone?"

"Something tells me a guy like Nelson Slate—and the company he keeps—has already signed on The Vacant's dotted line." She seems very sure of herself. "But if not, you get out of there before the blue fog gets you."

"What about you?" I ask.

"In a room full of deep pockets and trophy wives, I'll be the last thing The Vacant is worried about."

I can't sleep. Fire and glass cages again. One would think I'd remember everything perfectly, considering how many times I have the dream. But nope. It's all blurs and fleeting sounds when I'm awake.

I'm taking a stroll through the quiet city streets, and I'm visible this time. I don't like being seen, but Maria and Dr. Hughes seem to overlap on their advice occasionally. They say I need to transition to being visible in public more than transparent. I can't bring myself to go out in the daylight alone, but I can ease into the familiar shadows of the night.

Of course, even the shadows can't hide much from me, but I try to remind myself that no one else shares my hyper-sensitive vision.

I'm starting to consider that it's not just my vision that is hyper-sensitive. No one else in elementary school seemed to react to the same insults that I did. If I think hard about it, everyone got made fun of to a certain degree. It's just that I was the only one who'd turn red and cry. At that point I was still the fat kid who couldn't defend himself.

I'm still the fat kid, but at least now I shouldn't be afraid of anything. So why am I so afraid?

I mean, why do I care so much about being found out? Maria saw me naked when I was unconscious in City Hall, and she's still hanging around. That's about as "found out" as is humanly possible. She still hasn't said a word and has somehow made me feel like she doesn't look at me different. Maybe the superpowers are just the excuse I've been giving myself all these years to retreat from humanity.

Or maybe Dr. Hughes is in my head, forcing me to overanalyze myself. I've only seen him twice in the last week, and I feel like we've already talked about way more than we did after my parents died.

Of course, back then I barely said two words in the first few months. I remember he would give me puzzles when I refused to talk – like Rubik's cubes or the kinds with tangled metal rods that you're supposed to slip apart. Half of the time he'd just do a crossword puzzle and act like we were having a casual conversation while I tried as hard as I could to solve the puzzles without bending or breaking things. I ruined a couple of them, but he wrote it off, saying he'd had them for years and that they must've been worn out.

He would talk to my grandma after our time was up, whispering to her about how I was still repressing so much. I saw him for months before our conversations got much deeper than surface level.

He waited until I gushed all of my problems out like a toothpaste tube, squeezing myself until the opposite walls of my heart were touching each other. Even then, I hid what I was *really* worried about. Dealing with my parents' death was emotional enough without having to deal with a coming-of-age of epic proportions.

Maybe telling him the truth about me was what I should've done all those years ago. Maybe he could've helped me avoid most of my misery. What if I never really needed to live a lonely life of self-confinement?

Bah. That can't be true.

I try *not* to soften my steps on the pavement. I try to move my feet without restraint, as if I'm not afraid to create imprints of my shoes. But after I rattle several nearby garbage bins with shockwaves, I pull back to my normal self-control.

No, I still need to restrain myself. Physically. It's my mind I need to loosen up. I have two friends who know my secret. They haven't turned on me, or tried to use me. Dr. Hughes is legally obligated to keep quiet, and would risk destroying his reputation if he didn't. But Maria could do it easily enough.

There are a lot of moments when I want to ask her if she really likes me. But that's stupid – I can't ask her something like that outright. If I'd asked Vic that kind of question, he would've given me brutal honesty and admitted that he was only around me for the recognition that came along with it. It was obvious that we wouldn't have been real friends in any other circumstance.

Maria was much nicer. If I were to ask her that kind of question I wouldn't be able to trust her response. Of course she would say she likes me, and that she wasn't hanging around just because I had super powers. But I thought about it a lot. Why in the world *did* she hang around me? I'm not good looking or funny. I mean, *I* think I'm funny, but in a geeky way – not in a way that makes a girl like her laugh. Sure, she laughs at some of my jokes, but I can't trust that either.

Maria could get her big break by exposing me if she didn't care about me. But she hasn't. She hasn't even asked me to use my powers to do her a favor or anything. Is it possible that we're actually friends? That she's not expecting anything from me? That she's pushing me for my own sake?

"Got any change, mister?"

I look over at the bum with his outstretched arm, reaching into my thoughts to pull me back to reality. I don't usually carry anything with me, but I brought another one-hundred-dollar bill for just this guy. I've been leaving money here since the night of the drunk bully, sometimes following him after he celebrated the magically appearing gift. At first I was afraid he would just spend it on beer or worse, but instead I'd catch him buying food for a host of other homeless men and women.

He might be the best hope I have in humanity. Someone who has nothing but shares everything. After spending years with a guy who had everything and shared none of it, I try to convince myself that there are lots of people like this.

But this is the first time he's seen my face.

As I extend the green image of Benjamin Franklin, the guy's eyes get wide.

"Thank you!" he says excitedly.

I turn to leave – I don't need to know where he's taking the money anymore. I trust him with it.

"Are you an angel?" he calls out.

"No," I say.

I fight the urge to fly away.

In contrast to my previous night, I'm surrounded by expensive suits and diamond-studded everything. Nelson Slate would probably have a diamond rhinestone jacket if there were such a thing. I can feel the slime dripping off of him even though I'm floating several feet above his head.

Maria is magic with bouncers. If there was a list, they didn't ask if she was on it. She walks in like she owns the place – and from where I hover, she does. Her tight black dress with the familiar vanilla-coconut scent makes it hard to focus.

She grabs a drink and says hi to a few fancy looking people as if they're old friends. Maybe they *are* old friends. It makes me wonder what her life was really like before she showed up on my doorstep. What if she was on the up and up with her journalism stuff but didn't want me to know? I wonder if she was used to gatherings like this, but gave them up to sit in a poorly decorated tenth-floor apartment.

Nah. I don't think she's actually that humble. She's no Victor Boone, but she does enjoy letting me know when she's good at things, and when she's right. It would have come up in conversation, instead of her acting like she's still simply *trying* to be a journalist.

She's just got the same kind of confidence that Vic had. The kind that allows them to walk into the room not caring if every eye is on them. Vic just lacked the other nice qualities she has.

I see Slate before she does, but there's really no way I can clue her into his whereabouts. He's clad in a suit and alligator dress shoes that probably cost more than everything I own. She'll find him eventually, so I just wait and listen to the beautiful people banter about profits, synergy, and friendly competition.

"...closed the deal with Jacobs, because he promised to give them..."

"...hear about the merger between their two firms? That's going to really shake up the..."

"...offered me double my asking price. Double! I don't know what he saw in the account, but..."

Slate's is one of the few conversations that doesn't seem to be about business. Rather, he's whispering inappropriate things into the ear of a girl half his age. His slicked-back black hair and grey goatee just scream scumbag. The girl giggles, even though her heartbeat seems more nervous than excited. As if she's afraid of him, rather than smitten.

There are two men with earpieces within three feet of him, constantly scanning the room. They each have firearms strapped inside their suit coats, but neither smells of fresh gunpowder. Either these guys don't generally see any action, or Nelson is the kind of man that throws something away after he uses it once. I hope the girl is aware of that possibility.

Maria sees him, or at least notices the two bodyguards, and makes her way in their direction. She holds her glass of white wine like a movie star and slips through the crowd. It seems like Nelson catches her eye, then looks at the girl next to him in comparison. The two women are maybe a year apart in age, but Maria is prettier by far. At least, by my standards. Perhaps I'm biased.

"Hey Sara, how're you doing?" Maria says with a relaxed smile to Slate's arm candy.

"Hey Maria!" the girl, apparently named Sara, replies excitedly. She disconnects with Nelson for a moment to hug Maria. "What are you doing here?"

"Trying to see if there are stories to write about, I guess," Maria says. "Are you still working for Trace?"

Sara nods, her eyes darting between Maria and Nelson. "Yeah – she hired me right after graduation."

"My goodness, Sara," Nelson butts in. "When are you going to introduce me to your…" He pauses, searching for a word. "…delightful friend?"

"Oh, sorry," Sara says, slightly flustered. Her pulse quickens its pace just slightly. At least I think it's hers – there are a lot of heartbeats in the small area. "Maria, I'm sure you know Nelson Slate. Nel, this is Maria Truman. We went to school together."

Oooh... They're not just on a first name basis – she's shortened it to *Nel*.

Slate gently takes Maria's beautiful fingers, causing me to tense up. I expected the action, but for some reason his lips move in slow motion when he kisses her hand. I don't understand why, but I kind of have to hold myself back.

"Bonne soirée, belle," he says as he lets her hand go.

Maria giggles and keeps her fingers in the air for a moment. I hope she's faking her excited response, but I can't tell. I shouldn't care.

Why do I care?

"You mentioned you were looking for a story to write about," he continues in a hushed voice. "Surely I can find a way to—" pause "—satisfy your curiosities."

Grrrr.

He's already got a beautiful woman on his arm, and he's jockeying for mine now.

Wait— Mine?

Maria giggles again. Either she's really laying on the charm—or at least the *acceptance* of supposed charm—or she really is enjoying the admiration.

I need to get out of my head. Maria is free to do whatever she wants. I'm in no position to expect her to only have eyes for me or something.

"Well, you *are* a very interesting man," Maria replies behind a giggle. "I've read about all of the wonderful companies you've been involved with, researching illnesses and developing so many new medicines."

"You're interested in medicine?" Nelson says, scanning her up and down. "I have several new drugs in development that you might be interested in. Some that you could try tonight, actually."

Wow – what a ball of slime. Even Sara swats his shoulder as a response to what I think we all know he's insinuating.

Maria doesn't skip a beat.

"Wow, really?" she asks. "You have more pharmaceuticals in development beyond Delaproxin and Erizephenol? Those are incredible. I'm excited to see what happens when they're finally approved by the FDA."

Slate's face starts to sag as Maria speaks, especially as she enunciates the prescription names with perfection and ease. I'm pretty sure she could've made names up and he wouldn't have known. His frown is very pronounced by the time she finishes talking.

"Wow," he says as he rolls his eyes. "You sound like Bradford. Sara, why'd you introduce me if you knew she was no fun?"

Maria doesn't allow Sara to respond.

"Dr. Winston Bradford?" Maria asks quickly. "Are you still working with him? I was under the impression that you parted ways when he failed to deliver on a very *hush-hush* project the two of you were working on."

Slate curses.

"No, that peasant decided he could fund his own research better than I could. He was probably just waiting until he could get some big contract on his own the whole time I was bleeding money into his work."

"Do you know where I can find him?" Maria asks, a little more forward than I would expect could work. "I'm so impressed with the projects both of you did together."

"Last I heard, he bought the old diagnostics lab on Twenty-Fifth Street," Nelson offered while rolling his eyes again, giving answers almost too easily. "If you run into him, tell him that I'm still waiting for that strength enhancer that was supposed to make me a trillion dollars from the government."

Before he finishes giving Maria all the information we need, he grabs Sara and starts walking away. He looks like a frustrated father who's dragging his daughter away from a party with underage drinking.

"Warn me next time one of your brainiac friends tries to waste my time," he mumbles to her before getting out of Maria's earshot. "This place is dead."

He snaps his fingers as his date apologizes. Sara seems to forget about any allegiances to Maria, joining Slate in ridiculing her. The bodyguards react to the sound from his fingers and fall in behind him. Maria turns around and heads for the opposite door.

I debate on who to follow, Maria or Slate, but after hearing more berating comments from him and his date, I conclude there would be no further information to gather.

A few minutes later, I'm quietly hovering next to Maria in an alley way.

"You were *amazing*," I whisper to her.

"Thanks," she shrugs. "What a gross old man. I can't believe Sara is with him."

"You're not kidding," I agree. "We really lucked out that she was there, and that you knew each other."

"No, I figured she'd be there," she says. "She was sleeping with him when she was an intern."

"Really?"

"Yeah," she confirms. "He has, like, ten girlfriends. She talked about him all the time. She doesn't really like him, but she got used to a standard of living that an entry-level publicist assistant's salary can't maintain. If she wasn't there tonight, I was just planning on bumping into him and spilling my drink on myself or something to catch his eye."

I shake my invisible head in disbelief.

"You are such a good actor. For a minute there, I seriously was afraid you were about to—"

I cut myself off.

"What, sleep with him?" she snaps back after I don't finish my sentence. "Disgusting. Like I said, he's Victor Boone with money. Even if he wasn't almost sixty years old, there's no way."

I have flashbacks of the times when Maria would flirt with Vic after he outed himself as a "superhero." I felt the exact same way back then as I did tonight. I don't think I really believed it was all an act until I saw her turn it on, then off, with Slate.

I hear something stirring at the opposite end of the alley.

"Shh – someone's coming," I whisper.

Maria pulls out her phone, and after a second of delay starts speaking in a sort of happy sing-song tone. "Hey, Robby. Just walking by myself down a dark alleyway."

"What are you doing?" I whisper.

"Well, what do you want me to do?" she asks into her phone. "Stop talking until we see each other again?"

"Hey baby," a voice calls from several yards away. "I can walk you home."

"Oh, don't worry about me," Maria says, still having a conversation with me on the other end of the line. "There's a nice man here who said he'll take care of me. Don't wait up, okay?"

"That's right, girl," the creeper says as he strolls closer with a devious smile on his face. "I'll keep you safe from all the bad guys out here."

She tosses her phone in her purse.

"I'd stay away if I were you," she politely warns him. "I don't want you to get hurt."

He laughs, staring at her like a hyena stumbling onto dinner.

"What – you got pepper spray in that bag or something?"

"Or something, yes," she answers with a big smile on her face.

"Well, don't worry," he soothes as he moves within a foot of her. "You won't have to use it. There won't be no trouble."

"I know," she says with confidence.

I listen to his quickening pulse and prepare to deflect any of his advances. He picked the wrong lonely girl to mess with tonight, especially after one sleaze bag already tried to hit on her.

But I don't have to make a move.

Maria's knee rams into his junk as hard as she can force it.

CHAPTER THIRTEEN

"I want you to concentrate on the room in your dreams," Dr. Hughes says.

My eyes follow a green light that darts left and right, left and right in front of me. The bar of LEDs illuminates in a rhythm that might seem fast to some, but to me it's like watching a turtle crawling across a two lane highway. The device has two wires leading to my hands, and I'm holding two plastic objects that vibrate when the light reaches the corresponding side.

This probably works for most people. I'm sure it calms their brain down and allows them to get lost in the pattern of following the green vibration. I'll bet it allows them to sink deep into their memories without wondering when they're coming back up for air. But so far, there's no indication it's going to work for me.

"You're in the room at the beginning of your dream – how do you feel?" Joe asks, once again with a pen in his grip.

"I feel like this isn't going to work," I say.

He laughs.

"Sure, I'm not positive that you'll benefit from this like most of my clients," he admits. "I'm confident in the therapy, but not as confident it will work on you. The purpose of EMDR is not to trick you into revealing things you wouldn't otherwise. It's not like hypnotism. Instead, it is meant to allow your eyes and brain to act like you're asleep. Then, we can talk about some of the traumatic events that you're unconsciously trying to hide when you're awake. There's more effort to keeping it hidden than you might realize."

I shift in my seat a little.

"And when will we know that it's useless to do it?" I ask, glancing over at him.

"After we give it a chance," he says as he smiles, motioning back to the bar of moving lights. "Now, please just relax. Don't *try* to do anything. Don't even concentrate too hard on following the lights. Just put yourself into the room from your dream again." His voice slows down. "Think about the fire and the metal surfaces. When you're there, tell me what you feel."

I try to relax. I try not to watch every single LED bulb illuminate and then darken. I try not to notice that there's a significant delay—at least four milliseconds—between the vibrations from the objects I'm holding in my hands. I try to let the stupid turtle cross the stupid road, without subconsciously anticipating its movement. I try to let it drag me.

I think about the dream. The one that I can never focus on when I'm awake. The moments that are simply my sleeping mind projecting the memory of my parents' deaths.

"Don't try so hard, Robby. Just tell me the feeling that you have when you think of the room."

I stop putting all of my effort into the experiment, and just focus on the emotions I feel when I wake up from it. It starts as a blur – the same way it always is when I think about it. But then the edges of the green lights soften, starting to run together, and the room barely starts to gain clarity.

"Scared," I finally say as my brain resists the process a little less.

"Good," Joe says. "I'm here with you. Keep picturing the room. Lock onto that feeling of fear, and just let your mind wander. You don't have to speak, but you can if you want."

I try to embrace it, as if the fear itself is the key to unlocking the memory. I know fear well. It's the same as when I think about people finding out about me. The same as when I consider reporters and cameras cramming into the hallway outside my apartment to unveil me to the world. The same when I consider if Maria is planning on using me to catch her big break.

Wait – no. It's *not* the same fear.

I let myself get really scared again. Afraid for my life. I haven't felt scared like this since I was eleven. It's the *true* fear that I'm not safe; that I'm going to die.

Fire licks the walls of Dr. Hughes' office. The wooden desk turns into a metal table holding test tubes and beakers filled with bubbling liquids. The couch I'm sitting on melts into the smooth concrete floor. Then, through the haze of heat, I see Dr. Hughes sitting in the middle of the room.

I shake my head and drop the vibrating plastic, breathing heavily. Somehow I've soaked my shirt in sweat.

"You're okay, Robby," Joe says. "You're safe. Tell me what you saw and felt."

He leans over and picks up the vibrators, handing them to me as I steady my breathing. He flips a switch and the lights and vibrations stop.

"I saw the room, but we were both in it," I say. "You were sitting in the middle of it."

"That's ok," he says as he leans back in his chair. "How did you feel?"

"Terrified," I answer, trying to slow my breathing and my heartbeat. "I haven't felt like that—felt like I was completely powerless—in a really long time."

Joe pauses as he writes something down.

"It might sound strange," he says, "but this is excellent."

I snort a little at the idea that this feeling is anything but horrible.

"Robby, I want us to do this again a few more times. Instead of trying to get out of that situation when you feel overwhelmed, just talk to me."

It sounds insane, but I nod and watch the lights when he flips the switch back on again.

"Lock onto that feeling of fear," he says again. "Picture the room and just let your mind wander."

It's quicker this time. Fire licks Dr. Hughes' bookshelves and framed college degrees. Everything inside the room is replaced with lab equipment. I can't see him this time.

"Joe," I yell out, still staring at the burning room.

"I'm here," he says calmly from a world away. "Keep locking onto the feeling of being afraid and powerless. Just let your mind wander through the room."

I know he keeps repeating the same words and phrases, but it doesn't bother me. It's almost like they're magic spells that pull the curtains back from the windows inside my head.

"Everything's on fire," I say.

"Where are you?" his voice calls out in the distance.

"My dad's lab. The one at home, in the basement."

I look around and notice the caged animals. Most of them are already dead, but some of them are running around in circles.

I'm still terrified, but time seems to stand still. The animals claw at the wire doors separating them from the outside for what seems like hours. The second hand on the wall clock ticks back and forth, as if each second that passes undoes itself in the same amount of time.

"Are you alone?" Joe's voice says from another room.

"Yeah," I say, letting my mind take in my surroundings. I scan the walls and see my dad rushing around in slow motion. "No – my dad's here."

He runs to each of the doors that line the walls, struggling and tugging against them. They're all locked. Why would they be locked?

He resets, starting at the first door again and checks each as if if he's stuck in a loop – the same as the clock and the caged animals. Even though this is the third or forth time I've watched him struggle against them, he pulls with frantic hope. Each time he reaches a door, it's as if he truly believes it will open to freedom.

He's yelling something.

Patricia! Tricia!

He's calling for my mom.

When he lingers at one of the doors longer than the others, I focus on the small glass window at the top of it. Through the glass I can see my mom's dark hair covering one of the steps to the stairwell. I don't think she's moving.

Patricia!

My dad calls out—over and over and over—at the door, but her hair lies still on the stairs.

Smoke is filling the room, and it's getting harder to breathe. I cough against the thick air entering my lungs.

"Don't worry, Robby," Joe's voice calls out from far away. "You're okay. I'm still here – keep going."

I can smell something slightly out of place. Boiling chemicals, charred fur, and melting plastic mix with the smoke, but somehow I recognize a scent that shouldn't be there.

Almonds.

That doesn't make any sense. I don't see any nuts, or any discarded food in sight. Am I remembering something different at the same time? Is this a smell from a different memory? I push the thought out of my head. It's distracting, and I can't imagine that it's related to anything.

My dad finally breaks his loop and runs toward me. He's yelling my name now, asking if I'm okay.

I don't know what to tell him. I'm paralyzed with fear, knowing there's no way out of the room. I'm afraid that my mother is dead on the other side of one of the locked doors. The smoke is filling the room and our lungs, and there's nowhere for us to escape from it.

My dad grabs my arm and drags me when my legs don't seem to work. I try to walk, but nothing happens. He pulls me through a maze of hot metal tables, toward the glass box where my dream always ends.

Buddy, try to help me if you can, he says as he struggles to pick me up. I'm too heavy for him. It's as if my body mechanically knows what it's suppose to do, but my brain doesn't process it. I crawl into the opening of the glass box without knowing why.

Trust me, he says, sweat and tears dripping off his face. *No matter what happens, I need you to remember one thing.*

He shuts the fourth wall of the tiny glass room in the middle of the burning one, the space that I crawled in, and then seals it with large metal latches.

I love you, buddy, he says, pressing his hand against the glass. *No matter what happens.*

We're both crying. I have no idea what's going on, or why he put me in the glass cage. I'd seen animals inside the box, and he would slip his hands into the oversized gloves to interact with them inside it – but I never really knew what he was doing.

I watch his hand smack down on a red button near the foot of the glass, right beside where the gloves lay lifeless. The tiny room fills up with a different kind of smoke, and I start seeing movement through a small window to the outside at the top edge of the opposite wall.

I focus on the window as I'm surrounded by a dense fog. I thrash around, as if my motion could clear the air in front of my eyes so I can see. The movement outside couldn't have been my mom – I can see her motionless shoe on the stairs through the panel in the door.

But as I look back at the window to the outside, I see a shoe there as well. A man's shoe. Walking away.

I suck in the last bit of breathable air as I scream out.

"Robby, you're okay!" Dr. Hughes yells from the other side of the world. "Robby!"

My eyes, which had been open the whole time, refocus on the small office, my head surrounded by books. But Joe is not sitting in his chair anymore – he's behind his desk. Or – at least behind a piece of it.

"Joe – what're you doing?" I ask, feeling sweat drip from my skin.

"Are you okay?" he shouts, showing his own fear.

"Yeah," I say. "Someone else was there."

"But you're calm?" Joe questions, peeking his head out a bit further.

"Yeah – why?" I ask as I try to steady my breathing.

I look around the room as he nervously stands up. I'm hovering several feet off the floor, and all of his furniture is completely destroyed. The couch I had been sitting on is split in two, the chair that had been in front of it is in pieces in the opposite corner, and his desk has large chunks taken out of it. The bar of lights is in pieces.

I lower myself to the carpet, raising my hands to my head. I notice there are wood splinters stuck to my knuckles with sweat. A moment later, one of his assistants frantically beats at his door.

"Dr. Hughes?" the female voice calls through the thin wood. "Is everything okay?"

"Yes – everything's fine," Joe yells out as he stands, making his way to the door. He presses one hand on it, the knob with the other, as if to prevent her from barging in. "Everything is under control."

"Are you sure? Do I need to call anyone?"

"Everything is okay, Deborah," Joe responds through the door as calmly as he can despite his obvious stress. "I'll let you know if I need anything."

Dr. Hughes' quick heartbeat and heavy breathing is matched by several others' in the hallway. They linger for a few minutes, but eventually the people in the hall move away from the door, back to wherever they're supposed to be.

"Joe," I say just above a whisper, again looking around the room at the destruction I caused. "I am so sorry. I don't know what happened."

He raises his hands to me.

"It's not your fault, Robby."

"What do you mean it's not my fault?" I counter in a louder tone. "I demolished half of the room – of course it's my fault!"

He motions for me to keep quiet and flips an overturned chair upright. "No," he says, brushing off the cushion. "Have a seat on the—"

He stops himself, noting that the couch is in shambles.

"Find a seat wherever you can," he finishes with an almost embarrassed smile.

I don't know what to do or say. I just unconsciously obliterated his office, and it seems like he wants to act like it didn't happen. Like we should just continue our session.

"Joe, I'll pay for everything. I'm so—"

"Please, Robby," he cuts me off, again with his hand up. "No apologies are necessary. As I said earlier, I didn't know if EMDR would benefit you. This is simply an occupational hazard."

Something tells me this is not the normal risk a therapist takes. I want to argue – to whine apologies until he allows me to fix everything with cash and agree that we should never do any of this again. But he actually seems like he isn't angry. His heart rate has evened out, and it's almost as if he's doing Lamaze or Zen breathing exercises.

I finish breaking the couch, so that a portion of it is level, and have a seat. We both stare at each other in silence for a moment.

"We do need to acknowledge what happened," he begins. "As I said earlier, one of the purposes of EMDR is to bring traumas in the unconscious mind to the forefront, so that we can process them consciously. For most people, it's not unlike guided daydreaming.

"I've had clients who encountered a particularly traumatic event and had a hard time containing the emotions that it brought up. But yours wasn't simply emotional. Your memory is exceptional, once you can access it. At a certain point it seemed as if you could no longer hear me, and you were describing things in perfect detail. You wouldn't stop talking."

I didn't even realize I was talking. Not since acknowledging one of Joe's questions.

"I hope it was helpful," he continues. "I'm quite sure it was. And I would love to delve deeper into the true purpose of the therapy—to help you process your trauma and emotion— but there are other details that concern me. However, I think it's safe to say that we shouldn't do it again, at least not unless we find a way to put certain safety measures in place. Agreed?"

He smiles, as if we're both sharing a private joke. I nod, not matching his smile.

"I'm sorry about this damage," I apologize. "I'll pay—"

"Stop," he says firmly. "Seriously – don't worry about the damage. I have insurance, and I've grown tired of these pieces of furniture anyhow. Tell me what you remember."

"Everything. I mean, there are still blurry details, but for the first time I *remember* it."

I can still imagine the room on fire, the animals, my dad.

"There was someone else there," I announce after a pause.

"Yes, you mentioned that," Joe responds. "And you said the doors were locked. You also talked about almonds for almost five minutes."

Hmm – apparently my brain switched gears. Instead of one second feeling like five minutes, this time five minutes felt like one second.

"Those are the details that surprised me, because I read all of the reports of the…" Dr. Hughes paused for a bit before he finished his thought.   "…accident.   And I've never read anything about you being found in laboratory glove box, which is what it sounds like you were describing."

The glass cage is the least of my focus at this point.

"The locked doors and the man's foot outside…" I say. "Do you think it *wasn't* an accident?   Do you think someone killed my parents?"

Dr. Hughes picks his notepad off the carpet and dusts it off.

"Robby, do you know much about what your dad was working on at the time?"

The way he asks makes me feel like he knows a lot more about it than I do.

"Some sort of correction drug," I answer. "To cure genetic diseases, I think.   I honestly didn't pay much attention to *why* he did what he did."

Joe nods.

"I spent a lot of time with him, as well as others in his industry," he says. "He was indeed working on curing genetic diseases – to a certain degree.   And some of the investors in that arena required regular psychiatric evaluations to ensure that their money was in the right hands.   More specifically, they wanted to make sure the research and experiments being done weren't affecting the scientists who led them.   For your father, it was a humanitarian effort. But for the investors, they were more interested in its impact on the military. Whether by creating chemical weapons, or by creating stronger solders."

Dr. Hughes looks down and shakes his head. What he says sounds familiar, as if the same buzzwords were uttered in conversations I overheard as a child.

"Honestly, maybe I shouldn't be telling you this," he says. "In doing so, I'm somewhat betraying your father's confidence. He was a client of mine, after all. But— I feel like this is a gray area. I know he spoke of it freely with your mother, but I can only assume he wouldn't have kept it from you."

"Yeah," I agree. "Some of what you're saying reminds me of what my parents talked about sometimes. He was always upset when he felt like money or politics were getting in the way of his work, when he knew the results would help so many people. And he would complain about people trying to use his research to hurt. I guess I didn't pay much attention at the time."

"And nor should you have," Dr. Hughes agrees. "Those are not the kind of worries a child should wrestle with. He was a good man, your father."

"Yeah," I say, focusing past the destruction in the room. "I do remember that."

"But to get back to my point," he says, as if we'd gone down a path completely unrelated to my memories. "You spoke of almonds."

I know my face shows confusion. If salted nuts are the destination of getting back on track, then maybe Joe is too hungry to keep talking.

"My own father fought in the second world war," he says, seeming to change the subject again. "He told me a lot of stories of his time there. Strangely enough, something that stuck with me is his recounting the smell of almonds when he was in the aftermath of an explosion. After his service he would avoid the nuts at all cost, as if they made him nauseous. I don't know any details of chemistry, but it might make sense that the person that you saw leaving had planted a bomb. So, yes – I think it is entirely possible that the fire your parents were killed in was not an accident."

My head swirls. I came to therapy with the hopes of getting the nightmares *out* of my head. Instead, it seems that I'm adding to them.

"And it should've killed me, too," I say.

He's silent for a moment.

"I definitely wouldn't prefer to use the word *should*. But, logic would say that you might have died in it – especially if it wasn't only smoke inhalation and burns, but explosives along with it. Had you exhibited any of your powers before that day?" he asks.

I don't know why I never remembered the gas in the glove box so vividly. If I were to remember it for a moment after I woke up, I guess I just chalked it up to smoke filling up the rest of the room and combining it with the years I saw my dad messing with animals in the box with the gloves.

"No," I answered. "Not that I remember. But I didn't really notice them immediately after that. They kind of trickled in over the next year or so."

"Did they trickle in," Joe questions, "or is it possible that you only realized them over time?"

"Sure, I guess," I say. "Are you saying you think my dad gave me the powers?"

Dr. Hughes is quiet for a second, which makes me think the answer is *yes*.

"Your father had been on the brink of something for at least a year before he died," he says. "Sometimes during our sessions he would voice frustration because his animal test subjects would show some signs of improvement, but then would die within days. He either solved his issues just before the fire, or he simply took a chance."

"You mean he experimented on me?" I snap back. "My dad wouldn't have used me like a rat and risked killing me."

Joe looks at me calmly.

"You were both going to die," he soothes. "I'm sure he never would've done something so rash in any other situation. But if he knew, beyond a shadow of a doubt, that you would both die soon, perhaps he tried the last possible solution."

The words hit me differently than I expect them to. I feel like I should be angry—both at my father for possibly experimenting on me, and at Joe for accusing him of doing so. But instead, I'm relieved.

It makes sense, and I don't know why I haven't thought of it before. Sure, the dreams are always blurry, so I'd never completely remembered details like the smoke in the glass glove box, as Joe called it.

Instead of being angry, I feel like all of this is explaining why I am the way I am. Not as a curse, but possibly as the last-ditch effort of my father trying to save me.   Rather than saving himself.

CHAPTER FOURTEEN

I'm silent as I walk alone through the city towards twenty-fifth street. I guess I'm not really paying attention to the fact that people can see me, perhaps because I'm starting to get use to it with trips to Dr. Hughes' office and Maria's mandated outings.

No, I think the real reason is because I'm completely lost in my thoughts. Maria wanted to come with me to Dr. Bradford's last known address, but I lied and told her that I had a bad feeling, and that I didn't think it would be safe. I even used Vic's memory as a pawn, telling her I didn't want her to die because of me, too. She'd heard things like that from me before, I'm sure, but I really drove it home this time.

I'm not really concerned for her safety – I just need time to myself after my appointment with Joe this morning. I need time to consider what I think I already know to be true. I want a moment alone to feel like an idiot that I'd never figured it out before.

Of course I got my powers the day of the fire.

The ambulance that showed up on the scene gave me a quick examination after the firemen pulled me out of the charred basement. The other two bodies they fished out were beyond recognition, while my body was without a scratch. If it weren't for my sooty face and scorched clothing, no one would have guessed I'd been in the fire at all.

There's still a gap, though. Between the non-fire smoke filling up the glove box and my emerging with the firemen, time is missing. They didn't find me in the glass cage – they found me on the opposite side of the room, under a broken metal table.

Everyone assumed the table somehow shielded me from the worst of the flames. That it was just a fluke I survived – though no one said that part to my face. I overheard way more than I should've, but I didn't assume it was because I had abnormal hearing. I thought it was just careless adults treating me like a dumb kid who wasn't really paying attention when they were talking about me. Because people talked about me all the time.

I probably should've found out about my impenetrable skin immediately after the incident. Common practice tells me, in a situation like what happened, I should've been checked out at the hospital to make sure I didn't have lung damage from smoke inhalation or worse. I should've had a blood test or something.

But as soon my grandma showed up on the scene, crying and wailing louder than I'd ever heard anyone before, she ripped me out of the emergency responders' hands. She refused to let a doctor hurt me physically, since I was obviously so emotionally wounded. Her words. I don't think I really registered what had happened yet, because it was all a blank. I didn't recognize the burned bodies that they removed from the basement lab, so when someone told me it was my parents, it took a while for me to believe them.

It was hard to admit that I was in a fire with them, because I physically felt better than I ever had before – minus the foggy memory. Emotionally, I quickly became a train wreck. I stayed in bed for months, only getting outside for their funeral. My grandma never made a big deal out of the mornings I'd wake up with a broken bed or holes in the walls. She played it off, like it was normal for someone who endured what I had. She gave me a little time, but then figured it was time I re-integrated with my "friends."

When I reenrolled in school, I started seeing Dr. Hughes. If I didn't already feel completely different from everyone my age—no other twelve-year-olds I knew had a therapist—I started noticing the changes. I did everything I possibly could to hide them, and convinced myself for a while that it was all in my head.

I realized I felt no pain. Bullies' hands had no effect, and somehow I no longer fell if someone tried to trip me. I thought maybe it was just part of puberty, but that was a question I would *never* ask Grandma. And I didn't know what Joe would do if it wasn't normal.

The moment I knew beyond the shadow of a doubt that I was different was the first day I tried to shave. I broke four razors but didn't put a dent into my peach fuzz. After a certain point, I *tried* to cut my face, but my skin simply could not be penetrated.

I only found I could fly when I decided to test my limits. If I didn't survive the fall off of a cliff, then at least I wouldn't have to deal with anything anymore. The last thing I expected was to not hit the ground at all.

Of *course* it all happened the day I lost my parents. It's so obvious. And the fact that the fire wasn't an accident weighs heavily on my mind.

I wish I could focus on this mystery immediately, but The Vacant is the clear and present danger. The best I can hope for is that Dr. Bradford not only helps me identify the blue powder, but can also remember any enemies that my parents might've had.

The area of twenty-fifth street that was once alive with medical research is fairly worn down. Broken windows, faded signs, and the occasional official-looking document litters the landscape. I've been in the neighborhood several times to bust up drug deals. It's no wonder Dr. Bradford was able to afford the old diagnostics lab – the previous owner most likely gave it away just so they wouldn't have to keep paying the property taxes.

Standing at the heavy entrance door, I glance down at myself to make sure I'm presentable, feeling the need to straighten the wrinkles in my shirt. I haven't talked to Dr. Bradford since before my parents died. I feel like I'm dishonoring my dad's memory by showing up looking like what I am – a college dropout without a job or direction. I'm not content with how I look, but if I wait until I *am* content, I'll never move forward.

I push the buzzer next to the windowless door, marked with "Deliveries." I've already been around the block, and I found no other, more official, entrance. I guess he has his reasons to desire secrecy, what with his old partner getting murdered. Not that he knows what I now do.

I look up at the bricks above the door that once said "Gilmore Diagnostics" for a minute or so, then push the buzzer again. I take another moment to analyze the faded paint, wondering who Gilmore was, and if he was distraught when he threw in the towel at this location.

"What?" a voice crackles through the small speaker by the buzzer.

"Uh… Hi… Um… Dr. Bradford?" I say nervously.

For a moment there's only silence on the other end.

"Who wants to know?" the man on the other end replies curtly.

"Uh," I stammer. I don't know why I'm never ready with words when I practice conversations in my head long before I know I need to use them. "It's Robby Willis. I was wondering if you…uh…might be able to help with something."

Silence for another moment.

"Do I know you?" the voice demands. He sounds at lot different than I remember, harsh and unforgiving. I probably should've reached out years ago – maybe he needed someone after my dad's death as much as I did.

"Yeah, uh," I answer. "Robby Willis – I'm Eric and Tricia Willis's son."

Silence.

I follow up with, "Dr. Eric Willis – your old partner?"

I hear a faint crackle of him repeating my dad's name in a whisper.

"Eric's son?" the voice says with a change in tone. "You're alive?"

I'm taken aback a little. Is it possible that he didn't know that I survived that night? Not that he was supposed to seek me out – but maybe he had his own spiral of depression and lost himself to the outside world. Is that why I hadn't heard from him since the fire?

"Yeah," I reply.

There is silence again, and I try to think of something else to say. I don't know if he doesn't believe me, or is sobbing at the other end of the microphone, or what.

"Give me a minute," he says, much softer. "Please stay there."

"Sure," I say, noticing two cameras aimed in my general direction. One of them makes the tiniest sound of a lens focusing.

Maybe he's been in hiding since that night because whoever killed my parents is after him too? I know he worked with Nelson Slate for the last several years, but maybe he's been withdrawing deeper and deeper over time. Even this building isn't in *his* name, but under "WLB Ventures, LLC." All records for WLB Ventures, LLC point back to the building, and W. L. Brad is the only publicly listed board member.

Several minutes later, I finally hear sounds on the other side of the door. A heavy door opens and closes, and two feet squeak along a tile floor toward my direction. It's odd that I can't hear any other sounds in the building. Several locks twist and retract.

The door pulls opens, and Winston Bradford squints at the sunlight that floods into the hallway, seeming to use his lab coat to shield his thin body. He's much older looking than I remember, with only a few gray wisps of hair from one temple to the other. His skin is oily, as if he hasn't taken a shower in a couple of days, and he peers over his bifocals.

"Robby," he says after his pupils recover from dilating, looking me up and down. He wears a happy and surprised expression. "You're really alive?"

"That's what they tell me," I say with a smile. I've already decided that he's turned into a recluse, which puts me at ease.

"But how?" he asks, still standing in the doorway, dumbfounded.

It's kind of a strange question, and I feel sarcastic answers filling the back of my brain. The least sarcastic, *because I'm not dead*, doesn't seem to fit the situation of being reunited with my dad's old partner after a decade.

"What do you mean?" I ask.

"I thought," he says with his eyes wide, then blinks and shakes his head. "When your parents...*passed*... I thought you passed with them. No one ever told me—"

"Yeah," I interrupt. "I don't know how, but I made it out okay."

"I've regretted not attending their funeral for all these years, because I couldn't deal with my own pain," he continues, downcast. "If only I'd gone, I would've seen you— I could've helped you—"

"My grandma was overprotective, so I guess she didn't let many people know I still existed," I interrupt again. I wanted to give Dr. Bradford an easy out on why he didn't know I survived. It wasn't his fault that Grandma was finicky about letting me out in public for the first year or so after my parents died.

"Oh," is all he says. He stands in the doorway for another moment before all of a sudden being aware of himself. "Where are my manners? Please, come inside."

He moves to the side and motions me down a dimly lit hallway. He relocks two deadbolts and two sliding bolts before turning around, leading me toward another doorway at the opposite end.

"Sorry for the security," he laughs nervously. "I suppose I'm less trusting than I used to be. Especially as of late."

"I understand," I say, dismissing any of his worries with a motion of my hand. "I'm no stranger to locking myself in my apartment to keep the rest of society out."

We could start a club. Hermits Anonymous. The only problem would be getting us all out to the meeting.

He puts his finger on a softly glowing panel at the end of the hall, which blinks green and unlocks the thick door opposite from where we started. His security is impressive. With each new paranoia I pick up on, I feel more and more at home.

We enter a kitchenette with another doorway into a massive, pristinely-cleaned laboratory. There's a table in the center of the room, with only one chair, though there are numerous other chairs dotting the lab's workstations.

"Sorry for the mess," he apologizes. "I'm not used to having guests, but it's a pleasure to see you again."

Obsessive-compulsive cleaning is not something I share with him.

"Thanks, you too," I say.

"I'll retrieve another chair," he says as he puts his finger on another glowing panel by the door separating the kitchen from the lab.

I wait for his return, not wanting to assume it would be okay for me to use the chair currently at the table. I'm glad I wait, because when he gets back he immediately sits at his preferred chair.

"We have much to catch up on," he says as he spreads his hands out on the table. "But first, what brings you here today?"

"Well, a couple of things," I say, deciding on the priority of my topics mid-sentence. "First, I don't want to alarm you, but do you know if my dad had any enemies?"

There is a visible change in his posture. He sits up a bit straighter, as if he's being watched.

"What?" he asks with concern.

"Well, I've been trying to remember what happened on the night my parents died, and I think someone else was there. I think someone murdered them."

"Oh, no," Dr. Bradford whispers, his face dropping. "That's... That's terrible. What do you remember?"

"Not much," I answer. "I've been seeing a therapist, Dr. Joseph Hughes.   He worked with my dad's—er, your company—before it happened."

"Yes, I remember Joseph," he acknowledges.

"And he helped me remember that night, because I've always had trouble with the memories. A few details make me think it was actually an explosion, not just a fire. And I remember seeing someone's shoes through a window. Just for a second."

Dr. Bradford shakes his head and looks down. "You don't remember anything else?" he asks.

"No, unfortunately I don't."

Dr. Bradford looks back up at me with concerned wrinkles around his eyes.

"I've always feared it is as you say," he admits, rubbing his temples with a finger and thumb from his right hand. He pushes his glasses up, stretching the elastic strap that holds them to his head. "I never had proof, and I could never talk to anyone about it, but I've always been afraid that he was murdered. He was a good man. And your mother— It was so terribly unfortunate."

"So, you don't know of anyone who might have wanted to kill him?"

Dr. Bradford seems to almost laugh.

"*Any*one?" he says. "Everyone. They wouldn't have wanted specifically to kill *him*, per se – not for personal grounds. But our work had many parties up in arms. We tried to keep all aspects of our research quiet, but any time investors get involved... Well, that becomes very difficult. There were several other teams who were doing the same sort of research, vying for the same government contracts. Your father – he was perhaps one of the last great scientists. He cared nothing of the contracts or the money. He cared for the art of it: chemistry, biology, genetics. Science was his paint brush.

"I used to joke with him that he would've done the work for free. And come to find out, he did. While the rest of the team would go home and ease our minds with music or television, he eventually admitted to several of us that he was working on another project at home. Together, our work was for the military. But separately, his work was about medicine.

"When the investors found out, they were furious. They felt that he wasn't giving them his full focus, and threatened to fire him. But they would never do that – his skills were far too integral."

Hmmm. Bradford's explanation helps to support my theory that my parents were murdered, but helps with nothing else. I was hoping there would only be one or two people that I'd need to look into for motive and alibi, but it sounds like it could be an entire industry. Maria will be able to help with that, once I let her in on the revelation.

"I assume that's why you've added so much security, and now work on your own?" I ask.

He looks surprised for a moment, as if he thought his paranoia was discrete. "An astute observation," he says. "Yes, it didn't happen all at once. At first I simply added a few more safety precautions. As time went on, I found that I had added more layers of security than even I realized. And I no longer trust men and women who have too much money. They feel that their funds don't simply entitle them to your work, but to your whole self."

I've been a recluse for a decade because I was afraid of people finding out that I was invincible. He's a recluse because he's *not*.

"I have another question, Dr. Bradford," I say, my hand reaching into my pocket to grip the plastic bag containing the blue powder. "I have a chemical residue that I can't identify. I tried a handful of things that I knew, but I'm definitely not my dad. Can you help?"

I pull out the bag and place it on the table. His body slightly recoils for a moment, as if he's afraid I just opened a letter addressed to the President, spilling anthrax onto his kitchen table.

"It's no longer potent," I say. "At least I don't think. It knocked—"

I pause. I trust Dr. Bradford, but not enough to take him down a rabbit trail that would lead me to telling him about my abilities.

"It knocked some people out, and…a friend asked if I knew what it was because, well, they thought I have more of a background in chemistry than I do."

"Where did it come from?" he asks after he settles back comfortably in his chair.

"A crime scene," I say, finding myself unconsciously lowering my voice. "The Vacant used it."

His eyes widen over his bifocals.

"Did you get this from the police?" he asks. "I haven't heard anything on the news about a chemical being used."

"No," I answer. "My friend also thinks the police and the news haven't been too trustworthy lately."

He picks up the baggy, tipping it from side to side, watching as the powder avalanches from one corner to the other.

"Let us observe and measure, then," he says.

A few minutes later, Dr. Bradford and I are standing in front of a contraption that looks like a large copy machine. Tubes of various fluids are sticking out of the machine, one of which contains the blue powder which is now suspended in liquid.

I'd told him of the tests I tried to do on the powder, and though he applauded my effort, he warned me that doing such experiments on an unknown substance could be dangerous. Apparently, my foresight to wear gloves, goggles, and mask were not enough to protect me from blowing up the university's lab.

The device, apparently called a Liquid Chromatography and Mass Spectrometry—or LC-MS—machine, would vaporize the powder-turned-liquid, then shoot lasers through it to break it down into fundamental components. The computer would print out what the powder was made of. My dad definitely didn't have a LC-MS in his basement lab.

Dr. Bradford looks at the results appearing on the computer screen. Rubbing his temples again, he breathes heavily.

"Dear God."

CHAPTER FIFTEEN

Dr. Bradford stares at the screen, dumbfounded. It's as if he's trying to figure out how to tell me some terrible discovery, but he doesn't know the words he should use to make it hurt less. He looks like a proctologist who's been tasked with breaking bad news. Sad and disgusted.

"What is it?" I ask, fearing the worst. Whatever the worst could be when looking at a chemical that I've already inhaled.

"Where did you say you obtained it?" he asks.

"The Vacant used it at City Hall," I answer, adding the detail of specific location. "He used it to knock a bunch of people out when he killed Councilman Alvarez."

Dr. Bradford closes his eyes and rubs his balding scalp, as if to jumpstart the gears turning in his brain. He's silent for longer than what feels comfortable, especially when I assume the words he's looking for are simply names of chemicals or elements on the periodic table – the same things he works with every day.

"What is it?" I ask again after a long pause, causing him to open his eyes and peer at me over his bifocals.

"Strangely, your first question relates to your request," he flatly states.

"I don't understand," I respond, trying to tie together what we've talked about in the last several minutes. Most of the work he did with the machine was done in silence, except for when he explained his actions for my benefit. I don't remember asking anything or making any request since we started the process.

"You asked if your father had any enemies," he begins. After a short pause, almost as if for dramatic effect, he continues. "The chemical compound we're analyzing is extremely close to one of the formulas we worked on before he died. One that we abandoned, because it had the opposite effect of what we desired."

He explains what Dr. Hughes already told me, but in more detail – that they were contracted to create an inhalable chemical that would temporarily enhance a soldier's strength and focus.

"The particular failed formula of which I am thinking," he continues, "would actually *fatigue* a subject, though not quite to the point of unconsciousness. For several hours, they would become lethargic, and would forego eating or drinking. It was abandoned because the investors didn't think its effect was impressive enough for any of their clients.

"This powder looks to be almost exactly that formula, but with the addition of trace amounts of trichloromethane. I would say there is enough to render someone unconscious, as you say it did. Possibly added as a fail-safe, under the assumption that some subjects could be immune to the other effects."

This sucks. My dad's work was stolen and made into a weapon used on civilians. I'm not happy with the idea that his work would've been used as a weapon at all, but at least if it was controlled by the military I would *hope* it would be used wisely. Whatever that means. Maybe I'm just happy not knowing the political motives for my country's foreign policy.

"Who had access to it?" I ask.

"It was only your father and myself working on it," he says. "But even I don't have access to it anymore. From the beginning, we did everything on a work-for-hire basis. All of our results and formulas, everything was owned by—"

He stops himself, and I can visibly see the light bulb going off in his head. He swallows hard before finishing his sentence.

"By the investors," he finally completes.

The investors.

Nelson Slate.

I knew I could feel sleaze on him, but only the womanizing, *I'm-more-important-than-everyone-else* kind. I didn't realize it might be the kind that would indicate that *Slate* is The Vacant. The kind that would tell me he murdered my dad.

It explains a lot. The money trail we found, which funneled to all of the thugs, who could even double as his security guards by day if any payments were discovered. His access to the blue fog and the explosives he set up at the radio stations. Not to mention his obvious desire for power and even *more* wealth.

If he'd been funding military projects for decades, it would be easy for him to fund any of his own private projects without any question. If he were to spread his investments around enough, he could just play dumb and act like he only gave them cash to keep his publicist happy. No one would expect him to actually know what they were doing with the money. I saw his feigned ignorance firsthand.

And my father worked for the scumbag. No doubt his skill wasn't the only thing that got him on Slate's elimination radar, but also his conscience. Slate probably didn't like having someone on board that pushed back when the requests approached the borders of morality.

"Dr. Bradford," I say after we both have ample time to consider the findings. "You worked with Nelson Slate for several years after my dad died, didn't you?"

He makes a pronounced frown as if to show he's sorry for the fact, then nods his head.

"Were there any indications that he—" I stop myself, not knowing how to ask the question sensitively, in case Bradford still had any respect for Slate. "That he would do *anything* to get his way?"

"That's putting it very lightly, Robby," he answers confidently. "Nelson Slate lets everyone know he always gets his way. I'm ashamed to say that I compromised some of my own values in order to maintain his funding. I decided enough was enough, and I departed from his presence about a year ago. I'd saved enough money to shed the skin of comfortable research conditions. Everything I had, I put into this facility so that I'd never have to rely on a man such as him again."

"Do you think he could be The Vacant?" I ask abruptly.

I hope I'm not crossing a line; it was his former boss, after all. I've heard people say that someone can talk about their own family all they want, but as soon as someone else complains about the same thing, it's offensive. I don't have family anymore, so I'm not sure what is socially acceptable.

Dr. Bradford is motionless. He says nothing. His heartbeat stays consistent. He has already answered the question before he finally looks down and answers with a single word.

"Yes."

An hour later, Dr. Bradford and I are sitting at the table in his kitchen again, after he obsessively cleaned the instruments he used to identify the powder. He'd printed out the results of the tests done on the powder and given me a copy, never asking what I would do with it.

We spoke of Slate's propensity for questionable actions, and he gave me more than enough examples to back up my theory of the billionaire as The Vacant. One of which was the reason for the FDA shutting down the company my dad worked for.

Apparently, Slate was frustrated that the team—without my dad—was taking too long. He would regularly throw tantrums about losing military contracts because of missing deadlines. He forced them to test on humans before getting approval, telling them that if they didn't comply then they would all lose their jobs and he would destroy their reputations.

The tests didn't go well. All were volunteers, though Bradford always wondered if Slate merely paid them sizable sums, or brought them in from hospitals or homeless shelters. Many died, and any survivors ended up in comas.

Dr. Bradford explained that he continued working with him after the initial company went bankrupt because it was the only way he felt he could continue some of the same research he did with my father.

"I've always known he was a terrible man," Dr. Bradford said when first considering the connection between him and The Vacant. "I just never assumed he would go this far."

Presently, it seems as if Dr. Bradford is tired of rehashing his own connection with Slate, and changes the subject to a more personal conversation.

"What are you doing now?" he asks. "It's been over ten years – do you have any family remaining?"

"No," I answer. "My grandma looked after me until she passed away. She raised me until I was able to look after myself, but wasn't in good health for most of that time."

"A girlfriend, perhaps?" he asks with a slight nudge of his elbow, which gets nowhere near me. "You mentioned seeing Dr. Hughes, but surely he's not your only friend?"

I smile and fake a laugh.

"Uh, not really," I reply. "I've got a friend that is a girl, but we're not...romantic...or anything."

"Robby, you might have recognized that I don't have many friends myself," he admits. "In fact, a section of this building is also my living quarters, and I rarely get out. Losing your father was hard on me as well, though I would never say that my loss was equal to yours.

"I have no idea what you must have gone through. I feel quite embarrassed that I never confirmed whether or not you survived, and am so sorry that I didn't make myself available to you sooner. But if you ever need anything—anything at all—please let me know."

I say thanks as Dr. Bradford fumbles in his lab coat pocket. Not finding what he was looking for, he gets up and finds a pen and a sticky note, writes on it, then hands me the light blue paper.

"That's my number," he announces. "Not many people have it, but it will always reach me, as it forwards to my mobile phone when I'm not in the lab. I don't care if it's midnight – if you need something, call me. I don't have many other schedule requirements, so I should be fairly easy to reach."

"Thanks," I say again, putting the note in my pocket. I take another piece of paper and write on it. "I don't have a cell phone, but here's the number for my apartment."

He smiles as I hand him the paper.

"Dr. Bradford – you mentioned earlier that you think something was added to the original formula you worked on to knock someone unconscious, in case someone was immune."

"Yes," he says, his eyebrows raised.

"Is it something that someone can become immune to? Could someone build up a tolerance to the new formula so that it would no longer affect them?"

His eyes drift toward the ceiling as if the answer would be found printed above us. He rubs his balding head and looks back down before saying, "I suppose so. But it would surely take a very long time. Why do you ask?"

"Well," I respond. "The mask that Slate wears when he's The Vacant – it's skin tight. I don't think there would be any room for him to have an air filtration system or anything. I'm thinking he has spent the time to become immune to it."

"It's very possible," he says as he nods his head. "Though dangerous."

"How dangerous?"

Dr. Bradford narrows his eyes.

"*Extremely* dangerous, Robby," he says. "You don't know of someone who would attempt it, do you?"

Well, see I have this friend that is a superhero…

"No," I dismiss, trying to lie smoothly. "Just thinking out loud."

CHAPTER SIXTEEN

"How could you keep that from me?"

Maria paces my apartment with her arms flailing.

"You have a breakthrough in your memories, realize your powers came from a single moment, and discover that your parents were murdered," she yells, "and you don't tell me about it?"

She's far more focused on this than on the printout of the formula for the powder that I already showed her.

"I only just found all of it out," I reason with her. "It's not like I waited a month – it's been five hours."

"Yeah, but I asked you how therapy went earlier," she said, stamping her foot just a bit. "You said *fine* and went off to Dr. Bradford's by yourself because you said you felt like it was going to be dangerous."

I don't know how we've gotten so close over the last couple of weeks, to the point that me delaying a piece of personal information by just an afternoon is an atrocity.

"Sorry," I say. "I needed to think about it by myself for a while. You've been dealing with me having powers for a month, but it's been ten years for me. I've had a lot of questions that are kind of clearing up, but the same answers are bringing up new questions." I pause for a moment before finishing with, "I'm not used to having a friend I can talk to."

Maria slowly lowers her arms and her eyebrows. The look of anger she had on her face is replaced by what seems to be a visible indication that she feels sorry for me. She puts her palm against her forehead for a moment.

"No," she says, dropping her hand. "I'm sorry. You're right – this is your life, not just a story."

She sits in the swivel chair opposite mine and we're both silent for a moment.

"Well, is there anything else?" she finally asks a bit sheepishly.

There's plenty to unpack in the realizations of my memories, but I figure there will be more time for that – especially in the context of my next piece of news.

"I have a theory, and Dr. Bradford agrees," I say, "that Nelson Slate is The Vacant."

She doesn't react. Even her heartbeat stays consistent. Any movement she might have is deep in her thoughts, much like Bradford when I first offered the option. After a minute, her response is to acknowledge my words with a distant "*huh*."

I explain everything Bradford and I talked about, and the common threads between the powder, my parents' murders, and Slate. We talk further about how easy it would be for a man like him to move money around and get his hands on whatever explosives he'd ever want. She moves to my computer and does some surface-level searches online.

"If this is true," she starts, "then he's a genius."

"What?" I say, surprised at the compliment she pays him. "How does all of this make him a genius?"

"Not the good kind," she clarifies. "He's spent most of his life as just the right amount of terrible. He has a bad public image, but not so bad that anyone would think him capable of this kind of evil. Greedy, sure. Egotistic womanizer, absolutely. Murderous?"

"Doesn't that make it more obvious, though?" I ask. "That he's not trying very hard to be secretive? Of course he's not going to kill someone in public."

"Yeah, but The Vacant is really good at being secretive. I just mean I don't know if I can believe he's really that smart or self-aware," she says. "I'm going to do more research. We call this sort of thing a hunch, and I'm not ready to put all my faith in it. Not enough to post something on the internet or run it by editors."

"Okay," I nod. "I'll do some research of my own."

It's midnight.

If Nelson Slate isn't The Vacant, then at the bare minimum he's scum. I trailed him for a few hours, overheard his pitiful pick up lines in fancy bars, then hovered quietly through his mansion after those same lines apparently worked on a young woman—not Sara—and they confined themselves to his bedroom for forty-five minutes. I rummaged through his filing cabinets, trying to distract my sensitive ears from hearing the horrendous noises coming from the antique bed, but it was an impossible task.

At present he's in his study reading emails about problems at his various companies, typing harsh responses that don't seem to take into account that the people who work for him are, in fact, people. From my view over his shoulder, I watch at least two of his employees get fired while they sleep, and another berated for bringing up a question about ethics.

Maria ended the evening at her own apartment, using her own internet. Something tells me I need to give her some hard evidence to prove that Slate is who I think he is. So far he's only acted like the jerk we already knew him to be and nothing more. The socially acceptable kind of evil, as Maria put it.

Slate's cell phone buzzes with a text message. He looks at it, huffs loudly, and shoves it back in his pocket before I can see what it says.

His heart starts racing. He pounds a fist on his desk, then picks up the nearby landline phone.

"Yes, sir?" the voice on the other end responds, as if they were always waiting for the call.

"You get the info?" Slate asks.

"Yes, sir."

"Set it up," Slate responds, as if in the middle of a meeting. "I want to see the traitor first thing in the morning. I'm going to try to get some sleep – no further interruptions."

"Yes, sir."

He puts the phone down and leans back in his plush office chair. He takes a deep breath, closes his eyes, and sits still for so long that I expect him to start snoring where he sits.

Finally, he gets up and heads to a different bedroom than where his female companion is still sleeping. He falls on the bed without changing out of his clothes, his cell phone barely peeking out of his pocket.

Several minutes later, the snores begin. After I'm completely sure he's lost in dreamland, I try to slip the phone out of his pocket. Each inch that I'm able to move it is accompanied by a stir in his breathing or his body. It's a painstaking process, considering how much I have to restrain my speed. Eventually, the device is free, and it floats through the room in my invisible hand.

I fly into the hallway so that the light of the phone doesn't have a chance to wake him up. The screen illuminates when I push the main button, showing me the last message he received.

He knows.

It's not attached to a name – just the moniker of "Security."

I slide my invisible finger across the small display to try to access more information, but I can't get past the lock screen.

He knows.

No more information is available to me, but I know it was enough to get Slate angry. Considering I talked to Dr. Bradford earlier in the day, and we declared the secret identity of The Vacant, I have a good idea of the meaning behind the message.

He knows.

It's not about me. I'm a nobody – Slate has never laid eyes on me. If it were about me, there'd be more to the message, possibly some detail about an awkward, overweight guy. Instead, I know who it's referring to.

Dr. Bradford knows.

Slate must've bugged Bradford's lab. Of course he would – Slate probably assumed Bradford would find out sooner or later, piecing together some formula or project that could tie the man with the villain.

I quietly hover back into the bedroom and slip the phone beside Slate's pocket. He might be asleep, but something tells me his thugs are carrying out his wishes at this very moment.

I fly around Bradford's lab for about 20 minutes without seeing any indication of activity. I push the buzzer I don't know how many times. I'm not sure what I would do if he were to answer – either I'd tell him what I know while invisible and expose myself, or I'd stand there naked to talk into the camera by the door and literally expose myself.

I realize I can't do anything outside—he probably has some sort of night setting on his buzzer that keeps him from hearing me—but I have to get ahold of him. I remember that the paper with his phone number is sitting on my desk, so I start flying back to my apartment as fast as super-humanly possible.

The flight seems to take longer than usual, but I think it's just because my mind is running faster. I don't often break the sound barrier, but I'm sure I'm doing so right now. Still, every detail of the ground and sky seems slow and steady, as if I were taking a leisurely stroll. I don't know how long I have before Slate blows up the lab, and Bradford's sure to be stuck inside.

Slate's explosive skills have surely improved since he killed my parents. My dad's lab was destroyed by fire rather than detonation, as if the murderer hadn't made the correct calculations to topple the building. The AM radio station that crumbled had no such short coming.

Slate's henchmen are possibly moving through air ducts or sewer drains, silently placing bombs everywhere they can. I couldn't hear anything around the building because of Bradford's security system. The very thing that was meant to keep evil out is preventing me from saving him.

I finally get to my apartment, slipping into the always unlocked window of my my tenth floor bedroom. Well, *slipping* might not be the best way to describe squeezing three-hundred-and-fifty pounds through an opening that I could destroy with a shiver. Either way, I get inside the building and rush through the doorway, then over to my desk.

The piece of paper sits right where I left it – on top of one of Maria's doodle-filled notepads. I try to slow myself down to pick it up, knowing that one nervous movement could mean the destruction of my furniture or the computer that sits on top of it. I dial the number with extreme caution.

While it's ringing, I notice that my answering machine is blinking, letting me know that I have messages. I never have messages.

After the phone rings for what feels like forever, Bradford's recording plays, telling me to speak my piece after the tone.

"Dr. Bradford – it's Robby. If you're hearing this, get out of your lab. Call me back when you're outside."

I hang up the phone, and immediately dial the number again. When the answering machine picks up once more I restart the process.

I stare at the phone after the sixth or seventh time I try calling, realizing that he told me how easy he was to reach just hours before. He even said something about not caring if I called at midnight. Well – it's not long after, and the number that he was sure would reach him doesn't seem to be doing the trick. Was I too late? Did they already blow up his building?

Wait—no—Slate said he wanted to see *the traitor* first thing in the morning. Could it be that he would kidnap Bradford before blowing up his lab? Either way, I'd definitely hear an explosion of that size. Maybe I should go back over there and prevent Slate's henchmen from tossing him into a van or something.

I look back at my blinking answering machine, wondering if perhaps he'd already called to leave me a message.

"You...have...six...new...messages," the robotic voice announces after I click the button, seeming to take forever. "First...message...recorded...at...eight...thirty-six...pm..."

Get on it with it! I scream internally.

The excruciatingly slow pace of the machine's voice is maddening, but eventually it plays through two messages, both of one second of silence.

I wonder if Bradford tried to call. I wonder if he was trying to warn me of something but was too afraid of letting his voice be recorded. What if he's holed up in some unknown panic room in his lab, now waiting for the police, watching masked men on security cameras who are destroying his work while looking for him?

As soon as I've resolved to prevent the possible abduction, my phone rings.

Thank God – it has to be Bradford. My mind is quicker than my fingers, and I'm relieved before I click the button to hear the voice on the other end.

"Dr. Bradford!" I shout.

Nothing.

"Dr. Bradford – is that you?"

No – not nothing. Awkward breathing. Then a whisper.

"Robby," the voice states, barely audible above the static in the phone.

I'm not confident that it's him. The person on the other end is so quiet that there's no recognizable features in the sound of my name.

"Dr. Bradford – are you okay?"

The breathing continues, then changes as if the person is restraining themselves.

"Don't worry," the whisper reassures. "Dr. Bradford is in good hands."

The voice on the other end breaks out in laughter. At first it's as if they've recalled a slightly clever remark. Then they let loose.

I stare at the receiver as the laughter builds.

And my apartment explodes.

CHAPTER SEVENTEEN

Yup – Slate's abilities with explosives have greatly improved over the last decade. I must have been incredibly distracted not to notice the new chemical smell.

One moment I'm standing in my quiet, calm living room, and the next I'm surrounded by everything I own slowly hurtling towards me inch by inch. The drywall crumbles, first exposing the brick and then the night. Fire creeps into the cracks, its tentacles filling every available space from the outside. Then I have a terrible thought.

Other people live in my building.

There are nine floors below me and each is filled with men, women, and children who occupy one-bedroom apartments. Almost forty families went to sleep with no knowledge that there's been a superhero living above them, always putting them at risk in case he was ever exposed.

I've already wasted time standing there like an idiot, but I can at least save *someone*. Before my brain even starts any of those thoughts, my body is barreling through the floor and into the bedroom below mine.

After blasting through the ceiling, I grab the unsuspecting couple asleep in their bed, then fly backwards through the floor again, my body shielding them from the splintering wooden beams separating the building's stories. I try to handle them as softly as possible, but if I leave them alone they're dead anyway.

I do this through two more floors, gathering a young man and an old woman, before I burst through the outside wall. I'd keep going, but I can't fit anyone else in my grasp without probably ripping off an arm or leg in the process. I slump them into a pile on the sidewalk across the street, none of them yet aware of what's going on, then burst through a sixth-floor window.

Next in my arms are a mom and her five-year-old kid, another couple, then one more single man, again dumped on top of the previously made people pile. At this point, the top of the building seems to be gone, and I realize the explosion originated from the roof.

I return to the top floors, bursting through every wall like they're paper, and find three dead bodies. This fuels me even more, and if I wasn't already moving at my top speed, I am now. I don't know that I've ever felt this much adrenaline. My eyes can barely take in the destruction created by both the bombs and my body. My ears don't work because I'm creating so much noise that everything else is drowned out.

Until I hear another explosion detonate. Apparently each floor is wired separately, and a chain reaction has started.

With the top floor clear, I pummel through every wall, floor, and ceiling in the building until I'm certain that every living human being is safely across the street.

The almost-victims are standing on the sidewalk, staring at the building that they occupied only moments before. Fire licks the remaining walls and time seems to recalibrate a little closer to normal. Several of them are locked in embraces, and most of them are crying. A child is screaming about his cat, who unfortunately didn't make it out. When making choices between pets and people, I didn't really spend much time in thought.

After the main destruction is over, when the multitude of explosions cease, and the survivors realize what happened, I slowly reenter the wreckage. The dozen bodies that I'd passed over—those who's heartbeats were already gone by the time I came to their aid—I gathered up and laid one by one in the alley way. Most are unrecognizable – many are not even intact.

But these are the ones I couldn't save. The least I could do is give them the dignity of not being removed from a heap of rubble with machines. At least a human hand laid them here, even if it was invisible.

You can't save everyone.

Dr. Hughes' words echo through my head like a jackhammer as I stare at the remains of my neighbors. Neighbors I hadn't even met. Neighbors I'd avoided at all costs. Part of me thought that it wouldn't hurt so bad to lose people if I'd never made a connection with them. I thought it only hurt to lose Victor, no matter how terribly he treated me, because he was the last family I had. But it's not true.

This hurts. It hurts almost as much as Vic's death. It hurts because I couldn't save them.

I can't take the pain. I scream and pound my invisible fists into the pavement over and over. I'll never be strong enough, fast enough, good enough.

I stop when I realize that I'm not helping anything, but just destroying the concrete. I float over the bodies, giving them some sort of memorial service with my tears, as the building to my back completely collapses on itself. Ash and brick dust flood into the alley, and I watch as my deceased neighbors are given a thin burial.

After the commotion, my senses start to clear up. I hear the survivors whispering about how Victor Boone must've saved them, how he must still be alive. Why didn't a guy like Victor get my powers instead? Almost anyone else would be better at this than me.

I fly over the burning rubble where my apartment once stood, toward the ash-covered group huddled across the street. Their faces and hair are gray, with dark streaks of tears down several of their cheeks.

"There he is!" a kid points at me and yells at the top of his lungs. "There's Victor Boone!"

My eyes glance down to where my gut would be, afraid that I would see my naked body hovering above the group. Luckily, I'm still invisible. I glance behind me as if his ghost would be striking his confident pose. But nothing's there.

Several wide eyes start looking at me and mouths drop open. They can definitely see *something*.

"Thanks Victor!" someone else yells.

Soon it's a chorus of appreciation directed at the air that I'm filling. It doesn't make any sense. I raise my hands to double-check that I really am invisible, and it confirms what I already know to be true. I see no skin, no bone, no blood.

However, my eyes trail up my arm to my shoulder and see a thick later of dust covering it. I frantically move my eyes around, noticing that if I look through my gut and legs, the entire back of my body is painted in gray. I move my hands through the back of my hair, and when they return they're covered in ash. I again glance at the group, who seems to be overjoyed at seeing my indentation floating in the air, and I'm frozen.

I'm obviously not Victor Boone. If they can see anything that I can see—which, they should be able to see much easier than I do—then they'd be noticing a body that is nothing like the chiseled physique that he worked so hard to maintain. They'd be seeing flab and matted hair. They'd be seeing the body that I've spent so much time trying to keep hidden.

"Thank you Victor!" the crowd keeps calling out, waving.

I fly away at top speed.

<**•••**>

It's the middle of the night, so I have no trouble getting to the river without being seen. I create a frantic spin cycle in the water, washing all of the ash off my invisible body as quickly as I can. I'm sure that if anyone sees the commotion they would assume a whale is having a fight with an alligator or something, but it only takes a few seconds until the gray sludge seems to be gone from my skin and hair.

I air dry by flying to Bradford's lab, which is still completely silent. I'm sure it means Slate's men were able to get in without any issues to kidnap my father's friend. The security system he'd set up couldn't have been any match for the maniacal billionaire, who pretty much owned the man at one time.

The entire time I was scoping out the lab, Slate already had a crew setting explosives around my apartment building. In fact, Bradford probably spilled the beans about who I was early on in the night, before Slate even got the text or gave an order. My place could have been set to blow while I was watching him nonchalantly answer his emails.

But he doesn't know the truth about me. Bradford doesn't know my secret, so there's no way he could've given me away when he confessed that the two of us knew the true identity of The Vacant. Slate blew up my building because he thought it would keep me quiet.

Nelson Slate has taken away everything from me. He murdered my parents and Victor, kidnapped my dad's partner, and destroyed my home, killing my neighbors for no other reason than they were in my proximity.

What am I doing at Bradford's lab, when he's probably already dead? I shoot through the air like a bullet towards Slate's mansion.

My thoughts move even faster, deconstructing the timeline of the day, trying to remember every detail. Too much has happened in twenty-four hours. My heart is already pounding from adrenaline, but it sounds like it's beating out of rhythm because of nervousness.

Maria had been at my apartment for a bit after I left to follow Slate. If anyone followed me, maybe peered into my window, they would've seen her. If Slate hurts Maria, I will tear him limb from limb, and for the first time in my life I won't regret causing any pain.

But there's a chance that she's still unscathed by all of this. Even if they had followed me, they wouldn't have known which apartment was mine until they got the info out of Bradford. Slate obviously had my phone number, so Bradford talked for sure. But no one entered the building after me – I don't recall hearing any doors opening or closing. Maybe they didn't even bother to figure out which apartment was mine from the phone number – maybe they just blew the whole building up instead of wasting their time pinpointing my room.

But the call just before the explosion. They were making sure I was in the building. That's what the silent messages were before that – they were calling every so often, waiting to hear my voice before detonating.

I fly through an open window in Slate's mansion – the same one I flew out of an hour ago. I follow the labyrinth of hallways to the bedroom he had earlier collapsed in.

He's not there.

I guess I'm not surprised, but for some reason I was really hoping he was sleeping while his thugs were carrying out his wishes. I was hoping I could wake him up and find out where he was holding Bradford by smacking him around a bit, like a detective movie. But of course he would want to be in on the action.

The entire house is silent except for one heartbeat, one pair of lungs pulling air in and pushing it back out. It takes me only a moment to follow the sound, and I find the girl Slate had taken home. She's deep in a dream and has no idea what's going on.

No other sound in the house. I have no idea where Slate has taken Bradford, but it's not here. Even the security guards are gone, which means they're probably at some fortress that he has for times such as these.

Instead of trying to gather more information, which didn't help me at all when I was here the first time, I opt to start my trek to Maria's to make sure she's safe. I'm not so worried that she's a damsel in distress – though I don't hate the thought of saving her and having her latch on to me while I fly her through the air. But she'll know how to find Slate better than I do.

"Maria, wake up."

I've never actually been to her apartment, and now that I know she's safe, a weird part of me wants to rummage through her closet or something.

She did stalk *me* a little bit, after all.

But I keep to the task at hand and turn on the lamp by her bed. At first I try to whisper to get her attention, but she's sleeping heavily. Instead, I shake her by the shoulders and she dramatically lifts up from her pillow. Apparently by instinct, her first action is to grab a baseball bat leaning against her nightstand.

"It's me – Robby," I try to reassure her. "That bat isn't going to do anything anyways."

She stares in my direction with squinted eyes and a frowning pouty lip, still dead to the world. Of course, even if she was completely awake, she still wouldn't see me. I can't help but stare at her curly hair draped across her smooth, beautiful shoulders. Her white camisole tank top makes me lose my breath for a moment. If I don't speak soon, I'm definitely a creeper.

"Maria, are you awake?"

She takes a moment to look around, starting to recognize her dimly lit room, still holding the bat like her bed is home plate.

"Maria, can you hear me?"

She rubs her confused eyes.

"Robby?" she asks after taking a deep breath.

"Yeah," I answer.

"What are you doing here?" she says with a cute exasperated grunt.

"Slate blew up my apartment," I say. "And he has Bradford."

"What?" Her eyes finally come to life.

"Slate kidnapped Bradford, and they're not at his mansion."

"No – what'd you say about your apartment?" she corrects.

"Oh, my apartment building exploded," I say, releasing a breath I didn't know I was holding. Her body is completely covered, but I'm still having a hard time breathing. I'm don't know how I can be so distracted by how she looks when I just finished dragging dead bodies out of their bedrooms. "I got a bunch of people out, but not everyone. It's completely gone."

"Oh God," she whispers.

She lays the baseball bat on her bed and scoots to lean back on the headboard. She's wearing short red shorts that draw my eyes to her perfect legs, which she crosses after she kicks off the covers.

Focus, Robby, focus.

"I don't know that you're safe here," I say, trying my best to look away. "I don't think he knows about you, but there's a chance someone could've seen you leaving my building earlier."

She rubs her eyes again and runs her fingers through her hair to scratch her scalp.

"You mean we have to leave?" she yawns.

"Yeah," I say, "and you should pack a bag with anything you might need for a few days. I don't think we should come back here until we're sure that Slate and his men don't know anything about you."

She stands up and stretches her arms, yawning again. Her camisole clings against her body like plastic wrap and I can't help but stare at her again. She walks to her dresser and bends over, opening the bottom drawer.

"I'm sorry, Maria," I cough. "This is completely stupid, but would you mind going ahead and changing out of your pajamas first? I'll go in the other room."

She turns and looks towards me as I float through her doorway.

"I thought my clothes didn't matter with your X-ray vision?" she sleepily smirks just before I round the corner, closing the door behind me.

"Sorry," I say, mainly to prove that I'm on the other side of the door. "Do you have any cash? I need to buy some clothes, because everything I have was burned up."

"How are you going to buy clothes right now?" she yells, as if the door was enough of a barrier for me not to hear her clearly anymore. "It's two in the morning."

"I'll just leave cash at the register with a note," I say.

"Well, I don't ever carry cash anymore," she yells. "Just my card. You can leave them an IOU."

I make a quick trip to the closest store, which happens to be open twenty-four hours. There's a guy a few years older than me buffing the floor with headphones on, but I don't even care that he's staring wide-eyed at products floating off of shelves. I fill up a backpack with the essentials – packages of socks, underwear and t-shirts, a pair of jeans, and the cheapest pair of shoes I can find in my size. I don't need much arch support, considering my weight is never fully on the ground. I also toss in some toiletries so that I don't gross Maria out.

I wish I had payment, so that I could slip through the self-checkout line, but I make a mental note to come back later and make it right. I return through the open window in Maria's living room and her bedroom door is still closed.

"I'm back," I announce to her door, and head to her bathroom with my backpack.

"I didn't even know you were gone," she answers.

I get dressed, brush my teeth, and make sure to slather on deodorant since I don't have time for a shower. I figure my dip in the river will have to do for now. I shove the rest of my new gear back in the backpack, minus the plastic packaging and stupid thin tags holding the socks together. Even with super strength, those things are just annoying.

She opens her bedroom door, wearing clothes that are far less revealing, though still as beautiful as ever. She's shoving clothes and toiletries into her own backpack, then slips her laptop and charger into a padded bag.

"Where are we going, by the way?" she asks when she walks out of her room with the two bags on her shoulders.

"My parents' house."

CHAPTER EIGHTEEN

The flight is silent.

No doubt we have a ton of things to talk about, but I think Maria is focused on simply staying attached to my visible, clothed body. It's still dark, so I don't think anyone will see us, but I didn't even offer the option of her riding an invisible, naked version of me. I'm not sure that *I* could've handled that.

I've got our three bags in one hand and my other arm is wrapped around her. There's no possible way I'd drop her, but her heart is still racing. This is the first time she's flown like this, after all. I guess I've gotten used to watching streaks of street lights move beneath me like shooting stars.

When we're within a mile of the house, I descend and start to slow down. The layout looks mostly the same – small patches of farm land with the occasional subdivided lot. My parents' land—er, I guess *my* land—is still cut off from the rest of the world by tall evergreen trees on all sides. The trees have gotten a little taller since my parents died, though privacy was never an issue, considering the one-hundred and forty-five acres have been in my family for several generations.

I touch down near the house, setting Maria's feet on the ground as softly as I can, then slip the bags out of my hand. Her heart starts slowing down, but mine speeds up. I come back on the property as often as I need to take a chainsaw to my hair or beard, but I don't generally stray far from the shed. I don't know how long it's been since I've walked into the house.

I stand silently for a moment, as if paying respects to my childhood, then Maria timidly speaks up.

"I can't see anything, Robby."

Stupid me – everything looks as bright as day to my eyes, basked in the starlight, but she's waiting for me to prepare the way for what normal pupils see as pitch black.

"Sorry," I say.

I fly over to a small array of solar panels about a hundred yards from the house and carefully flip the cutoff switch. I flinch as power flows from the battery bank with a dangerous hum. I fly back to the house and turn on the main breaker, which illuminates several lamps on poles around the perimeter of the yard and a couple on the house itself.

I listen for any sounds of arcing, and sniff for electrical burning, just in case the wiring hasn't held up. The wires seem to be stable, but a couple bulbs blow as soon as the power reaches them. When a thick glow reaches the house, Maria timidly heads into the front door, then flips on the interior lights. I pick up the bags and follow.

The years have not been kind to the house. Cracks have appeared in a few of the walls, and there are several water stains from leaks in the roof. Sheets and plastic are draped over all of the furniture. Spider webs and dust cover every inch of every surface, except for foot prints on the ground and occasional streaks on tables.

"Stay close," I whisper as I step in front of Maria and point at the footprints. "I don't hear anybody now, but someone's been here."

"Robby, I tried to tell you—"

She pauses.

"Before The Vacant showed up, when I started explaining how I knew that it was you and not Victor..." She trails off, then speaks after another temporary silence. "I wanted to tell you that I'd been here."

I look at the footsteps and compare them to her feet. The sizes match. I think back and remember the awkward conversation of her pulling my records, just before I started hearing news reports of The Vacant. Sure enough, I got distracted when she told me she found the house. And I remember shutting her down in the DMV when she brought the house up again.

"Right," I confirm. "I forgot about that."

"Sorry," she says, her face revealing a look of shame as though I'm finding out she murdered my goldfish. "I meant to tell you more about it then. I wasn't trying to keep it a secret."

I raise my eyebrow.

"So you don't have a problem with breaking and entering, but you do have a problem with keeping it a secret?"

She smirks, visibly relieved that she's not going to have to justify her stalking actions again.

"Yeah, felonies don't bother me as long I can talk freely about them," she says. "And it wasn't breaking and entering – just entering. You should really lock your doors."

I shrug.

"This is the kind of place where you don't have to lock your doors," I smile, then motion towards her. "But I'll let the neighbors know they should worry about the riffraff that just moved in. You'll probably burn the whole county to the ground by sunrise."

She laughs, then grabs her laptop bag from me and says, "Can't – I couldn't find any matches when I was here last."

It's nice to have someone who laughs with me rather than at me.

"Well, we're here – what now?" she asks as she wipes off a spot on the sheet draped over the couch. A small cloud of dust surrounds her hand. "I understand the need for safety, considering your entire apartment building is still smoldering. But you can't expect me to hide in the shadows for long."

"No, I can't," I say. I know I need to stop Slate as soon as possible, or else Maria will try to do it herself. "I'm gonna try to get an hour or two of sleep. I don't know where he is yet, and he might act like business-as-usual in the morning. He assumes he killed me, so it's not like he's waiting for me to attack or anything."

She furrows her brow and shoots me a look.

"What about the people in *my* apartment?" she demands. "Are we just going to let them die, as long as I'm safe?"

"No, no," I reassure. "Slate called my place immediately before it blew. I'm pretty certain he was waiting to confirm that I was in there before detonating it. If he's aware of you—which I don't know that he is—it's a safe bet that he'd do the same thing. Otherwise, you'd get the word out after both of our buildings *coincidentally* blew up on the same night."

She frowns for a second, then relaxes her lips as though she might believe me. She puts her laptop on her knees and opens it.

"So the plan is I wait here while you fly around, hoping to find him?" she asks. "And then hope he doesn't gas you when you do?"

I roll my eyes.

"Well, when you say it like that," I mock, "it almost sounds like I didn't have time to make a plan while I was pulling innocent people out of my apartment building, looking for Slate, and trying to protect you all within the same span of thirty minutes."

"Okay, so the plan is a work in progress," she says, then follows it up with a sarcastic, "No WiFi I'm guessing?"

She pulls out her phone and taps on it a few times.

"Nope," I answer. "But I'm pretty sure my dad's old 56K modem is in the attic."

"Funny," she says, then starts typing. "I've got it covered with my phone."

She keeps typing as I slowly walk around the room. I pick up various picture frames, wipe the dust away, and stare at the three sets of eyes looking back.

I don't think I really understood how young my parents actually were when they died. They seemed old to me when I was eleven, but they were just over a decade older than I am now. I think, to a certain degree, I tried to forget their faces – as if that was going to make things easier. But looking at the photos, I remember. I can see them playing with me outside, reading me stories, laughing with each other around the kitchen table. In all of the pictures and in my memories, they're always smiling.

I'm always smiling.

The overweight kid between them in the frames looks so happy. He looks safe. Loved.

I think I'd convinced myself that I'd always felt alone, but the flashbacks wash over my mind like a tidal wave. I might've still had trouble connecting with other kids when I was young, but I was always loved.

My mom had a masters in computer programming, but even though my dad was still in school, she decided not to work after she had her baby – me.

My dad built a lab on the property, spending every penny they'd saved up, so that he could spend more time at home with his family – us.

I thought the reason I avoided coming back here was because the memories were too hard. Instead, it was because the memories were too *good*.

Everything changed that day in the lab. Not just because of my powers, but because my grandma tried to keep me from remembering. I don't blame her. She was afraid that I couldn't handle thinking about them. The reality is I couldn't handle *not* thinking about them. But I didn't feel like I was allowed to. I felt like I was supposed to be stable and in control, and—because I wasn't—I felt like I should fake it. And I was terrible at faking it.

God, what I wouldn't give to have them back. Screw the powers. Just to hear my dad say that he's proud of me again. To hear my mom say she loves me again. To feel as happy as the pudgy kid in the picture looks.

"What were they like?"

Maria's voice cuts through my trance, and I realize tears are silently rolling down my cheeks.

"My parents?" I ask with the steadiest voice I can muster, looking away for a moment while I wipe my face.

"Yeah."

I stare back into their eyes, encased beyond dusty glass and over ten years of time.

"They were perfect," I finally say.

I can feel Maria's eyes watching me, expecting more of an answer, but I'm afraid I'll weep uncontrollably if I try to describe them any more than that.

"It must have been hard. I don't think I've ever said it, but I'm sorry that you lost them," she says, as if that's the first thing that everyone should say when they meet me. *Hello, my name is Maria. I'm sorry that your parents are dead.*

"Thanks," is the only thing I can get out. I know she means well, but I really just want to run into a dark closet and sob with ten gallons of chocolate pudding. I fight the urge to turn invisible, and only decide against it considering I'm not naked.

The next couple of minutes are super awkward. I start to turn away, but I worry it might seem like I'm being a jerk so I just stand there. I keep looking at the pictures.

Maria's typing and clicking, though she's obviously concentrating on whatever thoughts are swirling around in her head – thoughts that are no doubt about me. Her throat makes noises like she's going to say something, but it stays stifled. Finally, the silence is broken by sounds from her computer speakers.

"The residents of this ten-story apartment building woke up confused this morning," Gar Wexler's tired voice says, giving just enough information to make someone wonder what he's talking about if they hadn't been at the scene. I'm pretty sure that's what the media prides themselves in the most: figuring out how to leave a trail of truth breadcrumbs that keep someone glued to their signal, without actually revealing much of the context.

"I don't know what happened," a woman's shaking voice chimes in. "I was asleep in bed, and I woke up on the sidewalk watching the whole building fall down."

I set the picture frame down and move behind Maria so I can see the screen. There's video of the smoldering space where my apartment used to be.

"At around two o'clock this morning," Gar's voice says right before he appears on the screen with microphone in hand, "several explosions brought the structure down. But that's not the strangest thing about it."

The video cuts to a young boy – one of the kids I remember saving.

"He was flying up there and he was invisible!" the kid exclaims with excitement, as if he already forgot his bed and toys are gone forever.

The screen transitions to an amateur video taken from a cell phone.

"Witnesses say that the silhouette of a large man hovered over the disaster, as if to check to make sure they were okay," Gar's voice says over the video.

I watch the dust and ash that layered the back of my naked body move, obviously showing an almost completely invisible *me* look around. The people assume I'm checking the victims – they don't realize I'm simply trying to figure out what they're looking at.

"It's Victor Boone, I just know it is," a guy in his early thirties says. "How else can you explain that so many of us got out of that thing alive?"

The screen keeps scanning the survivors and the attending first responders, editing in b-roll of the explosions from nearby traffic cams.

Gar returns to the screen.

"Yet another event where witnesses claim to have had a Victor Boone sighting," he confidently announces. "In such dire times, could it be that, indeed, Victor Boone will *still* save us?"

The video clip ends and Maria scrolls down on the site, clicking a few links.

"Gar's really going out on a limb for this, isn't he?" Maria rhetorically asks.

"What do you mean?"

"This isn't official," she answers, pointing at the screen. "There's news about the explosion on several sites, but even Gar's station isn't showing this footage. Something tells me he had someone put it together but the managing editor rejected it, afraid the wrath of The Vacant would come down on them. I'll bet anything that Gar leaked it after it was nixed."

For the first time, I notice the website that she's looking at is not a news site. There are no logos or indication, besides Wexler's involvement and the slick editing, that it was tied to any station. It's an embedded video in a random person's blog.

I sigh.

"They're still waiting for Vic to save them," I say with a bit too much exasperation in my voice. I don't know why, but something is bubbling up inside me.

"Of course they are," Maria responds, as if to defend anyone that I was frustrated with. "Nobody knew it wasn't him. To the rest of the city—no, the world—Victor Boone was a savior. The public knew he had his issues, but people gladly overlooked them. He was slowly creating a utopia – a place where people didn't have to worry about crime or violence."

Somehow, without my consent, my voice screams unconsciously.

"It was never *Victor Boone*!"

I'm afraid of my own tone. I stand still for a moment, waiting for Maria to become scared of me because of my outburst. She knows what I'm capable of. First it's an emotional display, then maybe she thinks I'll pummel the old house into oblivion.

Her heart beats faster, but she stays silent.

"I'm sorry," I say after taking a few deep breaths. "I don't know what happened just then. I'm tired, I think."

Maria's eyes soften, as if my outburst causes her to have compassion rather than fear.

"You're amazing," she says after a pause.

What? Her response to someone yelling is to compliment them? I stare at her with confusion, and try to form some sort of response. Nothing comes.

"You are absolutely amazing," she repeats.

"What are you talking about?" I ask.

She shuts her laptop and sets it on the couch beside her.

"You've been saving people for years," she says as she stands, moving toward me. "You've never asked for credit. In fact, you gave all of the credit away to someone who barely deserved a sliver of respect at all. None of the people you've saved have ever thanked you. I doubt Vic even thanked you."

She grabs my hand. I'm already in some sort of emotional spin cycle, and she's adding to the confusion. Her touch, her smell, her eyes, her words – it's hard to contain whatever it is I'm feeling.

"They've never said it, so I will," she says as she squeezes my hand. "*Thank you.*"

I burst into tears.

CHAPTER NINETEEN

"I'm sorry, I don't know what's happening to me," I sob, ugly-crying in front of the only girl who has really *seen* me in years. I don't think I've let anyone but Dr. Hughes see me cry since my parents' funeral.

"It's okay," she says as she hugs me from the side, still holding my hand. "Between this house, pictures of your parents, and the events of the last couple of hours, I think it's completely normal to be a little emotional."

"Normal," I scoff through my tears. "Nothing about me is normal."

"Maybe not," she smiles. "But that's good. Like I said – you're amazing. Extraordinary. Special. There are a lot of people that wish they could have what you have."

I shake my head.

"Maybe normal people want to be special, but this *special* person wishes he could just be normal."

Her hug relaxes into more of a soft repetitive pat against my back.

"That might be how everybody feels," she says. "Everybody sees greener grass somewhere else. I think if we all thought about it long enough, we'd realize that without ordinary, there is no extraordinary. And vice versa – no ordinary without extraordinary. Maybe we're all a little of both at different times. There's a whole lot of regular people that do incredible things, and incredible people who…"

She pauses.

"And incredible people who do mundane things?" I ask, feeling even worse while finishing her thought. "That don't live up to their potential? Like me, wasting my life in my apartment?"

"No, that's not what I meant," she tries to correct me. "Look at Gar Wexler. I know him – he's a pretty normal guy, and he just risked his life to let people know the truth. And then there are people like my dad. He never tells anyone this, but he had some insane robotics job offers when I was young. He turned them all down because my mom didn't want to move from our small town, away from family and friends. So he got a normal job as a mechanic."

She pauses for a moment, as if she senses that I don't know what point she's trying to make.

"Another word for extraordinary people doing ordinary things is *sacrifice*. Even if you don't believe it yourself, saving people for all these years without asking for an ounce of credit is something that a guy like Victor Boone wasn't capable of.

No one else even knows you exist, but you're the best kinds of both normal and incredible."

For a guy that has shunned recognition for so many years, I have to admit that it feels pretty good to hear her say nice things about me. But awkward at the same time.

"You never told me how you knew it was me and not Vic," I say, changing the subject somewhat. I'm already tired of wiping my face, and I know that further compliments will keep the tears flowing and my nose running.

She glances at me with narrow eyes, probably seeing through the terrible segue, but then lets it go.

"Actually, I can show you, since we're here," she says as she drops my hand and heads to the stairway in the corner of the room.

I follow her like a puppy with his tail between his legs, wondering what clues I left behind for her to discover. She makes a beeline to my childhood bedroom. It's exactly as I left it the last time I was inside the house.

Broken wood from my bedframe litters the room, surrounding the mattress that has been ripped into three parts. The legs on my steel desk are mangled, and a few indentations of my fists dot the surface. There's a hole in the wall where I threw my bulky computer monitor through the drywall and into the adjoining guest room.

"When I got in here, my first thought was that someone broke in to steal something," she explained as she moved through the destruction. "But absolutely nothing had been touched downstairs. Everything on the first floor looked like it had been preserved, like no one had been here, but that the previous owners expected to come back some day.

"If someone broke in to steal something, they would've left signs on the first floor, since that's the only path to get upstairs. I held onto my suspicion until I saw the fists in the steel desk. At that point I knew it had to be somebody with a huge amount of power behind their punches. And I highly doubted Vic would come to your childhood home just to tear it apart. Not that I doubt he would've been that mean, but I just doubt he would've gone that far out of his way to bully someone."

I walk over to the desk and trace the indentations with my finger.

"Yeah, this was a bad day," I say. "I'd already been living with my grandma for almost a year, and she'd had some guys do everything to prepare it for vacancy – drained the pipes, covered the furniture. I realized I left something behind, something stupid, and I came back for it without her knowing.

"Problem was, I couldn't find it. I looked through all of my stuff, and I got more and more upset. I just started breaking things in a rage. By the time I started punching the desk, I realized that I didn't feel anything. Like, my hands should've hurt as they were slamming against the metal, but they didn't. I kept punching it, hoping to draw blood or something. Hoping I could feel on the outside the way I felt on the inside."

I took another glance around the room.

"That's the last time I ever stepped foot in this house. Until now."

Maria walked around the room, probably not so much looking at her surroundings as much as envisioning the chaos that I was describing.

"What was it – the thing you were looking for?"

I stare into the hole in the wall, surveying the pieces of the old tube computer monitor that lay in shattered pieces all over the room on the other side.

"It's silly, really," I say. "A few days before he died, my dad gave me a piece of metal on a chain to wear around my neck. I don't know what kind of metal it was or anything, but he said it was a good luck charm. I forgot about it until that day, and all of a sudden it felt like the only thing I had left of him."

"Did you ever find it?" she asks.

"No," I drearily say, rubbing my breast bone where the charm sat for the few days leading up to the lab explosion. "Wait!"

I remember wearing the charm that day – the memories that flooded back to me in Dr. Hughes' office didn't focus on it, but for some reason I remember the chain being around my neck.

"What is it?" Maria asks, expecting me to explain my exclamation.

"I never checked the lab," I answer. "I'll bet it's in there, if it still exists."

"Wasn't the lab completely destroyed?" she asks. "I couldn't even find a way into a basement."

"It's not a basement under the house," I respond. "It's under the barn near the trees."

"Well, let's go check it out!" she says.

She's a bit too eager. She doesn't have the same memories I do. For her it's part of a scavenger hunt. For me, it's the place where my parents were murdered in front of me.

"Okay," I say halfheartedly.

My dad built the lab so far away from the house because—even though he wanted to be close to home—he didn't want any possible disaster to affect my mom or me. He didn't take into account the fact that I would sneak in time after time, until he eventually gave me permission to watch him work as long as I didn't "get into" anything. Of course, it didn't take long before I was helping him with benign experiments. My mom would often join us, either because she was bringing us snacks or because she was working on a freelance project and could type in a corner without being too distracted.

And he definitely didn't take into account that all three of us would be here when a murderous billionaire decided to blow it up.

There's a steady breeze in the stairwell leading down into the lab, as all doors were removed after the explosions. The emergency crews took them off their hinges because they were still locked when they arrived, and the bolts were too strong to simply force them open. They hadn't expected to find anyone alive inside.

There had been a short investigation, but it was quickly declared an accident. Simply a foolish scientist who didn't take the precautions he should have. I was no help, because I didn't remember a single thing about it. Not that I would've understood much of it back then. Instead, I had to deal with thinking my dad really was careless – that it was his fault I became an orphan.

Entering the lab isn't as nostalgic as I expected. Because there was nothing keeping the elements out, it's obvious that animals had made it their own. The only things that remain somewhat unchanged are metal tables flipped on their sides. Broken glass crunches under our feet, and charred drywall fallen from cinder blocks surrounds us.

Maria shines a flashlight around the scene, highlighting what used to be a workstation, or dry erase board, or computer. It's unrecognizable. I might as well have stepped foot into someone else's abandoned and burnt warehouse.

"No one cleaned it up?" Maria asks, picking up crime scene tape that had been dragged in from the open doors. "The police or anything?"

"No, they never do," I say. "After an investigation is over, when all the evidence has been gathered, the property owners are left to themselves. Unless there are dangerous chemicals or something, then they bring in a special crew. I'm sure Dr. Bradford must've helped them determine whether or not any of the residue was harmful. At least that's what happens at the crime scenes I've been to in the last several years – an expert is brought in. Sometimes I straighten things up for families after it's over, because I know that it's one of the hardest parts. I never even attempted it when it was my own family."

"You're a good man, Robby," Maria sighs absentmindedly as she pushes a piece of bent metal with her foot.

"What, because I didn't clean up and couldn't handle things when it happened?"

"No," she snaps back. "Because you help other people who are hurting – who are going through the same kind of pain you did. I threw Victor under the bus earlier – but I don't think I could do what you do and not expect credit, either. Heck, my whole life for the last few years has been trying to make a name for myself."

She keeps sorting through the rubble.

"You're nothing like Victor," I say without looking up. "Believe me – he was the only person I talked to for a long time."

She stops rummaging around in the wreckage and shines her flashlight in my eyes.

"Not everyone is like you, Robby," she says. "Actually, no one is. If pretty much anyone else was given your powers, they wouldn't stay selfless and humble. Victor wouldn't have. Honestly, I don't think I would've either. Maybe at first, but then I'd probably use them to *be* the news story rather than write about them – just like him."

"Don't be so hard on yourself," I say, brushing off a table that used to hold my dad's journal.

"I'm not being hard on myself, I'm just telling the truth," she responds. "You are the one that deserves these powers. You. If anybody else was completely invincible, it'd be easy for them to become a bully. You're the only person that has no weakness, but yet you only worry about saving everyone else from their weaknesses."

"Electrocution," I say.

"What?" Maria asks with a confused look on her face.

"My weakness," I answer. "I don't think it'll kill me, but even the smallest amount paralyzes me, and it hurts. Oh, and that fog that Slate released in City Hall, of course."

"You see what I'm talking about?" Maria asks, throwing her hands up. "Nobody else would correct me, telling me their vulnerability, when I said they were invincible. I don't know how you don't see it, Robby, but you may just be the *best* person alive."

I keep moving things around, somewhat ignoring Maria's compliments. I'm still surprised at the warmth that seems to spread over me from her words, but I don't know how to handle them. If I deflect them because I don't believe her, or because I tell her she's just being nice, she'll just keep complimenting me.

A moment later, we're both turning objects over in silence – her by the glow of her flashlight, and me by the moonlight barely slipping through tiny windows and the open stairwells.

"What exactly am I looking for again?"

"A piece of polished, rounded metal on a silver chain," I answer. I know it's probably lost forever, but I feel compelled to look. I don't know why I'm wasting my time in here while Slate is possibly torturing Bradford, but I doubt there's anything I can do in the city right now anyhow.

"What's this stuff?" Maria asks, lifting a long strip of yellow material from under some junk.

"I don't know, I've never seen it before," I answer. "Is it a table cloth or something?"

"Or something," she says. "It's just weird to see something so clean and undamaged in all this."

"Maybe an animal dragged it in?"

"Maybe," she shrugs, stuffing it into the empty bag hanging from her shoulder. "I'm taking it - I'm curious."

I shrug in return. Whatever it is, it's technically my property considering it's in *my* lab. She can do whatever she wants with it.

I move to the center of the back wall, where I remember the glove box would've been. There's no remnant of it – I don't even see broken glass. Actually, it looks like one of the explosions went off where it would have sat, because there are burn marks surrounding the walls and floor, emanating from where I would have been contained.

I wonder if it was from me? I wonder if whatever happened to me was violent and explosive? Not in the sense of blowing the lab up—I know it was Slate's fault my parents were murdered—but that my transition to *super*-me was an instantaneous eruption of energy.

Meh, it doesn't matter. Whether I burst like a Super Saiyan or just silently shivered, how I transitioned doesn't change anything.

I scan the room from the vantage point of the last place I remember, when my dad filled the glass box with fog. I don't see anything except Maria stepping over broken glass and mangled metal. I imagine my body exploding with energy and throw my head back like a cartoon hero.

And something in the ceiling flickers, catching the glow from Maria's flashlight. I hover to the top of the room, focusing on a thin crack in the concrete above the exposed beams.

"Maria, let me see your flashlight," I say. I can see in incredibly low light, but nothing's illuminated in the hole. Only a tiny piece of chain is exposed.

She tosses me her battery-powered torch and I shine it on the crack in the concrete. I can barely see the chain shoved into a slit exactly the size of the metal that my dad gave me. I tug at the chain for a moment, but it's caught. I don't want to break the chain and lose the chance for it to lead me to the charm, so I toss the light back to Maria.

"Watch your eyes," I warn, waiting for her shield herself.

I flick at the ceiling, careful not to destroy too much – it *is* the underside of the ground floor of a building, after all. Once the concrete crumbles away, the good luck charm falls, dangling from the chain held in my other hand.

"You found it!" Maria exclaims.

We both celebrate for a moment, and then I realize the achievement is fairly pointless. I have a gift from my father, long dead. A symbol of a happy past and nothing more. Even so, I note that the broken chain is much smaller than my current flabby neck.

I float back over to Maria and hand her the charm.

"You take it," I say.

"What?" she protests. "I can't take it – it's a gift from your dad!"

"Yeah," I acknowledge. "But it was meant to fit my eleven-year-old neck – it won't fit anymore. And, anyways, it was for good luck. I personally don't need too much luck anymore – you could use it more than me."

She hesitates, then reaches out her hand with a nod.

"Temporarily," she says, wrapping it around her neck and fiddling with the broken clasp at the base of her skull. "We'll get a longer chain for you. I'll hold it until then."

I shrug, not expecting it back. I squeeze the clasp with my fingers, bending it until it holds. Maybe I have a new good luck charm, and she's wearing my old one.

CHAPTER TWENTY

"Robby – wake up."

Maria's voice is calm as she gently shakes my shoulder. I wake up in my parents' bed, and for the first time in a long time I actually feel like I got real sleep.

"It's eight o'clock," she says while leaning over me. I realize light is streaming brightly through the window.

Wow, I slept for at least four hours and didn't have any nightmares. I'm not even sweating more than normal. Well – not that my normal amount of sweat isn't already too much.

My dad's good luck charm is hanging down from Maria's neck and the chain reflects the morning light. She stands upright and the charm lies softly against the skin framed by her collarbone.

I don't know why, but this feels like the perfect moment. The best in a decade, at least. Almost like the thing that I'd been avoiding for ten years—coming back to this house—was the very thing I needed.

I follow Maria downstairs and find a box of cereal and bottles of milk and orange juice on the kitchen table.

"What's this?" I ask, surprised. This definitely wasn't here when I went to sleep.

"I found a bike outside, so I took a quick spin and picked up a few things," she says casually as she sits down and pours a bowl of cereal.

"A quick spin?" I ask. "The closest store that *might* have been open is at least five miles away."

She nods as she takes her first bite.

"What else was I supposed to do for the last several hours?" she challenges. "I couldn't fall asleep after everything that happened last night. Besides, I'd already slept for a while before you picked me up at my apartment. I'm not tired at all."

I sit down and pour myself a heaping bowl of sugary cereal.

"What's the plan now?" she asks with her mouth full.

"I'm going to head back into the city and see if I can find Slate."

"And what do I do while you're looking for him?"

"You stay here," I answer.

She frowns.

"Look," I start to explain. "I don't know what's going to happen. I'll feel a lot better if I know you're safe. If I can wrap things up quickly, I'll be back by lunch. Heck, if I can't find him, I'll be back by lunch. Keep an eye on the news—both official and unofficial—and see if you can find some leads in case I can't."

"Sounds boring," she says, but doesn't protest.

<‹●›>

My time in the city is completely unproductive.

Slate's mansion is quieter than a church on Tuesday. The girl is gone – no doubt leaving embarrassed after waking up alone. No security guards, no kitchen staff. I don't know who would normally be there at nine in the morning, but I had assumed *someone* would.

The streets around Bradford's lab are quiet as well. I didn't think any activity would be buzzing there, but I needed to confirm my suspicion. I can't even find any evidence of him being taken – no forced entry, no tire tracks. Whatever Slate did to kidnap him was professional and at the highest level of discretion.

I spend a little time surveying the crater that was once my apartment. Emergency crews are spread out all over the area and crowds stand behind pop-up barricades, wanting to see what's going on. Several people are scanning the sky – waiting for me to make an entrance, I suppose.

I'm at a complete loss. Slate owns dozens of businesses and even more buildings – there's no way for me to know which one he's holding Bradford in. I consider Maria's friend, the one who is kind of dating Slate, and wonder if Maria would give her a call.

But before I fly back to the homestead, I decide on a slight deviation from the plan of finding Slate.

I drift into the back of a big box store, well away from any heartbeats of employees or customers, and find a phone on a manager's vacant desk. I dial the number for Dr. Hughes' office. After the receptionist greets me, I talk slightly above a whisper.

"Could I speak to Dr. Hughes, please?"

"I'm sorry, Dr. Hughes isn't available at the moment," she answers, chewing her gum through the receiver. "Would you like to leave a message?"

"No, um," I stammer, still keeping my voice low. "I'm a current patient of his – is there any way he has an appointment open today? The sooner the better. I can pay more if needed."

"I'm sorry," she counters again. "Dr. Hughes isn't in the office today."

"What?" I ask, surprised.

He made no mention of a vacation—not that he has to confirm his schedule with me—and he wasn't sick the last time I saw him. Wow, was that just twenty-four hours ago? It feels like forever.

"Dr. Hughes won't be in for at least the rest of the week," she answers, popping her gum. "We've been contacting his patients to reschedule. If you have an appointment with him later in the week, I'd be happy to reschedule now."

"Is he sick?" I question.

"I'm sorry," she says again – it seems to be her default response. "I'm not allowed to discuss the personal lives or schedules of our staff. Would you like to reschedule any future appointments?"

"Is he home?" I ask, starting to get a bit frantic.

"I'm sorry, sir," she says, raising her voice. "I can't discuss any of that with you."

I hang up the phone.

Then I realize that I completely destroyed his office during our session yesterday. Maybe he took the opportunity to take some time off, waiting until the room is refurnished to get back into the swing of things. Heck – maybe the event was much more traumatic for him than he let on.

Either way, I dial 4-1-1 for information, and get his home phone number and address. The lady on the other end of the line is far less concerned about privacy than Joe's office.

I dial his number and am met with an answering machine. I decide not to leave a message, and instead take a quick flight to his house.

There's a car and a newspaper in the driveway – good signs that he's home. I knock on the door with no answer, then peek through windows like a crazy creeper. Eventually, I find that the back door is unlocked, so I enter, hoping he'll forgive me when he finds out the kind of twenty-four hours I've had since I last saw him.

"Joe?" I call out after I close the door behind me. "Are you home?"

I hear someone talking quietly down a hallway, so I float towards the voice. I realize it's the TV, turned down to an almost silent volume, before I get there.

"Joe?" I call out again before knocking on the door. There's no response, but I open it anyway.

To my surprise, no one is there.

It's a den with bookshelves lining the walls. Several lamps are on, even though sunlight pours into the room making them a bit irrelevant. A chair sits in the middle, aimed in the direction of the quiet TV. There's a glass of watered-down Kentucky bourbon on a small table beside the chair, along with the half-empty bottle from which it came, and an ashtray containing the remains of a cigar.

He hasn't been here for a while. I assume there was a good deal of ice in the drink based on how much lighter the liquid in the glass is than the bottle, even though Vic would've disapproved citing that a real man never drinks bourbon on the rocks. I've never been a fan of any alcohol, so I didn't care to argue or research it. Vic would've also been mad at me for not remembering the *proper* word for a cigar's remains.

"What's the point in helping all of these people if we don't get to enjoy the perks?" Vic had said on more than one occasion.

"The perk is that we know the people are safe," I'd always say.

"I'm out there risking my life for these jerks," he said once while smoking a cigar from a man we'd saved a few days earlier. "Most of them ain't even hot ladies. I'm gonna enjoy these gifts, even if they come from dudes or frumpy chicks."

"It'd be ironic if you spent all that time risking your life for people and wind up dead from cancer at thirty," I reasoned. "Too much of that stuff can be dangerous."

"Dangerous?" he said with his head cocked to the side. "Danger is my last name."

"Your last name is Boone," I corrected. "And that's not even how the saying goes."

Could Maria be right? Could it be that *I'm* supposed to have these powers and not a guy like Vic? Is it possible that people didn't care that Vic was masculine and perfect, but that they actually only tolerated the part of "us" that was him?

Meh, no time for thinking about that right now. Right now, I'm looking at Dr. Hughes' empty den, and I don't think he intended to leave it the way he did.

I have a terrible realization.

If Slate has Bradford, Bradford might have told him about Dr. Hughes. I didn't mention Maria by name, but I *did* mention I was seeing Joe.

Crap.

I check a clock ticking on the wall above the TV. Almost three in the afternoon – I should be getting back anyway or Maria might start worrying.

Nah, who am I kidding? I don't think Maria is the type to worry. And even if she were, I'm invincible.

I leave the house the same way I came in and fly towards home.

"I couldn't find him," I call out as I open the door to my living room. "And now I can't find Dr. Hughes, either." It still feels stale, but the dust on the floor and furniture has shifted a lot since we got there in the early morning. Maria must have moved around quite a bit judging by the paths all over the hardwood.

Her laptop sits open on the couch with a black screen. A half-eaten sandwich sits on the coffee table.

"Could you find anything online?" I yell, not knowing where to direct my voice. "Maria?"

I glance in the kitchen, then the various other rooms downstairs. When I don't find her, I check each room upstairs as well. Still no Maria.

I rush outside yelling her name, noting the bike she used earlier lying in the grass near the front porch. I check the shed, the barn, and the destroyed lab.

"Maria!" I yell again. I'm loud, so if she's nearby she has to hear me.

I fly back over to the house, and knock a picture off a small table when I swing the door open too abruptly. I keep yelling her name without a response. I check every room again, even pulling open the shower curtains. I would rather both of us be embarrassed than not find her.

But she's nowhere.

Dear God. Joe's watered-down bourbon. Maria's half-eaten sandwich. She was taken, too.

I helplessly check each room one more time, screaming her name. When I fly into the kitchen, I stir the air enough to knock a piece of paper off the table. It floats slowly and I snatch it up long before it reaches the ground.

Its message is typed. It was not something handwritten in a hurry – it was prepared beforehand. It was premeditated.

Come to Dr. Bradford's lab.
I hear you're looking for me.
-V

CHAPTER TWENTY-ONE

I don't even remember the flight to Bradford's lab. My mind races with an amount of hatred I've never experienced before.

Slate killed my parents. He kidnapped Dr. Bradford and Dr. Hughes. He kidnapped *Maria*.

I don't care that I'm losing control. I don't care that the warmth bubbling in my chest is slithering its tentacles all over my body.

He will pay.

If she has so much as a bruise, I will break every bone in his body. If she has a tiny paper cut, I will tear his skin to shreds.

And if she's dead, he'll *wish* he was.

I'm standing at the door on twenty-fifth street before I even know I left. Something tells me that it's unlocked, but I'm not in the mood for subtlety. I rip the metal door from the wall, taking the frame with it.

He's standing at the end of the hall.

A single bulb hangs over him like a theatre spotlight, illuminating his fragile body. That detestable mask covers his face, a growth of skin sitting on top of a four-thousand-dollar suit. His expensive alligator skin shoes don't move, as if he doesn't care what's about to happen to him.

"Where is she?" I scream down the hall at the top of my lungs, laboring to take one step at a time. I have to contain myself, as I'm sure he's rigged some sort of trap to kill my friends if I do something wrong.

His body shakes as his laughter fills the hall.

"Where—is—she?" I scream again, hearing my voice crack with rage. Each step is a testament to my self control.

After I'm about ten feet into the hallway I hear a tiny click, immediately followed by countless gallons of paint spraying the interior of the passageway.

I'm no longer invisible.

I'm not completely covered, but enough so there'll be no way to for me to have any element of surprise. I turn visible and laugh like a naked lunatic.

"Do you think that will help?" I manage to scream through my laughter. "Do you think you can stop me as long as you can see me?"

The Vacant laughs louder, his body shuttering. It's almost as if he's squirming – fighting the urge to run, but at the same time sounding like he's having a jovial time. Then he shakes his head.

"No," his distorted, monotone voice rings through the hall. "I just wanted to confirm it was really you. I've been outsmarted by you for a long time, after all."

"Well, take a good look, because if you've hurt my friends this will be the last thing you ever see."

I don't know where this machismo talk is coming from, but I can almost understand why Vic would give similar speeches. The adrenaline is pulsing through my veins like a time bomb. Each of my steps feel like an inch taken off of a fuse.

"Your friends are safe for now," he says, his head shifting to the left and right. "I wanted to talk for a moment, though. Just the two of us."

"There's nothing you can say to me," I scream. "Unless you're telling me that you surrender. Tell me where they are!"

"Don't be so hasty, Robby," he says in a clinical tone as if he's concerned for *me* and *my* impetuousness.

"You killed my parents and kidnapped my friends," I scream as I close the gap between us with my steps. "There is nothing to talk about."

"You really do have everything figured out, don't you?" he asks with feigned amazement.

His fleshy skull taunts me, and I realize it is not acceptable for him to see me while I still can't see his face. I reach up and grab the mask, ripping it from his body.

Nelson Slate stares at me with wide, bloodshot eyes, as if he didn't expect that I would actually unmask him. His chin is extended but his lips remain closed. Sweat covers his face and he's bleeding from his nose and ears.

I hope it was Maria that gave him the bloody nose. I hope she did far worse than that.

And then I realize something.

He's *trying* to open his mouth. He's trying to tell me something. He's shaking his head left and right vigorously, as if the thing he wanted most in the world was for me to turn around and leave him alone. The mask must do something to his face – prevent him from speaking without a special device or something. Or he has something in his mouth that allows him to breath freely in the blue fog.

No matter.

I'll make him talk.

I reach to grab his chin, restraining myself so that I don't crush him in the process. My hand travels the space between, seemingly in slow motion. As soon as my fingers graze his skin, my body ignites.

I'm helpless as I tense up and watch his eyes roll back in his head. I can't stop my fingers from clenching around his chin, breaking his jaw almost immediately.

Electricity shoots through my body.

Real electricity – not a feeling or an emotion, not a thought. As soon as my body connects with his, he becomes a conductor, bringing whatever current is connected to him, transferring it to me.

I'm paralyzed. I fall onto him, supplying numerous more points of contact. I try to fight it, but my muscles spasm, contracting around him until there's no possibility of life remaining inside him. As his body slumps, I realize he's tied to a metal rod behind him.

We both slide towards the floor, though he doesn't get far. He remains vertical with limp arms and legs, his hands behind his back. I eventually sever our connection, though not by any act of will of my own – our bodies simply don't have the strength to remain in the same position. His upright against the rod and mine prostrate on the ground.

I assume the electricity will cease when we disconnect, but no such luck. He was not the source – merely the trigger.

Laughing echoes through the halls, competing with the buzzing in my ears.

"You *thought* you had everything figured out," The Vacant's voice rings, for the first time expressing joy. "But there's an important detail that you missed."

I hear a pair of rubber boots take squeaky, intentioned steps toward my face. I struggle to do anything at all – look up, reach out, roll away. My burning body is at the mercy of whoever owns the rubber boots.

He walks around my head and into view, allowing my eyes to struggle to catch a glimpse of my captor.

"Nelson Slate was never The Vacant," a man wearing a lab coat says. "It was always me. Winston Bradford."

CHAPTER TWENTY-TWO

My head is spinning. Every muscle in my body contracts and I feel like I'm on fire. At least, I think that's what it feels like - I haven't felt fire since the explosion in the lab.

"Whaaaat?" I force, drawing the word out like a crying child. I'm sure I sound like I have a mouthful of marshmallows.

Bradford laughs. He's not wearing the mask or distorting his voice, but it's obvious that he is, indeed, The Vacant. The laugh is the last confirmation – the fact that he's enjoying this.

"I don't fault you for being unable to arrive at the correct conclusion until now," he says in an understanding voice. "I've always seen Slate as the perfect scapegoat if anyone were to suspect me. If you follow the money on everything pertaining to my alter ego, it's actually all his. I gained access to a few of his accounts – he didn't even realize he was funding my research over the last couple of years. To say nothing of the fact that he was a terrible person with no remorse. His last wonderful act was to make me his sole beneficiary in the event of his death. How unfortunate that the actual event was only a few hours after he signed the document. All completely legal, of course."

Bradford grabs my twitching arm with his rubber-gloved hands and tugs on me as hard as he can.

"Wow, you are incredibly heavy," he says as he slowly gets my body to move against the slick floor. "This entire floor is an electric conduit, by the way, so don't expect to be liberated any time soon. The fact that you're naked is a bit awkward, but it means you have ample points of contact with the voltage."

He gets his momentum up and starts dragging me through the doorway to his kitchenette.

"Whhhyyy?" I drool, as if my face has been injected with anesthesia.

Bradford stops pulling for a moment, wiping his brow with the sleeve above his gloved hand. Apparently he's not used to doing the heavy lifting himself.

"That's a great question," he says. "And honestly, it depends on what context you're asking it in."

He picks up my arm and pulls again.

"If you mean 'Why did you kill Nelson Slate,' isn't the answer obvious?" he chuckles. "He was a huge bother and he outlived his usefulness. When you and I had that conversation about the noxious gas, Slate was my backup plan. Not to mention that you, in fact, were the one that caused his death directly.

"Actually, to tell you the truth, I had completely forgotten about you. I only vaguely remembered that Eric—your father, of course—had a son. When I acted surprised that you were *alive*— The reality is, I was surprised that you existed at all. I remember Eric rambling on and on about his amazing boy, but I ignored most of it. I do remember seeing you in his home lab just before I blew it up, but I never thought I'd see you again."

"Myyy mommm," I breathe against the vibration of my insides.

"Yes, that was rather unfortunate," he answers. "I actually had no intention of killing you *or* your mother. Wrong place, wrong time as they say. Obviously, I had to kill her when she saw me barricading the doors shut."

"Yoouuuu…" The noise escapes, but I have no energy to call him all of the names I want to. Not that speaking them would help the situation.

He drags me into the lab where we had determined the composition of the residue I brought to him. Only one day ago, when he acted like he wanted to help me.

We're not alone.

"Robby, you know Dr. Joseph Hughes, of course," Bradford says as he motions his free hand towards the opposite wall.

Joe hangs like a crucified trophy, bruised and broken. His hands and feet are bound with rubber ropes, and his body is pressed against a rubber mat secured against the wall. He barely looks up, squinting his swollen eyes. It's obvious that he barely has the energy for the effort it takes to move his head and look at me.

"As I'm sure you can already tell," Bradford points out, "the rubber keeps him—and me—from experiencing the same pain and paralysis you're experiencing. It's not quite enough electricity to kill any of us, but he's already been through quite a bit. Slate, on the other hand, I would've preferred to kill a bit slower, but I don't think I could've had better cheese for the proverbial mousetrap I set for you. Dr. Hughes has provided me with the enjoyment of torture."

Blood drips from Joe's face, and red stains patch his unbuttoned white dress shirt. His beard is caked with red as well. His head droops down, unable to force the muscles in his neck to maintain eye contact.

"*It's okay, Robby,*" Dr. Hughes whispers, quiet enough that Bradford can't hear. "*None of this is your fault.*"

"He didn't give me much information, though," Bradford continues, unaware of Joe's message. "I guess he really takes the whole doctor-patient-confidentiality routine seriously!"

He laughs hysterically at his own joke.

"*I heard you saved a lot of people early this morning,*" Joe's voice murmurs. "*I'm proud of you.*"

The compliment is strange, considering I didn't save all of my neighbors, and that they were only in danger because of me in the first place. And the same goes for Dr. Hughes. If I didn't exist, he would not be strapped against the wall.

Of course, if I didn't exist, The Vacant would continue to have free reign. Who knows who else would be tied up in the same position now or later.

"But honestly – you've got a good therapist there, Robby. Locked up tight," Bradford says as he pantomimes a key turning near his lips. "But I can't have anyone running loose that knows your secret, since it could eventually lead back to me."

Bradford drops my arm and makes his way over to Dr. Hughes. I concentrate as best I can to slow down time, or hover off the floor, or *anything*. Instead, the electricity continues to pass through my body in real time, allowing me only to observe.

"*You can't save everyone,*" Joe whispers as he musters up the strength to look at me with courage, slightly nodding his head. "*You can't save everyone.*"

"Any last words, doc?" Bradford asks, still unaware of his captive's messages to me. He pulls a gun from his waist and places the barrel against Joe's temple just as the broken psychologist draws a breath to speak.

"No, I'm only kidding," Bradford says nonchalant as he pulls the trigger without delay, causing red to spray the wall behind them. Joe's body slumps against the rubber restraints.

Tears involuntarily run down my face, but I still can't control a single muscle in my body. Bradford killed Joe for no other reason than he knew me. Really *knew* me.

"Whhhyyy?" I weep, not able to get out more than a single-syllable word.

"Why kill Dr. Hughes?" Bradford asks. "I just told you – I can't let anyone else know our secret."

He puts the gun away and scratches his head as if he's sincerely confused why I would ask the same question again.

"Or maybe you weren't referring to Nelson earlier...?" he ponders. "Perhaps you mean why did I become The Vacant?"

He walks back over and picks my arm up once again.

"I guess that's answered with the usual ramblings. Power, money, fear. All the things that *didn't* come with being a brilliant scientist. Once I saw the kind of power that Nelson commanded, I wanted it for myself. I grew tired of always being at the mercy of investors and managers who couldn't understand what my mind was capable of."

He looks at his free hand, considering it as if it were some alien object. "They couldn't recognize the power I held in my hands. They treated me like a janitor."

"Nooo," I pushed out of my lungs. "Whhhyyy... Daaddd..."

"Oh - of course!" Dr. Bradford points a finger up in the air like a light bulb went off in his brain. "Why did I murder your father? You should've been more specific about the context of your *why* question earlier, my boy."

He grabs my arm with both hands, walking backwards to pull with everything he has.

"Your father was just too smart for his own good," he explains. "Or should I say too...*good* for his own good? His work was incredible, but he insisted on trying to keep most of it hidden. In that regard, your father was just like the rest of them. I felt like I was in his shadow – that my work was never recognized or appreciated on the same level.

"And to top it off, he wrestled with all sorts of moral objections to our experiments and what they would be used for, which meant we'd never be paid what we were really worth."

My brain, on fire, can't comprehend how this man could work alongside my father for years, and yet resolve to kill his whole family just to be appreciated. How he could be friendly with my parents at Christmas parties, the whole time plotting how to remove us as a roadblock from his own version of success. Instead of simply looking for another job, or a way to outshine my dad based on merit, he destroyed him.

We pass through a small hallway, his rubber boots squeaking with each step, toward what looks to be a strangely familiar door.

"But perhaps a more interesting question is, how did I know about *your* secret, Robby!"

I hadn't really worried about how he figured me out – once I saw Dr. Hughes, I assumed that piece of information slipped out.

"It's somewhat of a long story, but I'll try to make it as brief as possible," he says as he presses a couple of buttons on a keypad with a gloved finger, then leans his head in for his eye to be scanned. "And I guess it starts with Victor Boone."

The keypad lights up in green and the latch on the door is released. The stairwell beyond is eerily recognizable – everything from the colors to the way the light is cast from bulbs sticking out of the ceiling. It's impossible, but I feel as though this is the second time I've been here today.

"When Victor Boone showed up, I was fascinated by him. I had actually planned on taking control of the city a couple of years ago, but he threw a wrench into my plan. All of a sudden,

I couldn't simply shield myself from consequence with money or hired hands – I had a true obstruction to remove.

"While I still had to act like a sniveling underling, I did everything I could to find out more about him. He seemed like a typical simpleton – accepted into college on a football scholarship and barely kept up, but dropped out when his powers manifested. Son of middle-class parents, no history of heroics off the field. He went from unknown to celebrity the world over in the course of weeks.

"At first, I bribed doctors and nurses for vials of his blood – which was strange, considering he seemed to be bulletproof. All of his results came back very healthy, but normal. Well, except for once when he tested positive for Trichomoniasis, but it disappeared from future samples. Ah, antibiotics... Isn't modern medicine convenient?"

Bradford walks down the metal stairs, dragging me behind him. If I weren't invincible – except for the electricity, of course – I would have felt the grating of the steps scratching at my naked skin, and my head banging with each stair we passed. As it is, I have no pain but the constant wattage keeping me company.

"I can't tell you how many tests I did on his fluids, at first to see if I could find a vulnerability. Then I realized he was vulnerable to *everything*, like any human. I started looking for any possible differences that could explain how he was doing what he was doing. I could discover none.

"I started hiring crews to attempt to kill him. Lowlifes, drug addicts... They would do anything for money with no regard for their safety. Victor never killed anyone, so at worst these pawns would end up in hospitals or jails. I used The Vacant so that nothing could be easily traced back to me.

"After watching endless recordings, it occurred to me that Mr. Boone had a force field of sorts. It's not that he was bulletproof, but that no weapons could get near him. However, it was common for him to cozy up with people as he saw fit. With that new knowledge, I knew my best chance was to attack him at close range. It took several attempts, but I was finally successful."

We get to the bottom of the stairs and Bradford drops my hand. He pauses to take a breath.

"I wasn't confident if I'd killed him for sure or not," he continues. "No, I'm not one of the crazy theorists who believed he would resurrect or something, but I wasn't confident. I waited months before I decided to reveal my alter-ego to the public. But once I did—specifically in City Hall—Victor Boone sightings gained credibility again.

"I was confused to say the least. But, my God. When you showed up at my lab, asking me to test the concoction that I modified from the formula your father and I created... Serendipity!

"The two of us worked on a serum that would create super soldiers, but it never worked correctly. The animal tests were sometimes momentarily successful, but always resulted in death. We could never find anything to stabilize the genetic transitions in the host. The living tissue would start to change, but would break down almost immediately. We were trying everything.

"He'd made several breakthroughs without telling me, the traitor. And I found out he built a secret lab on his own property."

His hand moves to another keypad by the door at the base of the stairwell, and scans his eye again. The familiarity of the surroundings is starting to make sense.

"I decided to bide my time," he says as the door unlatches and swings open. "I didn't want to destroy it until I could create this."

He moves his hand into the empty doorway with a smile stretching across his face, apparently excited to clear up the confusion my brain had been fighting.

CHAPTER TWENTY-THREE

I'm looking at my dad's lab. An exact replica. Perfect, down to the details of the formula written on the dry erase board. This room is as alive as my father was a decade ago in it, contrasting the burnt-out shell that Maria and I explored only hours before.

There are only two changes: the empty cages in one corner that should be filled with various small animals, and in the center of the room, where a large, empty glass case should stand. The container is there, but it isn't empty. This one holds within it an unmoving, beautiful, curly-haired girl.

Maria.

I try to scream her name, but the only thing that escapes from my open mouth is garbled noise.

Her hands and feet are bound, and her mouth gagged. She's unconscious, but I can see her chest rising and falling. In a normal situation it would be easy for me to hear her heartbeat, but between the emotional hurricane in my head and the literal electricity pulsing through my body, I'm having a hard time hearing anything. I can't smell the vanilla-coconut mix, either – only the burnt hair and boiling chemicals from my past.

My reality is confusing. This is the place of my memories, my dreams. It's almost as if my vision detaches from my head and scans over the room in an out-of-body experience. I can see my father with an open notebook, watching a mouse who has climbed to the top of a cage wall.

"Good job, little fella," my dad says to the white rodent while scribbling something on the paper in his hands. He then looks in my direction. "Robby – this is incredible. I think I might have figured the whole thing out."

Bradford drags me closer to the glass box containing Maria, leaning me against a table so I can have a better view.

"It didn't do me any good, creating this laboratory," he says. "I must have spent six months observing every tiny detail of the one he built, taking the best notes of my life. I knew that I wouldn't be able to remember it well enough – it took me years before I had the funds to buy this property and reconstruct everything from my records. I assumed I'd be able to recreate his results if I had his lab, but I had the exact same outcome. Everything died."

"Watch this," my dad says with a huge smile on his face.

He holds a piece of cheese at the top of the cage, at least two feet above the mouse's reach. The animal floats to the top, grabbing the cheese in its hands, then starts nibbling on it in mid-air.

"That isn't even something I planned on – him flying," my dad explains. "We were only focused on strengthening living cells to fight disease, retain energy, and solidify to prevent lacerations. I don't know what part of genetics would allow a living thing to float without wings or some sort of thrusting. So fascinating."

The mouse takes quick bites, breaking his dinner by looking up every few seconds. I mimic him, stuffing bites from a candy bar into my already puffy cheeks.

"If I'm correct," my dad laughs as he continues, "this mouse barely even needs to eat anymore. Once his body creates fat, his own metabolism will take an extremely long time to break it down. Of course, he'll need to eat an awful lot to actually create that fat because it'll be completely packed with energy. But even though his body can break down his fat to retrieve that energy, it would only be after he stopped eating. He would feel like he's starving. So I'll keep feeding him. But the implication of this is that we could possibly create superfoods – if we modified a chicken this same way, then only one chicken nugget would last us for days!"

I haven't seen my dad this excited in a long time.

⟨−−•⟩

"I don't know what Eric did differently," Bradford says, dissipating my foggy memory. "I'd stopped working in this lab at least three years ago – I'd given up. But now *you're* here! I'm inspired to do more research."

He walks over to the glove box, tapping on the glass. Maria doesn't move. For the first time, I notice that the box and its stand are on a rubber mat, which means Maria is safe from the electricity. I can't remember if that's how the original lab was set up – but because it didn't stand out, I have to assume it was.

"I was going to simply try the blue fog again, but I was afraid you'd have built a tolerance up to it like I have," he says, still casually tapping on the glass. "I didn't know you were susceptible to electricity until your girlfriend told me. Are you familiar with Samson and Delilah from the Old Testament?"

He makes a fist and beats on the glass until Maria stirs, slowly opening her eyes. Once she takes in her surroundings, her eyes grow wide and she starts violently shaking against her restraints, screaming through her gag.

"Samson was exceptionally strong, supposedly because the Hebrew God gave him all his powers," Bradford continues. "His enemies tried everything, but could do nothing to kill him. Fortunately for them, Samson fell in love with Delilah, who was one of their own daughters. They convinced her to find his weakness."

He pauses for a moment to smile at Maria.

"No, no," he says with a laugh. "This girl is not my daughter, nor is she working for me, if that's what you're thinking."

Maria keeps struggling against her binding, while I feel like I have less energy with every moment that passes.

"Several times she asked him about his weakness, and each time Samson lied to her, telling her vulnerabilities that didn't exist. They would try the thing he specified, and they would be defeated."

Bradford strokes his hand on the glass near Maria's face.

"This one tried to hold out, I assure you," he says with a devilish grin. "By the time I got her to talk, she started spewing lies about how I could *really* stop you. Unfortunately for her, I tried everything she said when dealing with Mr. Boone. I was very thorough, and none of them seemed to pierce his force field, which I now know to be you."

Bradford walks to the opposite side of the glove box, then flips a switch. A low mechanical hum cuts through the air, and an air compressor kicks on in a different room.

"But, both she and Delilah eventually get to the truth. For Samson, it was shaving his head. For you, it's electricity."

❮●●●●❯

"Did you see that?" my dad exclaims. "His tail just disappeared! I mean – I know it's there now, but I'm one hundred percent sure it was gone for a moment. If that's the case, maybe even the Mnemiopsis Leidyi genetics were successfully infused! Bradford told me I was insane for attempting it – said that cloth would never be more than an expensive electric blanket."

He motions towards a large piece of yellow material bunched up under a table, then looks at his watch.

"Two hours," he says. "None of them have lived past twenty seconds before now – the anchor has to be the key. Want to know how I think it works?"

I nod, still chewing on the chocolate and nougat in my cheeks. I have no idea what he's talking about, but I'm excited that he's excited.

"I guess you might think it's convenient," Bradford says as he moves towards me, again pulling me back to reality, "that this whole building is wired as an electrical trap, but really it's just convenient that that's your weakness. I can't tell you how many precautions I made when I renovated this place – gases ready to be released in any room, intense heating elements underneath each floor panel... If one of my experiments worked, after all, I'd need to incapacitate it, were it to attack me.

"It *is* consistent that electricity paralyzes you, as I assume each of your cell membranes are disrupted. We were using electroporation in many of our tests, but the host would never survive the amount needed. I wonder – did Eric figure out a specific wattage or voltage? But I digress."

He looks at Maria.

"Your Delilah was very helpful, once I revealed her parents' address and several of her friends' as well. I think she thought you were being humble, and weren't really so susceptible. Nelson was a wonderful volunteer to confirm its harm. Had it not worked, you would've killed your assumed villain, and the rest of the building would be on lockdown. The hostages would be killed, and I would be gone, leaving you to call the police and blame all this destruction on him."

He walks back over to the glove box, glancing back and forth between Maria and me.

"But as it is, you and I have many more experiments to run," he says. "Your girlfriend is no longer of any use to me, except to help me show you what has happened to all prior test cases. How will we learn if we do not observe, after all?"

He gives me a wink, then smacks his hand down on a red button at the foot of the glass. Maria struggles harder against her restraints as the box fills up with fog. The dense gas hangs in the space above her head, lowering with each millisecond. She coughs uncontrollably through the gag in her mouth.

I do everything I can to move towards her – it can't be more than four feet. I don't know what I'll do when I get there, but I have to try.

I'm not very successful. From my position leaned against the table, I fall onto the ground, knocking over several empty beakers and test tubes. Bradford simply laughs.

"You can't even sit up straight, Robby," he mocks, moving to the other side of the room to observe without fear of my action, as weak as it is. "What are you going to do if you reach her?"

Maria thrashes against the glass, her eyes wide. I can see the fog enter through her nose, and tears stream down her cheeks. The sight of her terror forces me to put my full effort on reaching her. I drag myself, inch by inch, trying not to focus on her movements.

Don't give up, Robby, my burning brain screams at me. *You might not be able to save everyone, but you've got to save Maria. Not just because you're the one that dragged her into this. Not just because she's the only person that has protected you. Not just because she has pushed you and helped you and made you better.*

My mind pauses as it makes the logical connection.

Because you love her.

I can't imagine waking up tomorrow without her. I don't care what weapon she's hiding in her purse or what uncomfortable things she makes me do – I have to keep her safe. If I don't, I might as well die on the floor right now.

My body and mind keep screaming at me with the voice of a drill sergeant as I continue dragging myself across the floor, finally touching the rubber mat with my extended fingers.

I'm here! I'll figure something out!

I look up, expecting to see that Maria is relieved that I'm going to help. Instead, she lies motionless with blood dripping from her nose.

CHAPTER TWENTY-FOUR

"Well," my dad says, pointing to the good luck charm he gave me only a few days before. "That right there is the anchor."

"You gave him a good luck charm, too?" I ask, pointing at the mouse.

"Yup," he says, slipping in and out of his science-speak to just be my dad. "Without it, every single test case failed. Basically, we have to make the cells really weak before the subject inhales the compound. Up until now, the cells would be *too* weak by the time the chemicals could get into the bloodstream through the lungs. I needed to find a way to harness the current so it would focus the charge on the cells. Otherwise, I had to use so much electricity that they would get burned up inside. With that charm," he says, pointing at the strange metal hanging from my neck, "I can use much lower levels of electricity, but it's amplified across the cells."

Wait – this means something. Something beyond just the mouse.

"Is that how it happened to me?" I ask, my eleven-year-old body floating so I could meet my dad's eyes.

"Yup," he says, again sounding like my dad rather than Dr. Willis.

"I don't remember the electricity, though," I say. "Just breathing the smoke in. I think I passed out."

"Right before you passed out," he prods, trying to help me remember. "What happened?"

My mind is blank.

"Do you remember the last thing I told you?"

"Yeah," I answer. "You told me that you loved me."

"I didn't say loved," he corrects. "I said *love*. Present tense. I love you – still do."

"I love you, too, dad."

"But you're right," he confirms. "I said 'I love you, buddy. No matter what happens.'"

I nod.

"You don't remember anything else?" he asks. "Just before you lost consciousness?"

I look over to the empty glove box and scrunch my eyes, thinking as hard as I can. I glance over the various controls and screens lining the panel below the glass. There are two large buttons: one red, which pumps in the smoke, and one yellow.

"You pushed the yellow button," I say, finally remembering.

"Yup," he nods. "But I had to wait until the smoke filled the chamber. Otherwise, if the compound hadn't gotten to your lungs, the electricity would've hurt you. And I was nervous that you'd already breathed in too much smoke from the fire to inhale enough of it."

I picture it in my mind, remembering him pushing the button and my body arching in the glove box. My lungs burned, but not as much as the skin at the top of my breastbone. All of the current seemed to pass through my skin and bones, ending at the charm attached by the chain around my neck. The last thing I remember is my dad collapsing on the ground, coughing.

"What happened after that?"

"I don't know," he says. "You passed out after that."

"I know *I* passed out - but what did *you* see?" I ask.

He cocks his head to the side a bit, as if he's surprised that I'm missing something.

"Well, I don't know, buddy," he answers, then motions around the room. "These are just your memories. I'm only saying things I've already said to you, and you're just remembering more."

"Wait, so—" I pause. "So we're not really here?"

He frowns and shakes his head.

"No – I'm sorry, buddy," he says with a disappointed look on his face. "You're in the other lab, with Maria in the glove box and that snake Bradford in the corner."

I gaze around the room with my own look of disappointment. For a moment it was euphoric to be talking to my dad in real time. I now realize it's just a cross between a memory and a dream. All of his answers are either an echo of something he'd said, or something that I assume he would say. My subconscious is filling in the gaps.

"Did you know Bradford was going to kill you?" I ask, playing along with my own charade. It might not be real, but it's a dream I don't want to wake up from.

"I started to distrust him," he answers in a concerned voice. "I don't think I knew he would do something so extreme. If I had known, I probably would've done something to prevent it, don't you think? Or I would've at least kept you and your mom safe."

Is that an echo of him? Or is it just my obsession with never feeling like I can save the people I love?

"What if I can't fix things?" I ask. "What if Maria dies, I stay paralyzed on the floor, and Bradford figures out how to give himself these powers by experimenting on me?"

The look on my dad's face morphs from concern into consideration.

"Do you remember what I used to tell you all the time?" he asks.

He used to tell me a lot of things – he always had a proverb or a lesson in his back pocket.

"I don't know," I sigh.

"Sometimes you'll fail...?" he begins, trying to jog my memory by raising his eyebrows and nodding his head.

"Sometimes I'll fail, and sometimes I'll succeed," I say, finishing his frequent phrase. "But you were always proud of me."

He nods.

"Yup, I am," he says. "Present tense. I'm *always* proud of you."

"But I've messed a lot of things up," I counter. "I've gotten a bunch of people killed."

"Robby," he says, putting his hands on my shoulders. "Listen to what Dr. Hughes said. Listen to what Maria said. *You* didn't get them killed. You've done everything you could to keep people safe."

"No, not always," I say. "I've been hiding in the shadows, afraid of everything. Afraid of everybody."

"Then it's time to step out of the shadows," he says firmly. "You're strong. And even if you've had some failures, I know you're capable of huge successes. But either way, you know what?"

"You're proud of me," I nod, barely believing it.

"Exactly. Your mom, too."

Just then, I hear my mom through the door. I turn to look at her through the window and see a frantic expression on her face. She's beating her fists on the steel, trying to get our attention.

"What's going on?" I ask.

My dad runs over to the door, trying to turn the knob without luck. I can't see through the window—my dad is blocking it from my vision—but I hear a loud pop.

A gunshot.

My dad screams and puts every ounce of his strength into opening the locked door. The vision has reverted to my memory alone, without my brain filling in conversation.

"Tricia! No!" he screams. "What did you do, Wins—"

Before he could finish what I now know to be Dr. Bradford's first name, an explosion reverberates through the lab.

CHAPTER TWENTY-FIVE

I wake up, jerked into the present by the disaster in my past. In the last moment, my dad knew what happened.

I stare at Maria's lifeless body above me. The yellow button to release the flow of electric current to the box is at least three feet above me – much too far for my weak arms to reach. I'm going to watch Maria die because of three measly feet of space, because the electricity pulsing through my body prevents me from disconnecting from the ground.

Wait – of course! I'm my *own* conductor. I don't need to reach the button.

I reach out to the nearest piece of metal under Maria's cage, wrapping my fingers around one of the stand's legs.

Nothing happens.

I hear Dr. Bradford laughing like a schoolyard bully at one of his victims, confident that any efforts I make will be useless. As if I needed any more motivation, his smugness pushes me on.

I force my other hand a few inches above the leg, gripping just above my already-connected fingers. Then I try to use the leg as a ladder, sliding my hands up an inch at a time. After several tries, my tired fingers finally reach a piece of metal that is definitely connected to the cage floor.

But I'm too late.

I can see the metal charm on Maria's skin starting to glow, but she has no reaction. I stare at her for several seconds, watching the charm get brighter and brighter.

And then it happens.

As if she were waiting for the metal necklace to build up the charge, her body arches inside the box. She thrashes, stirring the fog around her, looking like she's in a whirlpool of blue cigarette smoke. Her whole body glows along with the charm.

I don't know what to do. I don't know if I should keep my weak fingers clenched around the metal, or if I'm killing her by continuing the charge.

I stare at her, hoping that there will be some indication that everything is over and safe, like some sort of genetic egg timer telling me when to disconnect myself.

"What are you doing?" Bradford yells in fascination as he approaches us, eyes wide. "What's going on?"

I don't have the strength to respond, nor would I even if I did. I don't think Bradford knows about the charm—the anchor—and I'm not about to tell him. I have half a mind to try to reach out and grab his arm when he gets close enough, to give him a dose of the electricity I've contained in my body since grabbing Slate. But I'm not sure that I can multitask with my arms at this moment.

"She looks different," Bradford exclaims. "You're doing it!"

The scientist in Bradford must have taken over, because he's truly just observing the process without thinking of the consequence to come.

After at least a minute of lighting the Maria bulb, her skin is as bright as the sun. Bradford shields his eyes, still trying to watch, while I look directly at the object of my affection, afraid I'm destroying her.

Then the light explodes out of her.

It's as if I'm standing at ground zero in Hiroshima, watching the detonation of an atomic bomb. The glove box turns into dust, and the instrument panel and metal stand below her shatters into hundreds of pieces. Fire-like beams of light lick the surfaces that surround her, burning permanent marks into the walls, floor, and ceiling.

Bradford flies back as if hit in the gut with a wrecking ball. The energy pushes me back as well, forcing me to disconnect from the metal that is losing its shape under her. Chunks of the ceiling fall down around all three of us, and I watch as the charm shoots like a bullet away from her radiant skin.

For a moment, the room looks like the inside of a supernova – everything as bright as possible to the point of nothing being visible. As the light dims, I realize all the bulbs in the ceiling have exploded, and any electronic device is dead and smoking. And for the first time since touching Nelson Slate, I am free from the electric current.

As if suddenly pulled by a divine string, I stand, then hover an inch above the ground, just in case a backup generator is going to kick on.   My abilities have returned, but I'm exhausted.

Maria lies on the ground in the middle of radioactive stains left over from her explosion.   Bent metal and broken equipment surround her. Her clothes are singed, and her skin still puts off enough light to illuminate the basement so that any normal eye could see clearly. Her chest rises and falls, rises and falls. I can hear her calm, steady heartbeat. She's asleep.

I move close to her, touching her glowing face with the same precaution as an art dealer might handle an ancient sculpture. I doubt I could break her, though – even the blood that was dripping from her nose only a moment ago has retreated, forced away from her most-likely impenetrable skin in the blast.

Then I hear a groan from across the room.

I float over to Bradford, who is covered in debris and an overturned table. I move the objects away then pull off his rubber gloves and boots. At this point, I doubt a backup generator will kick on, but if it does I want to make sure he feels the same current I do.

Lifting him in the air with a fistful of his lab coat, I fight the urge to punch him in the face as hard as I can. He murdered my parents, Dr. Hughes, and an innocent Nelson Slate. He *tried* to murder the most beautiful-smelling girl in the world, who is the closest thing to a best friend I've ever had.

I refrain and drop him on the rubble. It's not up to me to decide punishment. But I *will* do absolutely everything in my power to make sure any judge or twelve-person jury in the world sees him for what he is. When his trial is over, The Vacant will be used as a synonym for an open-and-shut case.

I guess to make sure of that, I'll have to be okay with a camera or two.

I hear sirens in the distance, as well as a commotion beginning to grow outside. People have definitely noticed. I suppose ripping the entrance door off the building allowed for lots of different sounds to escape: gunshots, screams, a beautifully explosive woman.

I scan the room for anything to cover myself. Even though I can turn invisible again, I'm covered in paint, which will still outline every part of my body even if the flesh and bone behind it are transparent. I notice another yellow cloth—just like the one Maria found in my dad's lab—and wrap it around my body like a toga, tying a knot to keep it steady.

Bradford coughs uncontrollably, then blinks.

"What happened?" he finally breathes, his empty eyes wide open, looking for light. I think he must've been blinded by Maria's glorious supernova. "Is anyone there?"

I succumb to the urge. I flick Bradford in the forehead with my pointer finger, just enough to knock him unconscious again. I restrain myself from inflicting any further pain, but I hope beyond hope that his headache never goes away.

I'm distracted by Maria stirring from the tiny crater she created. I rush over to her, watching as the unnatural light slowly drains from her skin.

"Maria – are you okay?" I ask frantically.

"My head," she says. "What happened?"

"Dr. Bradford had you in a lab like my dad's," I explain, not knowing how much she remembers. "He tried to kill us."

"And you saved me?" she says with a drunken smile, sitting up.

"Well – actually, *you* saved *me*," I respond.

She smirks.

"Shut up and take some credit," she says, lurching forward to give me a thirty-minute kiss.

Well, probably more like a half-second peck on the lips, but I used every ounce of power remaining in me to savor each nanosecond.

CHAPTER TWENTY-SIX

"What went on in there?" a reporter screams out from behind a temporary barrier. She juts her microphone out as far as she can. We've only been outside in the streetlight for a few minutes, and already the news cameras are making me feel claustrophobic.

"Say something," Maria whispers as she nudges me, adding more force than she intends.

We're sitting on the curb, emergency crews swirling around us. Maria and I both refused medical attention at least ten times already. Dr. Bradford lies in the back of a police cruiser, still unconscious, with zip ties around his wrists. Fitting.

"What do I say?" I ask. "I've never done this before."

I fight against every part of my instincts to fly away.

"As much or as little as you want to," she answers with calm smile. "Get the truth out there, before the police shoo them away and try to edit the story."

As my dad—or at least the memory-dream version of my dad—said: "It's time to step out of the shadows." The only way I can be sure that Dr. Bradford's list of crimes are correctly attributed to him is to be an official eyewitness.

I stand, clutching the yellow material that covers my otherwise naked, painted body. I slowly make my way over to the chaotic scene of cameras, microphones, and the beautiful people that hold them. I think I would feel more comfortable if I were being lowered into an Olympic-sized swimming pool teeming with piranhas. Scratch that – I *know* I would feel more comfortable with schools of carnivorous fish.

"Can you tell us what happened?" another reporter yells.

"The most important thing," I preface, "is that The Vacant has been captured."

The piranha-reporters go nuts.

"How do you know he's been captured?"

"Who is behind The Vacant's mask?"

"Are you absolutely sure?"

I raise my hands and, somehow, they actually quiet down for a moment.

"Dr. Winston Bradford is the man behind The Vacant," I announce. "A corrupt scientist who has ruthlessly murdered several people, both with and without a mask on."

"The Vacant said he was responsible for the death of Victor Boone – is that true?"

I glance back at Maria, who urges me on with a motion of her hands.

"Yes," I answer as I turn back towards them. "Dr. Bradford is indeed responsible for Victor Boone's death."

"Who is responsible for discovering this information, and for apprehending him?"

I again turn back to Maria, who whispers, "Take the credit. I would've died if it weren't for you."

I smile. Not long ago, she said she would be just like Vic, taking credit when it wasn't really hers. She was wrong about herself.

I'm wondering how much she's been right about me.

I don't think she realizes how much of a part she played in Bradford's capture. If it was anything like my transformation, she's going to have trouble remembering the last few hours. She might not even know that she now has the same abilities I do.

"Dr. Bradford was apprehended by my friend, Maria," I firmly say as I hear her huff behind me, then after a beat of silence I add, "…and me."

At least four reporters say in unison, "And who are you?"

"I'm Victor Boone. Er—"

Crap.

I did it again, and this time it's not only Dr. Hughes I have to convince, but everyone who has access to a TV screen or computer monitor.

It feels like cameras flash by the thousands. The reporters shoot a flurry of questions, obviously confused by what I said. This time, instead of spending any time to convince them with words or violence to myself, I turn invisible.

I hear at least twenty gasps.

I assume they're all surprised at my ability to disappear, until Maria screams, "Robby!"

I turn around, still clutching the material around my waist and torso.

"The paint!" she yells at me.

"I know," I project back. "That's why I've got the yellow skirt thing on."

She shakes her head with a concerned look.

I look down to find the that yellow material that was supposed to remain disappeared when I did. For a split second, I recognize one of my father's last achievements: the material he created shares my invisibility, and maybe more. I'll finally be able to fly around without being naked all the time.

But immediately after that thought enters my head, I realize another truth. The only thing that remains in front of the reporters is the painted shell of my naked body.

After a million more cameras seem to flash, I launch myself into the air, as far away from humanity as possible.

Turn the page for a sneak peak of

VICTOR BOONE

MUST DIE

Coming 2018

CHAPTER ONE

"How far do you think I can throw this one?" Maria asks with a smirk. She's holding a rusty golf cart above her head with one hand, eyeing the the opposite end of the junk yard with a squint. As if squinting will help her focus.

"I don't know – at least a few inches," I taunt.

She stifles a fake laugh with a snort, which causes the golf cart to sway above her thin frame. Flecks of rust fall into her curly hair.

"Funny," she says dryly, then focuses back into the distance. "I'll bet I could get it past the outer fence if I wanted to."

She's definitely enjoying her new-found powers, even though it's obvious she's having a hard time adjusting to them.

"Come on, Maria," I say, feeling a bit like a nerd crashing a party full of popular kids, asking them to use coasters under their plastic cups. "The whole reason we're out here is so you can figure out how to restrain yourself – not to see what you're capable of. We both know you could get it over the fence."

Her eyes mischievously light up for a split second, then she sends the four-wheeled hunk of rust careening through the air. Immediately after it leaves her hands, she realizes she put a little too much power into it.

Sigh.

"You realize it's going to hit that freight train, don't you?" I ask. "The one that's just two blocks past the field?"

She stares towards the roar of sound that she only now notices.

"Oh God," she murmurs, then turns toward me. "Please fix it!"

I hesitate.

"Maybe I shouldn't," I say, rubbing my double chin. "I bet you would try to be a bit more careful if you accidentally killed a few innocent railroad engineers."

"Robby!" she screams, as the golf cart hurtles past the halfway mark to the speeding locomotive.

I used to move in secret, protecting unaware people from countless dangers. Now I'm having to save them from my girlfriend.

No, scratch that: my friend who is a girl. More specifically, my superhero friend who happens to be female. Nothing gives me a mixture of excitement and nausea more than the thought of Maria giving me another peck on the cheek. But that has as much statistical probability as me letting the golf cart actually hit the train.

I push off the ground, flying through the air with incredible acceleration. The distance is probably a quarter of a mile, but I've given myself ample time. I decide to reduce my speed just a smidge so that it looks like the collision is inevitable. I'd never use innocent lives to teach her a lesson, of course, but I can at least let her sweat a little.

Long before the rusty projectile meets slightly-less rusty projectile, I'm underneath it, changing its flight path from horizontal to vertical. The locomotive rushes on, none the wiser.

"Show off," Maria yells from across the junk yard as I make a wide one-eighty.

I take my time flying back to where she still stands with her arms crossed.

"Did you seriously slow down to try to freak me out?" she says with a raised eyebrow. "I knew you had it."

The vehicle drops from my hands with a dirty, metallic thud as I set my feet down on the ground.

"Did you seriously throw a golf cart at a moving train to try to impress me?" I counter.

She rolls her eyes.

"If I wanted to impress you," she says, her voice immediately dripping with seductive sarcasm, "I'd just wear a tighter shirt."

All the blood in my body rushes to my cheeks. Cue nausea. I turn invisible, just in case she didn't see my initial embarrassment.

"Very brave," she laughs. "Especially considering you're not wearing your suit, so I can still see your clothes."

I turn away, as if that would somehow hide me more.

"Come on, Maria," I repeat, trying to divert attention from myself. "I thought you wanted to learn how to control your powers. Isn't that why we're here?"

It's been several months since what the media is now calling the "Return of Victor Boone," when Dr. Bradford—otherwise known as The Vacant—tried to kill Maria, but instead imbued her with the same powers I've had since I was eleven.

Or, at least most of the powers. Either they're taking a while to fully develop, or the chemical compound was different than the one that changed me. Heck – the stuff had been sitting on a shelf for who-knows-how-long, so it's possible that it lost some of its potency. But it's a lucky thing, because even at the level she has them, she has accidentally destroyed all of the furniture in her apartment and split a cab in half with a sneeze.

"Let's try again," she says, her voice a little defeated.

I turn visible as I move about a hundred feet away.

"That's way too close," she says when I stop, facing her.

"Control," I remind her. "One day we'll race or see who can spit the farthest or something. Today it's about control."

Her eyes roll hard enough that I don't even need my hypersensitive vision to notice.

She picks up a nearby tire, then closes her eyelids. I listen to her heartbeat start to slow, and she breathes like she's in a yoga class. Bad guys never give us this kind of time to prepare, but we have to start somewhere.

After several seconds of mostly-silence, she opens her eyes and stares into me with those stunning green irises. It would be super awkward if I didn't know she was about to launch the tire at my face.

Her arm extends, and the rubber wheel releases from her grip. It careens for just a moment, then buries itself deep into piles of junk about thirty feet in front of me.

"That was great!" I yell, fighting the urge to jump up and down.

"Great?" she screams back. "That was terrible! It didn't even get close to you!"

"But it's the first time you threw short," I encourage. "Accuracy will come later, but for now I think it's huge that you were able to restrain yourself."

"Whatever," she mumbles as she picks up a radiator. She positions herself back in the previous stance, repeating the same process as before.

I let myself get lost in the throbbing coming from her heart, the *lub dub, lub dub* tickling the drums in my ears. If I were a composer, every piece I wrote would be set to her tempo.

...but there's something else there, fighting against her pulse. Something familiar, but completely different. Something I never thought I'd hear again.

Before I realize it, the radiator slams against my face. Maria squeals with delight.

"I did it!" she exclaims. "I did it!"

My hand goes up before I even realize it. "Wait," I say just above a whisper. "Do you hear that?"

I look up at her long enough to know that she has no idea what I'm talking about.

"You're just mad because you didn't react fast—"

"Shhh," I force out. "I…"

I can't believe I just shushed her.

"Sorry – I hear something and it's really confusing."

She looks in the air like that will help her focus in on the noise in my head. It took me years to be able to pinpoint a single sound, so I doubt she'll find it any time soon.

I hear it a little clearer this time.

"I'll be right back," I shout as I burst through the air in the direction of the…voice. I'm hearing a voice for sure.

It grows clearer with every mile closer I get, but something seems off. It's distorted and shaky, and higher-pitched than it should be. If it's a recording, it's one I've never heard. It doesn't make sense.

"…everything in…the bag…" There's a long pause, then a chuckle, as if the speaker is slowly letting a joke form together. Then the voice continues with, "…*douchebag*…"

No. It's impossible.

I set myself down in front of the bank with the same large glass windows that I broke less than a year ago.

That day. *That* bank.

I scan the scene like I'm watching a rerun of a TV show that had been copied too many times. The picture sags and the sound isn't synced up with the moving lips, but it's definitely the same program. Same time, same channel.

There's a man holding a duffle bag in one hand and a struggling woman in the other. His left foot drags as he walks and his arms have what seem to be burns or rashes all over them. Clumps of his hair are missing, and he looks like he spent the night in a hole in the ground. He's the last person in the room to notice that I've entered the building, and he turns slowly.

It can't be.

"You...want...trouble?" he says with tremendous effort over a drooping lip. "Trouble...is my...last name."

I know I should act. I should stop what is obviously a robbery in progress. Normally it wouldn't take any effort—there's only one criminal, and he can barely walk—but I'm having a hard time standing myself.

"You...want...trouble?" he repeats, louder, as if caught in a loop. "Trouble...is my...last name."

"Let her go," I finally say, blinking my eyes several times, as if the next time I open them things will make sense. "Let her go right now."

"Do you know...who I am?" the man says, swinging the half-full duffle bag to his chest.

Yes. I know who he is.

The man standing twenty feet in front of me is none other than Victor Boone.

ACKNOWLEDGEMENTS

Thank you to my wife, Holly, for standing by me through my many creative endeavors.

Thank you to my parents, my brothers, and all of my family – your support means the world to me, and sometimes the only reason I get anything done.

Thanks always to Jeff Brinkley, Jeff Hildebrand, Brad Lawrence, Matt Lawrence, and Andy Neale for your brotherhood in Manic Bloom, and for forcing me to grow creatively. We've accomplished more than I ever would have dreamed ten years ago when we first met.

Thanks specifically to Hildee for being my chemistry consultant. If it sounds like I know anything about a *Liquid Chromatography and Mass Spectrometry* machine (because I don't), then I owe you some skittles or something.

Thank you to Rob Harig and Stacy Stinson for your support and patience – it does not go unnoticed.

Thanks to my growing number of friends who are also writers, and and who encourage me, help me, and push me: Seth Ervin, Casey Eanes, Deborah T. Bickmore, Lydia Sherrer, all of the amazing folks in the Murfreesboro Writers Group, and the

awesome fellow writers that I rub elbows with at Cons –
whether on a panel together or hanging at our tables.

Tremendous thanks to my beta readers, who clean up what I
write to make it presentable:

Deborah Bickmore	Pete McNally
Mary Beth Clark	Ron Messier
Earl Cunningham	Dean Mobley
Julie Fisher	George Rapier
Angela Ford	Shannon Skillern
Brenden Fowler	Ann Stevenson
Bruce Harvey	Holly Stevenson
Christine Isley-Farmer	Kevin Stevenson
Jenilee McNamara	Nicole Stevenson
Greg Martin	Chance Torrez
June McCash	

I listened to a lot of ambient music while I wrote this book,
and I want to give a special nod to Dawn of Midi, Loscil, and
Hans Zimmer. There are too many others to name, but
Spotify puts them all at my fingertips.

Like Robby, I know a thing or two about insecurity. Life
would be much harder without my real-life Dr. Hugheses, and
I recommend counseling to everyone. In some ways, I want
this book to encourage all of us (me included) to step out of
the shadows. Whatever it is that you're made to do, do it.

Don't wait until you're ready, or for the path to be easy, or for the time to be "right." It never is.

I'm a deeply flawed man, in desperate need of grace. I owe my life to Jesus Christ, and I hope that everything I do—including this book—reflects my gratitude.

Lastly, thank YOU so much for reading this, and for your support. If you liked it, please write a review, tell your friends, share it online, and buy a hundred copies for birthday gifts. …but even if you do none of those things – seriously, thank you.

ABOUT THE AUTHOR

David Joel Stevenson lives outside of Nashville, TN with his wife, several chickens, and thousands of honey bees. He is the singer in the band Manic Bloom (www.ManicBloom.com), a songwriter, a computer programmer, and is irregularly documenting his quests in homesteading on his blog, www.GeekOffGrid.com.

For more information, visit www.DavidJoelStevenson.com

Made in the USA
Lexington, KY
13 February 2018